A Most Promising Planet

M.L. Williams

Copyright © 2020 All Writes Reserved Publishing

Cover art by Blair Gauntt

Editors: Barbara Malmberg and Marty Novak

ISBN: 978-1-68454-442-4

Books by M.L. Williams

Fiction

A Most Promising Planet

Ebook series of *A Most Promising Planet*:
The Architects of Sentience: Book One
The Architects of the People: Book Two
The Architects of the Word: Book Three
The Architects of Omnipotence: Book Four
The Architects of Revenge: Book Five
The Architects of Justice: Book Six

Seers of Verde: The Legend Fulfilled, Book One;
Return of the Earthers: Seers of Verde, Book Two

Nonfiction

Cornfield Chronicles: Featuring Snowball, Pony From Hell

Essay collection

Memoirs of a Meandering Mind

ACKNOWLEDGMENTS

No book is produced by one person. It takes a whole team of people. I want to sincerely thank "my team" for all their efforts in making this book possible.

First of all, kudos to Blair Gauntt for his fantastic covers for the print and Ebook versions. Hopefully the text lives up to his artistry.

Thanks to Emijah Jones, who suggested using "Architects" in the title. Her idea wound up being the section titles in the novel as well as the theme for the Ebook series.

Editors Barbara Malmberg and Marty Novak did their best to ensure my words made a modicum of sense.

I also greatly appreciate the time C.M. Williams, Jessica Carney, Julie Franklin, Dawn Goodlove and Chris Galligan put in to help with the project.

Just as important, a heartfelt thanks to all my family and friends who supported and encouraged me through the process that started in the fall of 2018.

To Mary:
Great to meet you!

CONTENTS

DEDICATION

To the Tewa Pueblo of New Mexico, whose creation story
inspired this book.
Also to the inspiration created by Harriet Beecher Stowe for
her book, *Uncle Tom's Cabin,* which lit the fire in the North to
right the tragedy of slavery.

A MOST PROMISING PLANET

FOREWORD

Inspiration sometimes arrives in mysterious ways. I was admiring the fascinating clay sculptures by Roxanne Swentzell during a visit to the Poeh Cultural Center near Pojoaque, New Mexico, a few years ago when stories started to explode into my consciousness.

I had been staring into the face of a hunter sculpture. His spear was raised, ready to throw. I stood mesmerized for a minute or two, then forced myself to walk to the next exhibit, which showed a Spaniard whipping a Pueblo man. I remember frowning at the cruelty of the scene. Suddenly images of people — some famous, some not — throughout history flowed before my eyes. It was an exhilarating sensation, albeit, a startling one.

Everywhere you go in New Mexico, you cannot escape seeing "The Land of Enchantment" emblazoned everywhere. Admittedly, vistas in the state are amazing. It's easy to see why artists flock there in an effort to capture the beauty of the place. However, the enchantment part was lost on me until I visited the cultural center. Nothing like that had ever happened to me.

Uncontrolled and unexpected visions swirled through my brain. For a moment, I lost all sense of time and place as I gazed at scenes only my brain could see. I chalked the experience up to the mystical feeling of the place and reserved judgment for later.

A few days later, my fellow group of travelers and I were enjoying a performance by Ron Roybal, a talented pipe flute player and guitarist from the area. The room was dark. It did not take long for Roybal's melodic sounds to ease my brain into a meditative state. This time whole chapters and names of people floated into my brain. I eventually awoke from this daydream and realized a novel had entrenched itself in my mind. I knew my next project was going to be this book.

This work contains several stories that "witness" the history of the Earth and mankind told through another perspective. While researching various periods of history, I wanted to bring to light some tales that fascinated me, such as the invention of writing in ancient Sumer as well as the first fictional story possibly to be written in that cradle of civilization. I also had fun reimagining a different origin story for some of the gods of mythology. The tale that inspired this book came from the Tewa Pueblo — the first American revolution in 1680 when an alliance of native people drove the Spanish out of North America for a short time. The only roadblock I experienced was how to end such a far-reaching effort. So many significant events have shaped our history. Which one could serve as a fitting last tale?

While doing research, I became fascinated with Harriet Beecher Stowe, the author of *Uncle Tom's Cabin*, the book credited with raising Northern consciousness about the plight of the slaves a decade before the Civil War broke out.

I always have had a soft spot for the famous author who, according to family folklore, was said to be a distant relative via my paternal grandmother, whose maiden name was Beecher. My connection to that family is strong because I was named after two Beecher relatives. Stowe, two of my great-grandfathers and another iconic historical figure — Abraham Lincoln — all lived during the same time and obviously were deeply affected by this tragic period in U.S. history.

More study revealed Stowe visited Lincoln in the White House during the war, but no records of their conversation were kept. Also, Lincoln and one of my great-grandfathers had lived in the same area of Illinois. This was all my writer's brain needed to spin the last section in the book.

I have striven to present each period of history accurately and be respectful of real people from the past as I interwove them with fictional characters created by my imagination.

During the final stage of writing, I felt Cousin Harriet watching over my shoulder. I hope she approves of the tale.

M.L. Williams

At first the people gathered and surveyed the world, but it was too hot.

So they waited.

The people returned again and surveyed the world, but it was too cold.

So they waited.

When the people revisited the world again, they found a great water covering most of the world. So they came through the water, found dry land and settled the earth. — An interpretation of the Tewa creation story at the Poaque Pueblo's Cultural Center near Taos, N.M.

I

THE ARCHITECTS OF SENTIENCE

1

Searcher appeared in the atmosphere of the newly formed planet. The entity flickered, its reserves spent from the interstellar trip. The trek only took seconds in real time, but it covered such a vast distance in space, the traveler could no longer feel a connection with Family. It missed the comfort of that vast cloud of Family as they fed off each other's energies.

Searcher surveyed the planet. This third world from its sun was positioned in a favorable orbit. When the planet cooled down in a few eons it would be warm enough to create and sustain life. Some minor adjustments to its core would create a radiation belt around the world to protect it from the sun's life-threatening solar flares. Its moon also was developing a favorable orbit to help stabilize weather patterns and ocean currents if water formed here.

Time to taste the planet. Searcher hesitated. This effort always took so much energy, and there were risks. A few of its fellow planetary scouts never returned to Family because they bonded with the planets they were investigating. They were seduced by the desire to conjoin with an ecosystem.

Every scout longed to feel the sun warm a body whether it was covered in scales, feathers, fur or skin; the exhilaration of breathing air through lungs again; the excitement of procreating; and the thrill of the fight for survival.

The price for this seduction was heavy — the permanent loss of self-awareness; the abandonment of the chance to achieve independent thought and self-determination.

Nothing could be done when rescue scouts discovered their lost comrades bonded in a world teeming with life. The family considered such a world contaminated and forbade any further contact other than the occasional observance to monitor its evolution.

If abominations developed from a scout's influence, Family could choose to cleanse the world by initiating some sort of catastrophe. Asteroids were the easiest choice. A gentle nudge would send one of those giant space rocks careening toward a life-ending collision course with a planet.

Searcher was determined not to succumb to such a temptation. Besides, it was too early in this world's formation to support life — yet. It commenced with the tasting. Searcher danced around the planet, dipping into lava pools, melding with rocks to determine the chemistry and mineral content of the place.

The planet did not disappoint. It had everything but amino acids to spark the formation of life. This was not a problem. Searcher knew where to look — the asteroid belt that encircled this solar system.

It rose slightly above the world, soaked in some of the small sun's energy and blinked into the asteroid belt, appearing in the cloud of floating space boulders almost instantaneously.

Asteroid tasting was not dangerous — just unpredictable. Sometimes it took thousands of tastings to find the right one with just the right chemical mix for the intended target planet.

It only took sixty thousand some tastings for Searcher to find an asteroid with acceptable and durable amino acids. It was probably a remnant from some lost world whose sun went nova, causing a cataclysmic explosion among its orbiting planets.

Now, a path needed to be cleared of the other asteroids so the life starter could reach the target planet. Searcher aimed most of those extra rocks toward the giant gaseous planet in the system. It would absorb them with no ill effects.

With the path cleared, Searcher gently guided the seeding asteroid toward the third planet and watched it plummet into the atmosphere and explode into millions of pieces, littering the surface with the elements of life.

Only one more addition would give this world a chance for life — water. Searcher rested on an asteroid and reviewed the path it had taken from Family to the unique star system. It had skirted many anomalies to reach the world in this spiral galaxy. After a short contemplation, Searcher remembered a frozen ice ball of a comet it had encountered.

Even though comets travel very slowly compared with the blink speed of a scout, steering one off course and realigning its trajectory to collide with a celestial body would require a lot of energy. More energy than Searcher had ever expended on such a mission.

The entity was committed. It had seeded the planet with the building blocks of life and now it needed water. After almost three blinks of travel, Searcher intercepted the comet. It took almost four blinks to nudge the comet towards the planet.

Two hundred blinks later, almost an eternity to the scout, the comet was on a direct collision course with the planet. Searcher rode the comet almost all the way to the surface, then released itself and watched as the missile gave the planet its first drink.

That was a fine recipe for life. Searcher paused and re-evaluated its thoughts. Recipe? Strange concept. Somewhere in its memory it had a fondness for the word. But why? It seemed related to some sort of physical sensation, but Searcher did not remember the importance of it. Too many millennia had passed since Searcher had known life. Maybe it would try that experiment again, if Family allowed it of course.

Almost drained of energy, Searcher aimed itself toward the second planet from the sun where it could rest and rejuvenate on the world's scorching surface and bask in the solar heat. With its last bit of energy, the entity sent a message vibration back to Family to report its actions, and then it rested. An eon or so would do.

Searcher was awakened by a familiar nudge of energy. It recognized Other, its companion from Family.

The two entities had been tied together in some kind of mysterious bond ever since they exploded into existence. They had shared countless experiences in organisms whose brief lives were always extinguished too soon. Memories of those lives faded away when they returned to Family, but Searcher and Other bonded more strongly after every lifetime.

They even added to their own small cluster in Family when offspring were produced from their corporeal lives. Their cluster was small, only in the thousands, compared with the countless billions that made up Family.

Other merged with Searcher for a nanosecond, a show of affection for a family member and just long enough to relay a message and to determine what its companion had accomplished.

Searcher acknowledged the message: "Return to Family. A world on the opposite side of the galaxy has been deemed appropriate for habitation."

When Family called, all its members returned for another habitation. Only the watchers — those higher energy forms that guarded planets being cultivated for habitation by Family — were allowed to refuse.

Searcher responded to Other with a vibration of welcome, then the two blinked to the third planet to examine the scout's handiwork. Life had taken root. Multi-celled bacteria swarmed throughout the oceans. The surface was cooling nicely. The land should be ripe for hosting life when the ocean creatures were ready to leave their liquid nursery.

The scout tasted the planet one last time and left a minuscule spark of itself in the ocean. Any other family members who tasted this planet would recognize the energy marker and leave the world alone unless Searcher had been made nonexistent by Family.

Searcher experienced a strange jolt — almost like an emotion. Maybe it was pride, satisfaction or even pleasure. It had been too long ago to remember what those felt like. Other transmitted its approval. It tried to merge with Searcher but withdrew from its partner's higher energy output.

Only a watcher emitted such a signal, but Family had not approved of this transformation. Searcher somehow had evolved on its own. Family would have to address this situation.

Other approached its partner and requested a merger. The two commingled slowly so Searcher would not accidentally drain Other's energy, and then the combined entities blinked back to Family.

2

The cluster created by Searcher and Other welcomed the two entities back amongst them by surrounding the travelers in an orb of collective energies. The younger members almost shyly approached Searcher to assess its new vibration. Just touching Searcher sent strange shock waves through them.

Members of the greater family swarmed around the orb, sensing a change in the cluster's vibration. Moments later, a few hundred guardians — those enforcers of Family's edicts — circled the cluster, then entered the orb. Each guardian touched Searcher and drew back in a surprised reaction to its changed vibration.

When the guardians finished their inspection, Searcher transmitted what it had accomplished on that far-away planet. The guardians swarmed together briefly then returned their verdict of Searcher — nonexistence.

They could not allow a renegade to evolve into a watcher without Family's approval. Besides, Searcher's vibration was worrisome. It was new and resonated with a foreign energy.

The guardians merged into a glowing mass in preparation to absorb Searcher. Its knowledge would be transmitted to another scout, one who had completed a successful planetary mission but returned untainted.

The executioner mass commanded Searcher to hold its position. In an unprecedented act of self-preservation, the entity transmitted a danger signal to its cluster.

Without hesitation, Other and the cluster merged with Searcher, forming an imposing defensive cloud. Glowing with the combined intense energy, Searcher advanced on the guardians and absorbed them.

A shock wave ensued from the unexpected collision of energies, hurling the other members of Family thousands of blinks away. Gradually, Other and the cluster disseminated out of Searcher and formed a cloud around it. The cluster had changed. It now glowed with the collected energies of the absorbed guardians.

Other beamed with a stronger, new vibration. Several hundred other entities of their cluster approached Searcher. It anointed them all as new guardians. The cloud glowed blue with approval. Searcher considered its situation. Their former family would eventually regather itself and return to the home coordinates.

Not wanting to face Family that no doubt would gather millions of its guardians to carry out the verdict of nonexistence, Searcher transmitted an order — return to the small planet and wait for it to become habitable.

Before departing, Searcher deposited a flicker of energy from one of the absorbed guardians and anchored it in place with a message for the old family: "Travel to your appointed world for habitation. Do not follow. My cluster will resist absorption. I am Sentinel." The entity then blinked back to the small planet.

After a thousand or so blinks, the old family gathered itself as a whole cloud and returned to its home coordinates. A small cluster of guardians warily surrounded the message entity and absorbed it. Family glowed red. If it had been a living organism, the mood would have reflected anger. It formed into a compact cloud and departed for the habitable planet on the other side of the galaxy.

Only one entity was left behind. A new watcher would wait until contacted by Family to pursue the self-anointed Sentinel. It could not allow the break-away cluster to remain in existence.

≫≫≫≫≫

The watcher had lost track of the time it had maintained its position, waiting to be contacted by Family. It almost had flickered out of existence a few times but forced itself to drop into a dormant mode to recharge its energy.

One time, the lone entity snapped awake when it sensed another presence. However, the watcher found nothing but traces of a vaguely familiar vibration which dissipated quickly before it could identify it.

How long had it been? Two eons? No, possibly three. The watcher grew weaker with each awakening. No other entities surrounded it to help it recharge. The message Family had imprinted on it grew dimmer. What was its mission? Hold its position until Family contacted it. Yes, that was it. But, Family had been gone so long and no contact came.

Something akin to loneliness started to seep into its being. Without being aware of its intention, the watcher transmitted a distress message to the last coordinates it could remember — the strange blue planet to which the renegade cluster, led by the mysterious Sentinel, had escaped.

Its energy was waning. If it went dormant again, the watcher would fade away, becoming just a brief spit of gas dissipating into the void.

With its strength ebbing, the watcher barely had enough energy to hold its position. It wanted to travel again, blink back and forth among the solar systems, analyzing strange planets, recharging itself in the glow of a distant sun.

The watcher was about to let itself drift off into nothingness when a blast of energy from five strange entities surrounded it. The newcomers did not approach the dying watcher immediately but regarded it briefly before two of the entities touched it and delivered a welcome jolt of life-giving energy.

The entities then absorbed the lone watcher. Finding no danger other than a message from Family, they signaled their traveling companions and all merged into one entity.

Recharged, the lone watcher now remembered the last coordinates Family had given it and transmitted them to the travelers. The newly formed tiny unit considered its options. Return to Sentinel and their cluster or investigate what had happened to Family. When the lone watcher's distress signal had reached the cluster led by Sentinel, it had imparted decision-making awareness on the five travelers.

The five entities released Family's watcher from the bond and offered it a choice — stay or come with them to investigate the whereabouts of Family. The watcher was presented with a conundrum — follow its orders or join the travelers, which had recharged it. The lone entity had tasted the others' vibrations and found them intoxicating. Self-awareness now throbbed through it.

Frustrated with the loneliness, the watcher signaled its decision. The travelers absorbed their new member, coalesced into a new unit, recharged each other and blinked off in search of Family.

It took seven blinks for the cluster's traveler orb to reach the coordinates — a habitable planet with three moons on an opposite spiral arm of the home galaxy — Family had left with the lone watcher. This was a long journey even for the combined energies of the entities.

Not wanting to appear in the middle of what could be a hostile Family that would absorb it before a message could be relayed, the traveler unit orbited near the giant red sun to regain its energy.

When refreshed, the travelers peered toward the planet in search of Family. Only sensing whispers of energy and not

Family's usual massive output, the orb dispatched its newest member — the lone watcher — to investigate the planet and search for Family.

In less than half a solar day, the watcher returned with a strange report. It had encountered a small cloud of unorganized family members. The entities offered no resistance to the newcomer as it searched the planet.

It had found evidence of Family. Familiar energies inhabited millions of small mammals. Curiously, the watcher sensed no self-awareness in the primates who lived in small clans, foraged for food during the day and escaped to the safety of trees at nightfall.

The unit reabsorbed the watcher and blinked to the planet. Before disseminating, the five original members bestowed traveler status onto the lone watcher and gave it an increased jolt of energy.

The six travelers now turned their attention to the planet in an attempt to discover why Family had bonded with the lower life forms. The remnants of Family, the small cloud of watchers, were no help. They swirled about in disarray. None of the members contained orders nor did they know their mission.

Assessing the planet and all the life forms offered no clues. The primates seemed to be stuck in an evolutionary quagmire. Traveler-4 decided to taste one of the countless giant trees that covered the landscape, keeping much of the surface in a permanent dusk-like environment. This was an unusual act for an entity because it normally would not bond with a plant, but the travelers were gifted with self-awareness and with that came curiosity.

Curious at what it had found, Traveler-4 pulled out and immediately set about sampling as many trees as possible until a viable conclusion could be extrapolated. The entity stopped after a half-solar day and one million samplings. It had the information it needed.

Signaling the others, Traveler-4 relayed its findings. About an eon ago, a flare from the unstable sun sent a radiation wave through the planet. All genetics were frozen in an evolutionary limbo.

The primates that were on their way to forming a society when Family's entities bonded with them had devolved into a pre-evolutionary stage. The radiation also erased the mission memories of the cloud of watchers that were supposed to act as sentries.

The travelers reconnoitered, considered their options and set off to recharge near the sun. Forming into a single unit once again, the entities set out to return to Sentinel and the cluster. The fate of the former family now would rest with the whims of the break-away group.

3

Sentinel pondered the fate of Family. The last time Sentinel, Other and their cluster were with the teeming cloud, they had fought off a non-existence edict, disrupted the group and escaped to a planet that held the promise of habitation — someday.

Now Family was in danger. Sentinel displayed no remorse for what it had done, but it acknowledged an obligation to the collective which had spawned it and Other. After all their incarnations in a myriad of life forms, Family always welcomed them back, recharged them and sent them off on the next mission across the galaxy.

Sentinel called for a merger. Other and the cluster complied. The newly formed collective considered Sentinel's verdict. It glowed in thought and reached a conclusion — depart for that far-away world to save Family.

Sentinel did not want to leave this new world, which it had seeded with life and water. Plants now flourished on its cooling surface. The oceans teemed with organisms. Some of the creatures had crawled out of the water and were gulping oxygen out of the air. In a few eons, perhaps it would be habitable.

Four watchers were selected to survey the planet and protect it from any interstellar threats. However, they were forbidden from shaping or controlling the evolutionary fate of the planet.

Sentinel was pleased with its work. Now it was time for the long wait — when that first spark of self-awareness flickered alive, giving the entities the chance to taste life again. The cluster bonded into one unit, absorbed the information from the travelers and blinked away to help the immobilized family.

Sentinel observed the planet the old family had inhabited with cold objectivity. It had called for volunteers from the cluster to find a group of creatures with the largest brains and bond with them in hopes of creating self-awareness.

Even though the cluster now numbered in the hundreds of thousands, Sentinel was reluctant to waste any members in an attempt to revive the old family. The likelihood of losing entities during a bond with a physical being was strong.

Several volunteers offered to rescue more of the original family members, but Sentinel forbade it. The gift of self-awareness had been bestowed to a few beings that may have the ability to evolve into worthwhile physical forms.

The obligation had been fulfilled. Now it was up to those lucky few that had been given the gift to evolve or slip back into subsistence survival.

Too much solar time has lapsed since Sentinel had visited that intriguing planet on the other side of the galaxy. It wanted to return. However, the cluster entreated Sentinel to stay and watch over the old family.

Sentinel acquiesced to the group's judgment. The new cluster had saved Sentinel when Family threatened it with nonexistence. The creatures on the planet would be given an eon to show evolutionary improvement or risk extermination. The cluster flashed its agreement.

Not interested in observing the day-to-day activities of those boring beasts on the planet, Sentinel willed itself into a well-deserved sleep mode.

Sentinel was jolted awake by a vibration nudge from Other. Instead of being welcomed by countless thousands of its cluster, only a few hundred were positioned around the entity.

An unfamiliar green cloud of entities swarmed over the foreign planet practically infiltrating the atmosphere. A lightning storm of energies flashed from the planet to the cloud and back again in a continuous stream.

Had tragedy befallen the cluster? Sentinel flashed its alarm. Other asked permission to bond. Sentinel agreed, then glowed red after learning what had happened to its missing cluster.

After the volunteers from the cluster had bonded with the creatures on the planet, the primate group thrived and quadrupled its numbers in two generations. When the first two generations of the primates died, their life forces returned to the cluster and shared their experiences through a mass bonding.

The intoxicating thrill of experiencing a physical life was too much for most of the younger members of the cluster to ignore. Before Other and the original cluster could object, a giant cloud of their fellow entities swarmed to the planet, bonding with every primate they could find.

When there were no primates left to bond with, the leftover cluster members linked with lower life forms. As more beings died and their energies rejoined the cluster, more members were drawn to the temptations the planet offered.

Sentinel emitted unfamiliar vibrations. Possibly anger. Most definitely disappointment. Nothing could be done now to rescue the truant members of its cluster. The new cloud's sole purpose was to absorb the spent life forces from the planet and spew new energies back into any newborn organism on the planet.

The old family would have sent a massive jolt of energy to neutralize the mutinous cloud, absorbed it and then perhaps prodded a giant asteroid toward the planet to cleanse it of the contamination. However, Sentinel had resisted the will of Family when it had been threatened with nonexistence. Now, extensions of its energy had done the same thing.

Sentinel called for a bonding with Other and the surviving cluster. It relayed its message — leave this corrupted planet to evolve on its own and return to the blue jewel it had helped form. That planet now beckoned it. Other and the cluster agreed.

Before departing for the other world, Sentinel studied the traitorous cloud for a solar second. The entity no longer throbbed with red but an orange hue still glowed within it.

Sentinel approached the green cloud, tasted it and sent a shock wave through it. Two-thirds of the cloud flickered and died. Sentinel left a lasting message among the surviving energies — bonding is only permitted with self-aware beings. The surviving cloud throbbed with the yellow light of pain and slowly regained its green shade. Message received.

Other and the remaining cluster beckoned to Sentinel to join them. The remaining independent energies melded into a giant orb and blinked away.

4

Monstrosities. Giant animals with no flicker of self-awareness now roamed the forests, plains, skies and oceans of the world Sentinel had seeded with life. The entity could not mask its surprise and disappointment. It glowed a dull orange.

Sentinel merged with the four watchers and learned the fate of the planet. One dominant species had sprung up from the various genetic mutations among the life forms and had outgrown, outfought and outeaten its competitors.

Now these giants had evolved into a bizarre ecosystem. Some of the predators were capable of hunting and bringing down the moderately sized beasts but even larger plant-eating monsters were only slowed down by age or lack of food.

Other joined its companion in surveying the world. It ignored the dominant species and observed some small, interesting creatures. These warm-blooded animals scurried about from burrow to burrow, eating seeds, plants or gleaning the carcasses of the dead giants.

Sentinel called for a meeting of its cluster. The entities swarmed together to consider the planet's fate. Extinction would have been the immediate verdict of the old family. The abominations would not have been allowed to thrive.

All the entities in the cluster — except one — agreed extinction was the only viable solution to cleanse the planet and start over. Other was the exception. Sentinel transmitted its surprise but waited for Other to make its case for leniency.

Other did not argue against extinction for the giants and their smaller ilk. It offered another solution. A cleansing explosion that would eliminate the unprotected large beasts on land and in the oceans but small enough to give a chance of life for those interesting, scurrying animals.

Something about those tiny life forms intrigued Other. It had tasted a few thousand of those and found a genetic code that was ripe for evolution into higher life forms.

Sentinel was pleased at the compromise Other presented. It did not relish extinguishing all the life it had seeded on the planet. However, Other's plan would be difficult if not impossible to carry out.

Never before had an entity attempted a near extinction of life on a planet. The results had always been a complete annihilation, leaving the planet devoid of life. Only a few planets had recovered to start over. At best, the surviving life forms were rudimentary organisms in an ocean or deep underground.

The four watchers Sentinel had left to guard the planet approached Sentinel and asked to merge. The entity agreed and immediately glowed green with excitement after they relayed a possible solution.

During the cluster's absence when it left to help Family, the watchers had deflected three large asteroids that would have been planet killers. After sampling the space missiles, the watchers discovered one had life-starting amino acids and the other two still harbored water in their cores. So, the watchers nudged the asteroids toward the fourth planet from the sun and carried out an unplanned seeding.

Sentinel released the four watchers and emitted a vibration of surprise. It had tasted that planet and found it lacking a stable magnetic core. Life evolving there would face an uncertain future.

Curious, Sentinel and Other blinked to the fourth planet. To their surprise, the planet had a rich atmosphere. Water flowed through its valleys and bacteria could be found everywhere. So far, the weak magnetic core was holding its own in protecting the world.

Other tasted the soil and water, then transmitted a solution to Sentinel. Those small, warm-blooded life forms could be transported to this world where they had a chance to flourish. Some of the cluster could monitor and stabilize the planet's magnetic core just long enough until the third planet was ready to have life reintroduced to it.

Sentinel considered Other's proposal. Never before had an entity transferred life from one world to another. Not even Family had carried out such a bold plan. The two entities blinked back to the cluster and reported their findings.

The cluster divided into two groups — one to carry out the transfer of life from the third to the fourth world and the other to monitor the fourth planet's magnetic field. Sentinel then turned its attention to the asteroid belt. This time it needed to find a space rock just the right size and aim it at an ideal spot for the cleansing but leaving the planet with enough resources to once again host life.

5

Other supervised the transfer of the small creatures from the third planet to its neighbor. Thousands of the cluster's entities gulped air and created huge bubbles of oxygen. Dozens of other entities united in smaller units and flitted through the environment, gathering as many of those fur-bearing creatures as they could find.

With great care, the creatures were deposited in the oxygen bubble, where they hung suspended twitching and squirming trying to swim out of this strange environment. Once the bubbles were filled with the creatures, more entities surrounded them to form protective shields, and the masses slowly drifted to the fourth planet.

The transport bubble could have blinked to the fourth planet, but the first attempt to transport the creatures had ended in a disastrous loss of life. All the specimens had exploded from the pressure of blink speed. Many failed transport experiments later found the life-sustainable speed to be one-thousandth of a blink — two solar hours — an interminably slow speed for an entity.

Once the bubble transport reached the planet, it slowly deposited the animals across the fourth planet's surface, then released the oxygen which helped enrich the atmosphere. The small creatures scrambled to safety and burrowed into the soil of their new home.

The cluster had spread seeds from the third planet. After only a dozen decades or so, the plants now were flourishing and giving off oxygen. About half of the creatures survived the move, which Other considered a success.

Sentinel searched among the asteroid belt until it found the perfect life-extinguishing, but not planet killing, rock. And then it waited. After a little over a hundred solar revolutions, Other blinked alongside Sentinel and reported the transfer of the organisms to the new planet had been completed.

With a small nudge, Sentinel sent the asteroid on a collision with the world it had so carefully seeded. It seemed only a blink or two ago that it had pushed a life-giving rock toward the planet and now it was killing the monsters that roamed the surface.

Sentinel rode the asteroid all the way down, guiding it to the spot where its cluster had determined would complete its terrible task. The explosion, as explosions go on a planetary scale, was magnificent. Even Sentinel was impressed.

The fireball almost reached the outer atmosphere. The asteroid hit with such force, pieces of it were launched into the sky and came hurtling back by the thousands only to blanket the surface with flames.

The abominations on the planet didn't stand a chance. Those that were killed by the initial blow and shock wave either succumbed to the fires or starved to death when the planet-wide cloud smothered the atmosphere killing all food sources. The great extinction was complete, and now the planet had to rest and hopefully revive to the point where it could host life once again.

Sentinel watched the destruction. A great emptiness gnawed at the entity. It had given life to the planet, and now it was the architect of all the destruction that was taking place. This small, beautiful blue world was now cloaked with a swirling black cloud. It needed time to heal.

Sentinel blinked over to the fourth planet to check on the transition progress. Other darted here and there overseeing the temporary nursery world like a dutiful parent. The entity tasted the atmosphere and then flew to the surface to monitor the creatures which had been transported.

Water flowed through valleys, and belts of green were slowly taking over the landscape. The sky was a light blue, not quite the same hue as what had enveloped the third planet, but close. A few wispy clouds floated through the atmosphere, which was growing richer in oxygen every day.

Life could be sustained here with careful monitoring and adjustments by the Sentinel's cluster. The goal was to keep the planet alive until its nearby sister had revived after the extinction event.

Sentinel waited patiently for Other to finish its patrol of the planet. The entity flashed its approval of the efforts being carried out. Other beamed with gratitude and then briefly merged with Sentinel, feeling its sadness from carrying out the destruction.

In a surprise move, Other asked permission to visit the third world. Sentinel agreed and the two blinked to the wounded planet. Other tasted the atmosphere and then visited the surface. After returning, it offered an opinion.

The planet would need a massive drink to cleanse the atmosphere and give life a boost. Sentinel knew what had to be done. Find another ice comet, albeit much smaller than the first one, and guide it back.

It had taken more than 200 blinks the first time the entity had carried out a similar mission. A second effort could take as long or longer — thousands of orbits around the sun in planetary time.

Other vibrated its approval. This mission would keep Sentinel occupied for a long enough time to let the third planet from the sun recover from the killer asteroid and be ready to accept life once it was baptized again.

Sentinel flashed yellow with concern about the unstable fourth planet even though it was hosting life — for now. Other vibrated assurance that it and the cluster were well up to the task of monitoring the world.

The two entities merged one last time before Sentinel turned its attention to the mission. It blinked away to find just the right size comet to bring that precious little planet back to life.

6

The alien ship slowly approached the third planet from the sun in the small solar system after dropping out of intergalactic speed. The robot crew scanned the world but found only death and a swirling black cloud that choked out most of the sun from the surface.

Only one planet — the fourth one from the sun — remained in the life-sustainable zone. The crew had been endowed with problem-solving skills, so they turned the ship toward that planet and maneuvered it for a closer look. The coordinates did not exactly match the orders from the masters, but life was abundant on the fourth world.

An energy scan revealed the telltale sign — a cloud of entities swarmed over the surface and throughout the atmosphere minding the planet like obsessive gardeners. This obviously was the planet to which the renegade cloud had fled. The masters had downloaded the troubling history concerning these traitors.

After hundreds of years traveling at intergalactic speed, the ship had found its target at last. It took only seconds for the interconnected crew to confer.

Order number one, achieved — find the renegades' planet.

Order number two, achieved — confirm life.

Order number three, achieved — confirm the existence of the traitorous cloud of entities.

It was time to carryout the most important commands:

Order number four — exterminate all life on the planet; and

Order number five — extinguish as many of the entities as possible, especially the leader that called itself Sentinel.

The crew raised the anti-vibration shield around the ship to prevent an attack from the entities and aimed its weapons.

A guardian had just reported the appearance of a strange metallic object orbiting the fourth planet to Other when the firing commenced. Missiles were launched from the object and were speeding toward the surface, not unlike killer asteroids.

It only took Other a nanosecond to recognize what was happening — an attack! In another nanosecond, Other commanded a wave of Guardians to intercept the oncoming threat. It also sent a distress signal to Sentinel.

The missiles never reached the planet. The flurry of Guardians smashed into all incoming weapons causing hundreds of flashes not unlike lighting strikes.

The mechanical crew of the ship reconsidered their tactics. Since the entities had taken the fight to them, it was time to initiate order number five. The planet could wait. It would be defenseless without its protectors. Order number four would be carried out once those enemy entities were destroyed. It was time to launch the negative vibration orbs.

After the initial attack, Other and its cloud surrounded the planet in a protective blanket of energy. In response, the ship launched thousands of metallic balls, which spread in an ominous cloud.

This time Other's cloud of entities intercepted the oncoming orbs. The reaction of the entities striking negative-vibration balls lit the void like a new sun being born. Each orb exploded with a crackle of energy that exterminated any entity that came into contact with it. But the entities persisted. They attacked every one of those killer objects.

After the brilliant flashes of light abated, Other took stock of its situation. Only a few hundred of its cloud were left. The survivors swarmed around Other in a protective shield. The alien ship and Other's small cloud faced off in a stalemate.

The crew of the ship analyzed their situation. The explosions of the negative-vibration orbs had severely damaged their shields. A scan of the surviving entities found a minuscule cloud that barely registered on their instruments.

Their orders were clear. They must complete their assignment. The masters had programmed the crew to take vengeance on these traitors which had left the original family.

Family had survived and finally evolved on that far-away planet. The combined life forces on that world had eventually taken over the small cloud that Sentinel had left to oversee it. One thought burned bright with the entities all those hundreds of thousands of years — Sentinel and the other escapees must be eliminated because of their original betrayal of the nonexistence order.

Navi-bot clicked questions to the crew. Weapons-bot answered first. "All weapons deployed. First wave ineffective. Planet unharmed. Second wave, success. Entity cloud decreased by an estimated ninety-nine percent."

Defense-bot reported. "Shields down to twenty percent. Probability of surviving attack from remaining entities — 77.895 percent." Engineering-bot confirmed that all systems were performing up to acceptable parameters.

The four lead robots ran the probabilities of the only recourse left to them. Navi-bot clicked, "Consensus has been reached. Final solution will be initiated."

Other and its cloud felt energy radiate from the ship's engines as it started to slowly approach the planet. The entity issued a command to its surviving cloud. The ship was now picking up speed. Other's cloud formed into an orb and sped to the surface to protect as many organisms as possible.

The two adversaries squared off in a cataclysmic collision just beyond the atmosphere of the planet. Other jettisoned itself into the ship at blink speed. The aliens' shields sizzled out and the engines were damaged. The impact with the negative vibration shields careened a depleted Other helplessly away, unable to mount a second attack.

Weapons-bot and and Defense-bot went offline after the impact with the entity. Navi-bot tried to reroute its message four times before it finally connected with a partially fried Engineering-bot. Assured the engines had enough power to complete their mission, Navi-bot relayed the final coordinates and steered the crippled ship toward the planet.

The masters had downloaded one more order into the robot ship — launch a canister filled with their genetic material onto the third planet's surface. Engineering-bot barely had enough circuits left to complete the task but gave itself one last surge of power, opened a portal and fired the canister toward the sister planet before sizzling into uselessness in a cloud of overheated wiring.

Not unlike an asteroid, the alien ship plummeted out of the sky in a giant fireball. It struck with such force, it gouged a huge elongated crevice into the surface. Like the killer asteroid which struck the third planet, the ship accomplished its mission. Debris exploded into the atmosphere and once again, a giant cloud smothered a planet teeming with life.

The damage was irreparable. With no entities left to protect the atmosphere or keep the inner core stable, life was swept off the planet with a sad groan.

A massive bubble created by the surviving entities slowly drifted down to the surface of the third planet. It settled in a valley where foliage somehow managed to survive. With a gentle whoosh, some of the contents spilled out as a few hundred of the furry creatures scrambled to safety among the rocks or furiously dug into the soil to escape.

The orb repeated this feat many more times around the planet until all its living contents were distributed in the most livable zones it could find. Now, it was up to those creatures to fight for survival.

A small cloud of entities emerged out of the orb and blinked back to the dying fourth planet in search of an important member of their cluster.

7

Sentinel positioned itself between two solar systems waiting to steer a comet of the right size toward the planet to help bring it back to life. It had been two or three eons since the entity had traveled through intergalactic space. Locating a comet was proving to be difficult.

Waiting was not Sentinel's favorite pastime. It wanted to supervise the return of life to the planet it had so dutifully cared for in its early stages of development. Life would have to be nurtured to recover after the killer asteroid had done its job and wiped out the monstrosities that had evolved in Sentinel's absence.

The entity was about to relocate when it felt the whisper of a familiar vibration. Sentinel tasted Other's message over and over. The vibration was so weak, the message was barely decipherable.

After enhancing the minuscule blip with gradual energy surges, Sentinel finally understood. The comet would have to wait. Other and the cloud were in danger. Sentinel blinked back home.

Sentinel appeared just above the fourth planet. Its cloud was not there to greet it. The planet sat lifeless. A giant dust storm swirled overhead from the catastrophic collision with an alien craft that lay in a crater still smoldering from the impact.

The entity tasted the strange object. No life signs were detected, but something was familiar about the chemical signatures of the wreckage. Family! There was no mistaking the taste of the far-away planet Family had attempted to colonize but became stranded in an evolutionary quagmire until Sentinel and its cloud rescued it.

Now, Family had sent an instrument of destruction to the solar system Sentinel had been caring for. This was in direct violation of Sentinel's command to cease interference. Now, there was no trace of Other or its cloud.

Sentinel started to glow a soft yellow, which slowly morphed into a dark orange then exploded into fiery red. The forgotten anger of a thousand lifetimes was now coalescing. The entity remembered the pain of losing long-forgotten family members: parents, siblings, mates and offspring.

Now, that anger was focused on Family — that swarming cloud of entities which cast cold, calculating verdicts of life or death among its members. Family had issued another order of nonexistence. Once again, Sentinel had escaped and now Family would be the recipient of its judgment — total annihilation.

Sentinel recalculated the coordinates of Family's planet. Before blinking off on its mission, the entity emitted thousands of message vibrations of its plan that only its cluster could decipher. If remnants of its cloud were still conscious somewhere out there in the void, perhaps they would intercept one of the vibrations and rejoin Sentinel.

The entity made a quick visit to the third planet. The signs were encouraging. It sensed life, barely, struggling to survive. The giant cloud of dust and debris already was showing signs of dissipating. Sentinel left a tiny watcher energy behind to act as a beacon and then plotted its course to the planet occupied by Family.

Sentinel blinked into orbit around one of the rogue planet's three moons. It wanted to assess activity on the planet before taking action. The planet was a hub of activity. Dozens of flying objects were entering and leaving the atmosphere. Hundreds of satellites orbited the world.

One of the ships cruised by the moon Sentinel was using for cover. Curious, the entity followed the slow-moving object. It got close enough to sense the vibrations of the occupants. Several hundred living creatures were going about their business. Sentinel detected no threat, so it decided a tasting was in order.

The ship's systems all exploded in a zap due to the power surge from Sentinel's presence. The creatures inside the ship started to emit high-pitched vocalizations as smoke filled the compartments. Satisfied the object posed no threat, Sentinel sent another energy jolt through the ship. Everything went still at once inside the strange metallic container. Sentinel let the ship drift off into space.

Now, it was time to check out those small objects orbiting the planet. Sentinel tried to taste them but they kept exploding from the power surges. The entity felt vibrations coming from the surface. After a nanosecond or two of meditation, Sentinel determined they were rudimentary communications.

It waited for retribution to see how the planet's inhabitants would defend this obvious encroachment on their territory. Nothing came. The communication vibrations grew more numerous and intense, but no more than that.

With nothing to prohibit it, Sentinel proceeded to destroy every satellite in orbit. It took almost no energy, just a few vibration jolts here and there and then silence. No annoying buzzing back and forth from the planet.

Sentinel turned its attention to the asteroid belt. Its next action would leave no doubt as to the fate of the planet. The entity had declared the planet to be full of abominations. The verdict — nonexistence.

8

Sentinel rested on the huge asteroid. It was almost the size of one of the planet's moons. Memories from past military campaigns floated back into the entity's consciousness. Send in a scout to check out the opponent's capabilities. Yes, that would do. Sentinel gave the giant rock a pulse of energy and sent it hurtling toward Family's home world.

The planet's reaction to the threat from space was interesting. Dozens of those flying containers swooped up from the planet and streaked toward the asteroid on an intercept mission. The defenders closed in on the space rock and started firing forays of projectiles until it exploded into thousands of pieces.

Like gnats swarming to a wound, the flyers chased down the larger chunks and proceeded to fire more projectiles until they had broken up into harmless pieces that would disintegrate in their planet's atmosphere.

Sentinel emitted a soft blue glow as it watched the defenders' action with an odd sensation — amusement. Another interesting sensation it would hope to feel again if it had the chance to experience life in a biological form.

It took many solar hours for those mechanical insects to finally quit chasing and firing at the remnants of the asteroid. Half of them returned to the planet, but the others stayed in orbit in an apparent defensive maneuver.

Sentinel could have tasted the defenders and exterminated them with massive jolts of energy, but the entity had other plans. It blinked back to the asteroid belt, gathered thousands of the space rocks and nudged each one on an intercept course with the rogue planet.

Before the armada of asteroids reached the outermost moon, hundreds of the flying defenders rose from the planet in an effort to ward off the attack. Sentinel left nothing to chance this time. It gave energy jolts to hundreds of the rocks, increasing their incoming speed a thousand times.

The defenders had no answer for the asteroids which were now careening past them at a speed they could barely track. The ships tried firing at the incoming rocks but were ineffective. Many of the flyers were struck and exploded in brief flashes of fireballs.

The surviving containers hurtled themselves at some of the larger asteroids in futile suicide interception attempts. But their efforts were for naught. Most of Sentinel's missiles broke through the atmosphere and ripped into the planet with such tremendous force that it shuddered and wobbled slightly off its orbit.

Millions of pieces of debris were ejected off the surface from the concussive force of the asteroids. After circling their home for hundreds of solar years, these chunks of debris would plummet back home in round after round of destructive collisions. The planet would never host life again.

Sentinel watched the scene impassively. Almost lost among the planet's destruction was a fleet of ships that tried to escape. All but one of those flyers were hit and destroyed. The lone ship, a massive vehicle, much larger than the defenders, gathered speed and sped away from its home world. Sentinel marked the ship's course. It would be easy to intercept later.

Sentinel waited for the life forces of those millions of sentient beings to coalesce. The individual energies would be in a state of confusion at having been ripped out of their bodies in such a traumatic event. They would be like moths drawn to the flame of his massive vibration.

It contemplated what to do with this new host of entities. Sentinel could form them into a new family or it could destroy them once and for all. The entity had given Family chances to exist peacefully, but at every opportunity, the cloud had sought to enact revenge on Sentinel.

Now, the entity emitted a strong vibration. Within seconds, the energies from those biological forms on the planet started to swarm around Sentinel. The entity invited them to bond and then dined on their energies, carrying out its verdict of nonexistence.

Glowing with an even stronger vibration after its feast, Sentinel set out in search of the ship to finish its mission. The entity was impressed at the speed the flying container had achieved. It had traveled almost one-millionth of a blink away from the planet. Impressive for a physical object.

Just as Sentinel was about to taste the flyer, a small glowing orb intercepted it. Sentinel paused, sensing a familiar vibration. The orb dissipated into a small cloud surrounding a larger energy force, which slowly approached Sentinel. The vibration was weak but there was no mistaking it — Other.

Sentinel glowed with white energy. It felt another surge of a forgotten emotion — happiness. It would have to research this feeling further. Other tentatively approached Sentinel, aware of its higher vibration. Rushing to bond would have fizzled Other into nonexistence.

The two entities swirled around each other barely touching like long lost lovers. Sentinel detected that Other's vibration was much weaker than it remembered, but it was still the same partner it had shared all those lifetimes with.

Sentinel sent a series of micro charges into Other and let the entity slowly regain its former energy signature. What seemed like an eternity — which was only a few seconds in solar time — Other had regained its original vibration and was ready to bond.

The two entities merged. The combined orb glowed white again. Sentinel tasted Other. It learned the remnants of their cloud that survived the robot ship attack had tracked down Other and found it hovering almost a blink away barely emitting a vibration. What was left of the cloud fed their energies into Other until they could perform a viable orb capable of blink travel. The renewed cloud intercepted one of Sentinel's message vibrations and blinked away to find the entity.

Learning of Sentinel's actions, Other broke the bond and blinked yellow with disappointment. Sentinel flashed its intention to finish its mission — send any entity connected with Family into nonexistence.

Other communicated it wanted to taste the life forms in the escaping ship. With its reason for revenge abated, Sentinel acquiesced to the request. All the entities blinked after the ship.

The last time Other came in contact with a ship, the effort almost destroyed the entity. It approached the flyer but didn't taste the foreign object. Other could sense the energies inside and read their vibrations.

Returning to Sentinel, Other reported the highest vibrations it sensed were fear, the instinct to survive and last of all, hope. Sentinel and Other bonded once more and debated the fate of the survivors of the destroyed planet.

When they parted, Sentinel called in the remaining cloud and issued its edict. The entities — Sentinel, Other and the cloud — merged into a glowing white orb and blinked back to the third planet from the sun in that out-of-the-way solar system.

The flying container was allowed to continue on its mission of survival to succeed or fail on its own.

Sentinel's cloud — more like a wisp, now — thoroughly examined the third planet. The great cloud spawned by the asteroid impact was dissipating nicely. More sun was breaking through the atmosphere.

Plants were flourishing. The small creatures that had been transported back to their home world were spreading out and growing in size and numbers. Only time could heal the planet now. It would be hundreds of thousands of solar years until the creatures would be capable of experiencing self-awareness.

Sentinel glowed with the excess energy of all those entities it absorbed after destroying Family's planet. It was time to recharge Other and the remnants of its cloud.

The entity vibrated its wishes to revisit the second planet from the sun so its cloud could soak in the energy and wait for the right time when they could conjoin with those biological organisms and experience life once again.

9

The leader of the small group of primates munched on a large piece of fruit as he crouched on a limb overlooking the small valley. He was watching over his family unit as they grazed and searched for any tasty morsels they could uncover from underneath rocks and fallen trees.

He carefully scanned the horizon, looking for signs of predators. Grass moving against the breeze or scolding birds would be a signal for him to emit a throaty growl that would send his troop racing to the safety of the giant trees.

An unfamiliar noise, a crackle like dozens of twigs being snapped at the same time, made him flinch. The hair on his body stood out all at once. His skin felt like it was being pricked by a thousand biting insects.

The male started to scratch himself to relieve the annoying sensation when a flash of light blinded him. Feeling himself growing limp, the leader let out a whimper, made a feeble attempt to grasp the limb, but fell, collapsing in a heap on the forest floor.

Sensing something was wrong, the alpha female paused from her search for food and looked up just in time to see her mate plummet from his perch. She woofed a warning to the troop, but before any of the members could react, flashes of light exploded all around, blinding them. As if in a choreographed move, the troop fell to the ground in unison.

The leader groaned in pain as he slowly uncoiled from the fetal position he had curled up in after toppling from his perch in the tree. His head throbbed with an unfamiliar pain.

He rose and set out on wobbly legs to search for his troop. Hearing or seeing nothing, the male called out a frantic bark. The leader had never been out of sight from a troop member. The thought of being alone terrified him.

A soft whimper from nearby drew his attention. The male stumbled toward the sound and discovered the bodies of his fallen troop. Seeing his mate lying in a heap, the male scrambled over and stroked her face. She twitched slightly and tried to lift her head toward him but could not move.

Fearing for the vulnerable position of his troop, the leader barked out a sharp warning. As if a switch was turned on, members of the troop all started struggling to rise to their feet. His alarm call had triggered their flight instincts and now their bodies were finally responding.

In a rare show of concern, the leader ran to each member of his troop, nudging them, encouraging them to get to their feet. Several minutes later, the troop scurried back to the safety of the trees, unharmed but frightened from the strange experience.

The leader of the primate group hadn't slept well after the strange incident that had knocked him and his troop out. He awoke with a start. His troop members stared at him with frightened eyes. He had been twitching and growling in his sleep. The male had never experienced such a vivid dream.

He sat up and stretched. The scene from his dream replayed itself. It was a memory from when he was young, barely weaned. He and one of his siblings were fighting over food when the other youngster picked up a rock and struck him. The action of the blow replayed in slow motion over and over again.

The large male climbed to the highest point in the tree that would support his weight and surveyed the landscape. His troop had been hiding in the foliage for almost a day.

Seeing no danger, the leader barked the all clear signal. The troop uncharacteristically clung to their hiding places afraid to leave the safety of the trees. A growl in his stomach reminded the leader of his hunger. He looked around for his mate but didn't see her with the troop.

Ignoring the others, the leader scrambled to the ground and went to find her and possibly food. Not long into his search, he heard a sound like the wind whistling through the trees, followed by a series of thumps. Crouching in the grass, the male slowly made his way to the source of the noise.

Peeking over a large fallen tree trunk, he was astounded at the sight. His mate stood on top of a pile of logs and was using a stick to knock down fruit from branches that normally would have been impossible to reach.

He stood up and greeted her with his signature woof, but it sounded more like a question than a command. She cooed a greeting and proudly brandished her long stick. Her lips curled up in a strange contortion that usually was reserved for tasting honey — that treat which was hard to find and painful to extract.

The male sauntered over to his mate to examine her handiwork. She climbed down from the logs pile and demonstrated how she dragged the pieces over and put them together. His mate was just about to show him her fruit-collecting method when a rumbling growl made them freeze in fear.

A large spotted feline slowly crept forward out of the underbrush, then launched itself at the pair. Instead of running, the male grabbed the largest nearby rock and swung it at the cat's head. The resounding blow crushed the attacker's skull but not before it collided with the male, sending him crashing to the ground underneath the spotted body.

The female primate let out a scream of fury and proceeded to beat the feline's twitching body with another shorter and stouter stick. Her blows were for naught. The cat was already dead. With a groan, the male shoved the carcass away and rose to his feet.

The two primates stood staring at each other in shock and surprise. She clutched the stick, and he still grasped the blood-soaked rock. The pair gazed at each other for a moment, then tenderly stroked each other's faces. Recognition of something deeper, something familiar, passed between them.

The male let loose with a mighty howl of triumph that echoed through the trees. Shortly afterwards, the other members of their troop joined them and examined the bloody scene. All but one of Family's members avoided the feline's body. Most of them eagerly snatched up the fallen fruit and began to eat their fill.

One of the fruit gatherers studied her pile and began to break off tender twigs from nearby bushes. She started to weave a small replica of the nests the troop fashioned for themselves at night to keep them from falling from the trees.

The pieces of fruit looked like eggs to her. She began to plop them into the little nest. The female admired her work, picked up her fruit-filled basket and carried it back to the trees to feed her offspring.

A lone member of the troop poked at the warm carcass. She swiped a finger over the skull and smacked her lips as she tasted the blood. The troop had witnessed the attack and their leaders' response.

The female picked up a small rock, then sat down and proceeded to strike it against a large boulder. She hammered away with her small rock until a sharp point was formed. Returning to the carcass, she knelt and started scraping until finally cutting through the fur and skin. With a woof of pride, she managed to peel away the outer layers to reveal muscles and tissues.

Other members of the troop stopped eating and watched the new cleaning and skinning procedure with great interest. After satisfying their hunger, the troop split up into groups and mimicked the workers.

All the fruit soon was gathered into those small nests for easy transport. With the help from more hands and freshly pounded out sharp edges, the carcass was cleaned and meat divided among the members.

As they worked, the members of the troop grunted with pleasure and eyed each other with pride. Even a booming crack of thunder and sudden dousing of a heavy rainfall did not deter them.

Something had changed in this small group of creatures. They saw themselves in a different light. The world would be theirs to conquer.

THE ARCHITECTS OF THE PEOPLE

1

Other approached Sentinel, requesting permission to merge. Sentinel flashed an affirmative. After five nanoseconds, the entities separated. Other had relayed information that the sentient creatures on the planet were getting close to a watershed moment.

The two species they had been monitoring were getting close to meeting. This would be an important interaction. Sentinel considered the circumstance. Perhaps it would be an opportunity to bond again with the organisms to shape their evolution and once again feel the exhilaration of life.

Other flashed its approval. Now, they had to wait for the right moment. Sentinel disliked this part. Planetary time was always such a short experience.

The young woman pushed her way through the long grass near the river looking for reeds she could use to make her sought-after baskets. She paused intermittently and listened for any signs of danger.

Rabbitcatcher-Son-Spearmaker stood watch nearby. Hearing her stop, he checked his sister's position, then whistled the all-clear signal. Ever since one of those terrifying huge cats killed a ten-year-old girl from their family group, all errands were done in pairs for protection.

The young man was bored. He agreed to accompany Basketweaver-Daughter-Oldmother only when Spearmaker-Family-Father whacked him alongside the head. His ears were still ringing a bit from the blow. Rabbitcatcher knew the smack from his father's hand could have crushed his skull. It had just been a wordless do-as-I-tell-you command.

Rabbitcatcher stood under a huge oak and gazed at the geese across the river. His mouth watered at the thought of raiding one of their nests and snatching a couple of eggs to suck out that delicious juice inside. The geese had abandoned the near side of the river ever since Spearmaker's family group migrated to the area two months ago.

Basketweaver reached down to pluck out one more thick stem to add to the pile she cradled in her opposite arm when the geese across the river exploded in a flurry of wings and frightened honks. Instinctively, she and Rabbitcatcher dropped to protective squatting positions.

Laughter and shouting erupted from the opposite bank as several young men waded into the water and pulled out two geese felled by spears. The hunters were making strange, high-pitched sounds. Their words sounded like squirrels chattering.

Basketweaver stared at the others in wonder. They were taller and darker skinned than her people. Their faces were an odd oval shape and lacked the prominent eyebrow bridge of her people. The hunters climbed out of the water and held up their trophies in a triumphant gesture as others from their party gathered around.

A soft series of whistles broke Basketweaver's concentration. Rabbitcatcher was signaling it was time to leave — quietly. She rose slightly but still hunched over and made her way silently out of the grass. Rabbitcatcher intercepted her route and gave his sister a hard shove to make her move faster. He was worried about those strange-looking people. They would have to tell Spearmaker about what they had seen.

More shouting and splashing made the two siblings freeze in their tracks. Rabbitcatcher tapped his sister's head, softly this time. The gesture meant "stay down." He rose slightly just so he could peer over the top of the grass.

Despite himself, he let out a grunt of surprise. The people on the other side of the river had waded about half way across and were shouting and moving their hands back and forth.

"Brother, what are they doing?" Basketweaver asked. After determining the others had stopped and weren't pursuing them, he shook his head and gestured for her to take a look. She rose and saw the group of about twenty all waggling their hands over their heads and shouting. The strangers were laughing and pointing at her and Rabbitcatcher.

"They are not making war sounds," she said. "I do not understand."

Taking a last look, Rabbitcatcher shrugged and turned away. "Go. We must find Spearmaker."

Naroo was yelling triumphantly as he held up the goose his spear had successfully brought down. It had been over a day since his clan had bagged anything. They were getting hungry and anxious.

He gave his prize to one of the women to admire when he noticed movement across the river. Two people were sneaking away from the water. Naroo could barely make them out as they slunk low to the ground, but there was no doubt. People!

Naroo pointed and shouted with glee. These were the first people they had encountered in two full moons. Tajeer looked to see where his brother was gesturing. Soon all the clan members scrambled into the water in their excitement of seeing others of their kind.

Their shouts grew happier when the two people stopped to look their way. But the cheers turned to groans when the pair turned and disappeared into the trees.

"Did we scare them, my brother?" Tajeer asked while shading his eyes with a hand. "They were fair skins like the others we saw two moons ago."

Disappointed, Naroo put his arms down and shook his head. "We must frighten them. They are different, not of our clan or our people. The others we saw disappeared into the mountains. We must be careful if we meet again."

Tajeer poked his brother in the arm. "Come, let us find a place to camp. Our people are hungry. We will look for the others later."

Spearmaker-Family-Father frowned as he listened to the excited siblings. Rabbitcatcher and Basketweaver had seen strange people across the river. Taller, dark-skinned people not of their family.

Basketweaver painted the outlines of the stranger on a rock. Then she gathered some ashes from the fire pit, smudged them with water and filled in the outlines with the dark stain. Other members of the family gasped in shock.

Oldmother listened carefully and rocked back and forth, trying to let a memory resurface. "We have heard stories of these tall ones. Foxhair-Family-Father discovered some dark skins two seasons ago."

Spearmaker nodded. "He spoke of this at the last gathering of the peoples. It was a good story. One for a long campfire." Spearmaker was silent for a long while as he gazed into fire blazing in the pit.

"We will welcome these strangers if we see them again. They killed geese with spears. I have not done that. We will see if they come in peace. Good hunters will be welcome."

He turned to Rabbitcatcher. "Watch these strangers. Do not cross Mother Water. If she swallows you, Rabbitcatcher will dwell in the darkness forever."

The young man swallowed hard but nodded. "Yes, Family-Father, I will do as you ask," he answered, unconsciously rubbing the side of his head.

2

Rabbitcatcher watched the strangers from across the river as best he could. The tall dark skins foraged and traveled up the river. He was impressed by their hunting skills. They were catching fish and killing game successfully.

He could see their fires at night. Rabbitcatcher wondered how the strangers could manage so many fires. His family had to maintain one constantly burning fire in a pit. If it went out, they were left without light, warmth and a cooking source until they found flames after a lightning strike.

After following them north for four days, Rabbitcatcher turned back. The dark skins were leaving Spearmaker's territory and entering the hunting grounds of Elkhunter-Family-Father.

Rabbitcatcher would not be welcome in the other family's territory. The strangers may not fare well if they were discovered by an Elkhunter party. The other family aggressively protected their area.

He carved a mark on a large tree to show where he stopped. It was time to go home. Rabbitcatcher was hungry after dining only on roots, grubs and a few rodents he had managed to catch.

The young hunter also was exhausted from trying to keep up with the strangers. He could match their walking pace, but if they broke into a run, especially when chasing game, Rabbitcatcher could barely keep up. His lungs burned and his shorter legs ached from the stress when he finally caught up to them.

Rabbitcatcher turned to leave when he froze at the snap of a twig and then another and another. Three older hunters carrying heavy clubs emerged from the trees. They were from the Elkhunter clan. Seeing he was outnumbered, Rabbitcatcher dropped his spear and held out his hands with palms up to indicate he did not intend to fight.

"You must be lost, little brother," one of the brutes said as he walked to within one pace of Rabbitcatcher. The speaker bent down, picked up the dropped spear and examined it closely. "Ah, the workmanship tells a story. You are from Spearmaker's clan. You hunt alone and far away from your family."

Rabbitcatcher took a deep breath, trying to control the fear that was roiling in his guts. "Greetings, hunters. Yes, I have traveled far from the Spearmaker clan. Forgive me, I did not know I walk on your ground. I do not hunt. I follow dark-skin strangers across the river. They do not look like they come from the people."

The one who spoke stared at Rabbitcatcher for a long while. "All ground Elkhunter clan hunts is ours," he snarled. "Dark-skin strangers? Show me young one. You will live if you speak the truth."

Rabbitcatcher pointed toward the river. "Family father commanded me to follow them. I have watched them for four sunrises. They hunt birds and large animals near the water. They eat, camp and move quickly."

The leader cocked his head to one side and gestured for Rabbitcatcher to lead the way. The young man turned and walked toward the edge of the tree line where he had last seen the strangers. He knew his life depended on finding the dark skins. Remembering the friendly shouting from the strangers the first time he saw them, Rabbitcatcher hoped they would show themselves again.

Tajeer climbed down from where he had been keeping watch high in a pine tree, then ran to find his brother. "Naroo, the young one who has been watching us has returned, but others are with him. Three large males. They push him with their clubs. He is standing at the water's edge, not hiding."

Naroo frowned as he considered this change in the light skins. His clan was aware they were being watched from across the river. Tajeer had seen a shadow duck around trees, then got a good look at the young man when he came to the water's edge at dawn for a quick drink. It looked to be the same young man they had seen with a girl four days ago.

"Our friend is being threatened. Why?"

Tajeer shrugged. "He has been watching us quietly. Now others threaten him. They all are looking across the river."

Naroo paused. "Our people. They must be looking for us. Let us show ourselves."

The three hunters who captured Rabbitcatcher stood gaping at the sight. Across the river, a large group of tall, dark-skinned people were laughing and filling water skins. The strangers made a lot of noise. Some waded into the water and washed.

Rabbitcatcher was never happier to see the others in his life. One of the tall men waded a distance from the others bobbing up and down in the water. He dove under the surface, then came up with a splash, shaking his long hair as water flew everywhere.

The stranger caught Rabbitcatcher's attention and gave an almost imperceptible nod. The two locked eyes for a moment. Rabbitcatcher walked to the river's edge, lowered himself on his haunches, cupped his hand, dipped it in the water, took a drink and looked up. A relieved smile creased his face.

Naroo turned and waded back to shore. He surveyed his clan for another moment, then called them back to their camp site.

The leader of the three hunters walked over and stood beside Rabbitcatcher. He gazed across the river and watched the dark skins melt back into the woods. "You tell the truth, little brother. Who are those strange ones? Where do they come from?" His words bore no malice this time.

Rabbitcatcher shrugged. "I do not know. They appeared across the river when I was watching my sister gather plants. They yelled strange talk at us but did not attack."

The leader glanced at his captive, then continued staring across the river. "You live another day, young one. Return to Spearmaker. Tell him Elkhunter family will chase these intruders away if they dare cross Mother Water."

Rabbitcatcher nodded. "Yes, elder." He gazed at his spear the leader still held. The older hunter gave the weapon one more admiring look and tossed it back to Rabbitcatcher despite the grunts of disapproval from his two companions.

He frowned at the others. "We do not steal from babies." Turning toward Rabbitcatcher, he gestured for him to leave. "Do not return. These are my family's hunting grounds."

Rabbitcatcher stood frozen in his tracks. "You are Elkhunter?" He almost choked on the name.

The other man nodded. "Leave now, little brother." Rabbitcatcher needed no further incentive. He backed away a few feet, then jogged away as fast as he could.

Tajeer smiled from his hiding spot behind a fallen tree as he watched the drama unfold across the river. The young man, who had been following his clan, had been set free. It was obvious he was frightened of his captors.

The three other men walked to the water's edge and continued staring across the river. Tajeer's eyes widened in surprise as the largest one of the three waded part way into the water and pointed to where Tajeer was hiding.

A large growl emanated from the man in the river. He lifted his club over his head and struck the water with a large splash. Tajeer frowned. He knew a threat when he saw one.

Tajeer rose from his not-so-hidden spot and strode a few feet into the water. He raised his spear in a defiant gesture. The two men stared at each other for a long moment, then returned to their respective people. Both would have dramatic stories to tell over the campfires that night.

3

Naroo and the other men sat quietly after hearing Tajeer's tale about the encounter with the large light-skinned man across the river. The farther north their band trekked, the more mountainous the terrain became.

The few groups of light skins they had met had reacted with fear or with threats. The farther north they explored, those strange people seemed to grow more aggressive.

"We find land that gives us better shelter when we travel north up the great river, but the light skins do not welcome us," Naroo said, shaking his head. "I do not wish to fight them."

Tajeer studied the fire as he poked a long stick into the embers. "We may have a friend to the south. The young one who was captured and then freed will remember us."

Naroo looked at the others. "What say you, my brothers?" The three other men sitting around the campfire voiced their agreement. Naroo nodded and picked up five sticks. "I will ask the others at the fires, then we will count the sticks."

The next morning Naroo's group gathered their belongings and made plans to head south. No one at the other fires had cast a stick to continue traveling north. At least the terrain would be familiar, and the light skins may be less war like.

When the women returned to the river in the morning to replenish their water supplies, they were greeted by threatening shouts from three large light-skinned men across the water. A young girl was dispatched to find the men. Naroo, Tajeer and the other men came running to discover three new light-skin men striking their clubs into the water and howling like the wolves they had to guard against at night.

Naroo raised his spear and shouted. His men formed a circle. They began to twirl, thrusting their spears into the air and shouted in unison. The dark skins moved faster and faster. Their twirling became hypnotic and the crescendo of their voices were joined by their women.

The three light skins stopped and watched the dancing strangers in awe. They had never seen such a coordinated display before. Without warning, the dark skins shouted in unison, rushed into the river and thrust their spears at the light skins.

Instinctively, the three light skins backed out of the water and scampered back to the tree line. The retreat produced a chorus of laughter and taunts from the dark skins. The three men of Elkhunter's family stared at the whooping strangers, then disappeared into the brush.

Tajeer laughed as he saw the three light skins leave in haste. "Look, brother, we frightened those rabbits!"

Naroo called for the group to gather in traveling formation. He squinted across the river one more time. The leader could barely make out the three shapes, but they were there still watching.

He smiled and gestured north. "We will give those brave warriors something to think about." The travelers set out, walked until the shade changed directions on the trees, moved out of sight from the river and turned south.

Elkhunter was so enraged at the news, he cuffed one of the three scouts in the head, causing the man to crumple to the ground. "No one challenges Elkhunter clan," he growled.

The leader pointed to a young man, who stood frowning nearby. "Wolfkiller-Son-Elkhunter pick two more of my sons and follow those strangers. They will be trophies on our spears if they walk on our land."

Wolfkiller gestured at two men about his age. Without another word, the three set out to find the strangers. Elkhunter turned to the original three spies. "You three stay with the women when the men go hunting." He snorted with disgust as the man he struck sat up with a groan and swayed dizzyingly from side to side.

Five days later, Wolfkiller's group stumbled into camp. The bedraggled hunters said nothing as they plopped down by the fire pit. After hearing of their return, Elkhunter snarled at the young men. "Why do you return? Did you find the dark skins?"

Wolfkiller rose and confronted his father. "We watched and waited. We traveled north for three days and saw no sign, heard nothing. I do not know where the strangers walk." He braced himself for a likely attack. Family-Father did not like bad news.

The two men locked eyes. Elkhunter would have punished any other man in his family, but Wolfkiller was coming into his full maturity. He was as tall as his father and perhaps even broader. The young man was almost ready to lead his own group or challenge his father for leadership of the established family. Elkhunter was reluctant to spark that confrontation.

"The strangers walk away. I am pleased," Elkhunter said and nodded toward Wolfkiller. The younger man let out a sigh of relief and plopped back down among his brothers to rest and eat.

Spearmaker listened intently to Rabbitcatcher's story. He knew his son was fortunate not to have become a trophy for the enemy clan. "The dark skins showed themselves to Elkhunter?"

Rabbitcatcher nodded. "Yes, Family-Father. He saw them. I left when Elkhunter told me to go. I heard him shouting war talk. I was too far away to see."

Spearmaker cast a quick glance at the young man. He was surprised and pleased his son had lived after confronting the old enemy. "A wise move. It is always best to walk away and live to see the sun rise over the trees again."

Family-Father reached down to pick up a stone he had been carefully chipping away at to fashion one of his trademark spear heads. "I would not be sad to see Elkhunter killed by the dark skins." Everyone at fire pit grunted in unison.

4

Naroo and Tajeer peered out over the bend in the river. Naroo glanced at his brother. "This is the place where you first saw the watcher with the young female?"

Tajeer nodded. "It is a good spot for fishing and hunting. We can build huts and make it our home on the high ground not far from the water. The light skins will find us one day, then we will worry how to cross this water."

The family group had been at the site about a week when a familiar figure appeared across the river. A larger man was at his side. But this time, the other man did not look threatening, only curious.

Tajeer smiled and walked into the river, laughing as he bobbed up and down in the water. The young light skin also grinned, walked to the water's edge, knelt and scooped up a drink with his hands. The two men were repeating the actions of the last time they saw each other.

Naroo watched from the bank, picked up a fish as long as his arm and waded in next to Tajeer. He bowed and thrust the fish toward the light skins in a gesture of sharing.

The larger light skinned man gestured toward his companion. The young man reached behind him and pulled a dead rabbit out of a fold from the crude fur skin covering his torso and handed it to his elder. Spearmaker took a few cautious steps into the water and held up the rabbit.

Naroo and Spearmaker nodded to each other and retreated back to dry land. The gestures of food sharing were understood by both men. Spearmaker handed the rabbit back to his son. "The dark skins come in peace. That is good. If they live through the great cold and walk across Mother Water when she turns to stone, we will welcome them."

That summer and into fall, members of Spearmaker's clan occasionally visited the bend in the river to watch the dark skins go about their daily lives. The children, especially, stared in awe as the strangers frolicked and washed in the river, something their people would not do. Too many times one of their people had been snatched by Mother River's watery embrace, never to return.

The visits to watch the strangers grew less frequent as the air turned colder and leaves fell. All of Spearmaker's clan spent the time either hunting, gathering berries and roots or collecting dead wood to keep their lone fire alive.

Naroo's family had survived through three snowy winters since they left their warmer homeland in search of more game and land that did not die in the baking sun of summer. They had learned to build solid shelters of bark and skins that would keep them warm along with the fires they could start from nothing but a stick and grooved stone.

Winter arrived without warning. The first blizzard lasted for days, almost burying the huts of Naroo's people. It was fortunate the men had successfully hunted throughout the fall. Food was plentiful for the two first months, but the cold held onto its grip, and snow fell almost every other day.

The dark skins huddled by their fires and watched the food supply dwindle away day by day. The snow was so deep, the hunters had to trudge through waist-deep drifts. Game was scarce. Not a bird sang nor animal moved.

Frustrated by sitting at the fire and not being able to hunt, Tajeer gathered an elk blanket around himself and tromped through the snow toward the river. It had been almost three full moons since he had seen the light skins. He doubted they would be near the water this time of the year.

Tajeer stopped at what had been the water's edge and stared in wonder. No sound of running water greeting him. The hunter stared across what had been the river. Only a great expanse of white and silence stretched out before him. This was the farthest north his clan had traveled and set up permanent dwellings.

No familiar faces of the light skins were to be seen, only the lonely silhouettes of trees. Tajeer sat for a while studying the white landscape until the cold started to seep into his muscles and bones.

He started to turn back to seek the warmth of his hut when movement on what should have been the river caught his attention. Instinctively, he hunkered down out of sight to watch the figures moving towards him.

An elk was running through the snow on top of where there should have been water. Its tongue was hanging out of its mouth as the animal desperately tried to stay ahead of a wolf pack that was keeping a silent but determined chase.

Tajeer watched in wonder as the wolves slowly gained on the panting elk. He could hear the labored breathing of the elk as it struggled through the snow. The leader of the wolf pack now was less than a length away from the elk when it lunged for a leg and bit into it.

The elk bellowed in pain, turned and tried to defend itself. Another wolf leaped in from a different direction and clamped on to another leg. The lead wolf grabbed for the bleeding leg. With a chorus of snarls, the remainder of the pack closed in and brought down their exhausted quarry.

Tajeer had seen wolves bring down prey before but never on top of a river. The frozen water held up to the combined weight of the elk and wolf pack. The animals seemed unconcerned about falling into icy water.

The wolves hadn't been at their feast long when they were spooked by a series of howls and clanging of rocks. A group of people, covered with animal hides, moved slowly toward the pack. The light skins were wielding clubs and short spears.

Most of the pack slunk away, snarling their displeasure through blood-stained muzzles. Only the pack leader stood his ground. His hackles were raised and lips turned up to reveal an impressive set of killing fangs.

As the people closed in on the carcass, Tajeer recognized the light skin watcher and the older man he had seen before. Six other adult males joined them as they slowly advanced on the elk kill.

Spearmaker and the others halted a short distance away. Without a signal, the eight men closed ranks, thrust out their spears and advanced on the dead elk and lone wolf. The pack leader glanced back only to see the other wolves retreating even further from the light skins. With one last snarl, he turned and joined them.

The light skins whooped and yelled even louder when they reached the carcass. The wolf pack stood and watched from a safe distance for a moment then turned and retreated into the safety of the trees.

Tajeer had unconsciously stepped out of his hiding place to get a better look at the amazing scene of people and animals standing on the frozen water. A grunt from one of the hunters caused the entire group to turn and look at him. They eyed him for a bit then proceeded to cut up the meat.

One of the men walked slowly toward Tajeer. He then knelt and took a scoop of snow in his hand and raised it to his mouth. Tajeer smiled and slowly strode toward the young man. He paused, shrugged, plopped down in the snow, took a few handfuls and flung it over himself.

Rabbitcatcher laughed and called out to his companions. "Spearmaker-Family-Father, this is the dark skin from the river. He came when Elkhunter found me."

Spearmaker rose from the elk carcass he had been helping butcher and looked at Tajeer watching them work. Seeing hunger in the young dark skin's expression, he tore off a large hunk of flank meat and called Rabbitcatcher over.

The two light skins exchanged a few words. Rabbitcatcher took the hunk of meat and walked toward Tajeer. This was the closest the two men had ever been. Rabbitcatcher stopped within a few yards of Tajeer and held out the meat.

Tajeer was stunned when he realized the light skins were offering food. He held his hands out to show he had nothing to trade and shook his head. Rabbitcatcher cocked his head and turned back to look at Spearmaker.

The older light skin had been watching. He called out to Rabbitcatcher, and patted his head. "Trade for the fur on his head. I have never seen such a thing."

Rabbitcatcher turned back toward Tajeer and pointed to his fur hat. Tajeer sighed when he understood what the light skins were offering in trade. He liked the hat, which Naroo's mate had made for him, but his people needed food and they had plenty of furs.

Tajeer pulled off his hat and gave it to Rabbitcatcher. The young light skin took the hat and handed over the hunk. Tajeer's stomach growled loudly when he smelled the fresh meat.

Rabbitcatcher frowned when he saw Tajeer's reaction. "Family-Father, this dark skin is hungry. His people must not have food." Spearmaker grunted, tore off another hunk of meat, walked over to Tajeer and handed him the second piece.

Tajeer bowed and took the second piece. "Thank you, elder," he said tapping his heart. Spearmaker used his spear to trace a stick figure of a person in the snow and pointed at Tajeer. He then drew a group of stick figures, pointed to the meat Tajeer was holding, swept his arm toward the dark skin camp and patted his stomach.

The young dark skin studied the figures in the snow and the gestures the light skin was making. His stomach growled again. The two light skins pointed to him and patted their stomachs.

Tajeer finally understood that the light skins were asking if his people had enough food. He shook his head.

Spearmaker grunted, pointed to the stick figures in the snow and gestured toward his people. He then called to the group. A man almost as large as Spearmaker stopped what he was doing and joined the three men.

The leader of the light skins pointed at the wolf tracks, tapped his nose, gestured toward his two companions, then pointed at Tajeer. The dark skin shook his head in puzzlement. Rabbitcatcher picked up a stick, drew three stick figures walking and pointed at himself, the new light skin and Tajeer.

The dark skin hunter finally understood. "Ah, you are worried the wolves will smell the meat and attack. You want Watcher and this new man to accompany me. Very good! Let's go."

Rabbitcatcher looked at his companion. "I think he understands. His talk sounds like a squirrel scolding." The other man shrugged.

Spearmaker turned to his two kinsmen. "If you can make him understand, tell the stranger his people are welcome at our fires."

Tajeer waved for the two men to follow, picked up the chunks of meat and headed back to his people's encampment. When the three men neared the huts, Tajeer called out a greeting.

Dark skins emerged from four large round huts. Rabbitkiller and his companion hung back as Tajeer's people welcomed him and rejoiced at seeing the meat he carried.

Tajeer told his people about what he had seen and the generosity of the light skins. Naroo's mate ducked into one of the huts and emerged with two large elk hides. Tajeer took the hides and gave them to the two dark skins.

The large light skin rolled them up. "This is a good trade. But we cannot eat these when the people are hungry," the older light skin man said.

Rabbitcatcher looked at his companion. "We will find more animals to hunt. Let us return to the others." Before he left, the young man pointed toward Tajeer and his people, tapped his chest then waved toward the river. He repeated his gestures, smiled, then turned to follow his companion.

Without another word, the two light skins trudged back through the snow to help carry the bounty of meat back to their people. Naroo grasped Tajeer's shoulder. "It is a good thing what they have done for our people. But their talk sounds like a wolf growling."

Tajeer nodded. "My brother, I think the light skins want us to come with them. Perhaps they have better shelter and more food to share."

Naroo watched Rabbitcatcher and his friend disappear from sight. "We will discuss this over the fires. But first we eat!" The two brothers laughed and returned to the warmth of their hut.

5

Sentinel flashed its displeasure at Other's suggestion. Its companion of eons proposed the leader of the cloud of entities locate Searcher within itself— its original vibration — and split from it. Other argued Sentinel's higher vibration could kill a sentient on the planet when it attempted to bond with one of them.

The creation of two energy beings from one entity had never been done before in Sentinel's vast memory. Would the two entities be able to reunite? Would the new entity be more powerful than the reborn Searcher?

But the desire to bond with a sentient was powerful. Other was determined to bond, and Sentinel wanted to experience life again.

Sentinel examined all the entities it had assimilated until a familiar vibration emitted a greeting to the combined consciousness. The original Searcher considered the message.

Searcher experienced something like sadness. It would miss the higher vibration and the energy that had evolved into Sentinel. But it was time to taste life again with its gamut of emotions.

Sentinel flashed a rainbow of colors as it struggled to search within itself. Sensing an impending explosion, the entity blinked away into empty space. The explosion that ensued was not unlike a very small star going nova.

A few solar seconds later, two entities blinked back to the cluster. One of the entities emitted a blue glow. It approached Other and sent a vibration of greetings. Other tasted the new entity and flashed white when it recognized Searcher. The two entities encircled each other in a dizzying dance.

After the greeting, Searcher approached what was left of Sentinel. The former entity was glowing yellow, a sign of confusion. Recognizing Searcher's energy signature, it vibrated, "Who am I?"

Searcher sent a message of assurance. "We were Sentinel and many others of Family before I left us."

The new entity considered its plight for a few solar seconds. "I remember a name that seems familiar — Guardian." Searcher flashed its approval. "A being of your powerful vibration will be a vital protector of the cluster. Welcome Guardian." A flash of white showed Guardian approved of its name.

Other was sensing the messages between the two entities. Searcher's old companion vibrated its approval. "Come, the sentients we have fostered on the planet are ready for us. It is time to taste life again."

6

Naroo and his family group had been trudging through the snow for almost a day. His brother, Tajeer, had found the first sign — a large gash in a tree trunk — that apparently pointed the way toward the light skin encampment. However, his people were growing weary of treading through the deep drifts as they carried their belongings with them.

Tajeer had gone ahead to locate more of the directional markings in the hopes of finding the light skins. Carrying no extra weight, only his spear and the furs he wore, he soon outpaced the others and disappeared into the forest that rose slowly up into a mountain range.

Using his shadow stick to mark time, Naroo noted the line on the ground had grown longer at least twice. The sun's light soon would drop below the tree line, and they would be left in the cold and dark without shelter.

Naroo stopped and looked back at his people. The exhausted women were struggling to keep up. He dared not let his people see how worried he felt. If they sensed his desperation, it would only sap more of their energy.

The leader was about to admonish his group to keep walking when a call from a familiar voice echoed through the trees. "Ho, brother!" Naroo smiled and shouted an answer, "Ho, brother, we are here!"

Naroo waited anxiously and was about to yell again when Tajeer called out, "Brother, wait there. We are coming." The leader exhaled a large sigh of relief. His brother must have found the light skins.

Before the shadow grew longer from Naroo's stick, Tajeer tumbled through the snow and shouted a greeting. "I bring friends. Do not be afraid." Ten broad-shouldered light skins stopped behind him. The two groups of people stared at each other for a moment.

Without a word, the light skins took the bundles from the women, hoisted them on their backs, turned and headed back into the trees. "Come, come," Tajeer urged his people. "It is not far now. The light skins have shelter and food."

Naroo grasped his brother's shoulder. "Do they have enough shelter for all of us?"

Tajeer smiled. "Yes, brother. And once we get our fires started, you will be warm again."

The leader gave his brother a quizzical look. "They do not have fires?"

Tajeer shook his head. "No, they have not learned how to create fire. We can teach them how to create fire from our sticks. They have many things to teach us as well."

≫≫≫≫≫

Naroo's people paused at the cave entrance. They knew bears and those fearsome giant cats made dens in such places and were reluctant to enter. Tajeer looked back and shook his head. "Come, there is no danger. Only the light skins dwell here. I have seen it. Food and warmth wait for you."

The dark skins followed Tajeer inside. In the middle of a large space was an empty pit, which should have had a fire blazing in it. After their eyes adjusted to the darkness, Naroo's people saw several dozen light skins sitting quietly, eyeing their every move with suspicion.

Naroo's mate stumbled forward. Heavy with child, Ife rocked back and forth, exhausted from their trek. Cooing with sympathy, Oldmother rushed over and eased the pregnant dark skin down to a comfortable spot on a fur blanket.

The other light skin women followed her example. Each one took charge of a dark skin female and bundled them in furs.

Spearmaker rose from his spot where he had been sitting and gestured to the dark skin men to join him. Naroo looked at Tajeer who nodded his approval. "It is safe. They offer us hospitality."

Tajeer picked up a long, skinny stick and called for one of the men to join him by the pit. "Do you carry the fire starter?" His companion pulled out a fist-sized stone from a pouch tied around his belt and handed it to Tajeer.

The young man scraped some wood shavings from a nearby pile into the pit, placed the stone in the middle of them, sat down and began twirling the stick into a groove in the stone with two hands. His hands moved up and down on the stick, making it spin in an even motion.

Tajeer paid no attention as the light skins gathered around him, watching intently. After a minute or so, a small ember flew off the end of the stick and landed in the shavings. Tajeer lowered himself to the pile and blew gently on the ember.

Ever so slowly, it flickered and almost went out, but Tajeer kept softly puffing. He turned his head away when he needed to breathe, then returned to puffing. Smoke started to rise out of the pit after the ember made contact with one of the shavings. Tajeer slowed his blowing to a few controlled puffs, then sat back and watched.

Even more smoke poured out of the pile of shavings, then a small blaze erupted. The light skins shouted with surprise at the magic that had just been performed. Tajeer called for dry wood and soon the entire pit was ablaze with life-giving warmth.

Oldmother shuffled over to the fire and patted Tajeer on the head. She called to the other light skin women who grabbed a bundle of blackened sticks and soon two spits full of meat were cooking over the fire.

Basketweaver knelt by the fire, staring in wonderment at this wonderful trick. When she and Tajeer locked eyes, both felt their bodies burn from a thousand bee stings. Their hair swept from their faces like they were facing into a gust of wind.

Tajeer groaned as if he'd been stabbed, wobbled and fell toward the fire. The last thing he remembered was seeing Basketweaver collapse on the cave floor.

When Tajeer finally woke up, a concerned-looking Naroo was staring at him. He propped himself up on one arm and looked around. Five more large fires blazed throughout the cavern warming it up and spreading light.

"What happened?" he croaked. One of the light skin women offered him a bowl of water which he gulped down.

Naroo looked relieved when he saw his brother move and drink. "You almost fell into the fire, but their leader grabbed you by the hair and pulled you away. What happened? You and the light skin woman fell at the same time."

Tajeer shook his head, trying to get the cobwebs out. He was still a bit dizzy. "Bee stings. My skin was on fire from the bee stings." Tajeer examined his arms but saw no swelling.

"Bee stings?" Naroo sat down by his brother. "There are no bees here. They do not fly when the snow comes."

Tajeer shrugged. "I do not know. My body burned then I fell asleep. I remember seeing the light skin girl fall. How does she fare?"

Naroo looked at the cluster of women who were attending to Basketweaver. "The light skin is moving and talking. She said the same as you. It felt like bee stings to her. Maybe a poison plant was in the wood when you started the fire and breathed its smoke."

The dark skin leader handed his brother a nicely cooked piece of meat. Tajeer took a nibble. His stomach growled in anticipation, and he tore into the rest of it with great gusto.

After the meal, he sat cross legged on a fur with his back against a large rock. Basketweaver sat on the opposite side of the cave. She was still being fussed over by several older light skin women, but she waved them off.

The two locked eyes and stared at each other for several minutes. Both felt their hearts skip a beat as they sensed a deep familiarity in their souls.

7

It did not take long for the two groups of people to assimilate. This was never more evident than during the hunting forays. Spearmaker's men were adept at following game trails and finding prey. Naroo's men were highly skilled with their spears and brought down enough game to feed everyone.

Tajeer and the other dark skins showed the light skins again and again how to start a fire with just a stick and a grooved stone. The task seemed difficult for the adult light skins. The sticks would either break or fly from their hands, and they would tire of the task and walk away with frustrated growls.

Basketweaver, however, did not give up. Her skill at weaving served her well, along with Tajeer's encouragement. The dark skin hunter was reluctant to leave her side. The young woman basked from the attention.

After dozens of attempts, Basketweaver shouted with joy when an ember from her stick finally ignited a blaze. Oldmother swayed back and forth. The two teeth in her mouth gleamed as she smiled with pride.

Not long afterwards, another young light skin girl imitated Basketweaver's method and also started a fire. An even younger light skin boy finally created a spark and another fire. Spearmaker's people would never sleep in the cold and darkness again.

The affection Tajeer and Basketweaver were showing each other became a topic of discussion around the fires of both peoples. One night after everyone had satiated themselves after another successful hunt, Spearmaker arose from his fire and approached Naroo.

The light skin leader pointed toward Tajeer and Basketweaver and clasped his hands together. "Dark skin, my people have talked and agree that your hunter and Basketweaver-Daughter-Oldmother of my people should bond." Naroo shook his hand, not understanding.

The two races of people still did not make sense of each other's speech. They communicated by rudimentary hand signals and gestures. Basketweaver giggled and gazed at Tajeer. He smiled at her, then addressed his brother.

"I believe their leader said they give their blessing to my taking Basketweaver as my mate."

Naroo stared at his brother in wonderment. "You can understand them? How?"

Tajeer shook his head. "After I awoke from the bee stings, I began to understand some of their words, only a few. Every day, I hear more. I cannot speak them very well. Basketweaver can understand some of our talk as well."

The young light skin woman nodded. "It is true, Naroo," she said in the dark skin language.

Naroo looked from his brother to Basketweaver to Spearmaker. "If this is what you wish, then so be it," he said. "We will hold a ceremony in the spring when the women can gather flowers, and we can dance."

Basketweaver clapped her hands with joy. "Spearmaker-Family-Father, the dark skin leader agrees his brother may bond with me." Spearmaker nodded with approval.

Tajeer arose. "Thank you, Family-Father," he said slowly, trying to enunciate the difficult light skin speech. Spearmaker gazed at the young man and almost smiled. He understood Tajeer, but his words sounded like a toddler trying to talk.

Spearmaker then gestured for the couple to approach him. He turned toward the people who now sat silently at their fires, watching the scene. "This man and woman wish to be bonded.

I, Spearmaker-Family-Father, say it is a good thing." His people shouted their approval.

The light skin leader turned and looked expectantly at Naroo. Basketweaver whispered to Tajeer. "Brother, I believe you are expected to give your blessing."

Naroo sighed, walked over to the couple and placed a hand on each of their shoulders. "I, Naroo, agree. This man and woman are now paired." He turned to his people and announced, "But we still dance in their honor when the flowers bloom and the river flows again." His people arose as one and broke into song, much to the wonderment of Spearmaker's clan.

Tajeer and Rabbitcatcher struggled through the snow drifts during one of their hunting expeditions. Even though the two men barely understood one another, they had become close friends. They worked well together. Rabbitcatcher seemed to remember every game trail he had ever seen, and Tajeer was more than happy to lie in wait for game to bag and bring home to the cooking fires.

The young light skin stopped and held up his hand. Tajeer followed his companion's gaze and saw three does on the next ridge slowly making their way toward them. The two men crouched down and moved slowly behind two large trees just above the trail. It would be a perfect ambush.

As the deer drew closer, Tajeer steeled himself to be ready to step out and throw in one motion. The animals only had to traverse one more ravine before coming into view.

Savage screams cut through the cold, crisp air causing both hunters to drop into the snow. One of the deer bounded into view at full run. Its eyes were wide with fear as it leaped through the drifts. Howls of excitement followed.

"Not animals, people," Rabbitcatcher whispered to Tajeer. The dark skin hunter nodded and frowned. "Come, we must see who it is. Move quietly my friend."

The two men stepped carefully through the snow and kept low as they crept toward the top of the ravine. Rabbitcatcher took a quick look at the bloody scene and ducked under cover.

Four men were clumsily gutting one of the deer. The animal was barely dead, but the men already were cutting into the carcass and shoving chunks of meat into their mouths. Tajeer peered through a thicket. The men were gaunt. Their eyes were hollowed out like walnut shells that have had meat removed.

Rabbitcatcher was trembling, not due to the cold, but from fear. "Elkhunter's men!" He mouthed, daring not to make a sound. "They hunt on our land. We must tell Family-Father!" Tajeer held up his hand and stole another look.

The four hunters had taken to the butchering with savage efficiency. The carcass already had been cut up. Three of the men gathered large hunks of meat and were bundling them up. The fourth man, a huge brute, strode over to a brown pile, plucked it out of the snow and flung the body of another deer over his shoulders. Without saying a word, the four hunters set off in the direction of Elkhunter's land.

Spearmaker frowned as Rabbitcatcher retold the story of the trespassers' foray onto the land his clan claimed. The young light skin paused. "They looked to have been without food for many days."

Family-Father nodded. His eyes studied the dancing flames of the fire as he weighed the ramifications of the intrusion. "It is not good. Elkhunter's people hunt within a half day's walk of our dwelling place. If they have traveled that far, they will walk farther next time."

Basketweaver listened and translated the best she could to Tajeer and Naroo who sat nearby. The two dark skins understood the threat Elkhunter's clan posed to the people who had accepted them into their midst. The strangers would compete for game that already was getting scarcer from the harsh winter. The two hunters also remembered how roughly Elkhunter and his men had treated Rabbitcatcher and then threatened them that day across the river.

Spearmaker rocked back and forth on his haunches as he thought. "It is not good they hunt on our land. We have moved from the Elkhunter clan before. This land is good to us. There is plenty of game."

He paused and waved towards Naroo and his people. "We have new hunters, and they bring strong magic. Will the dark skins leave when Elkhunter's clan finds us?"

Basketweaver translated, then sat back with a worried expression. It had never occurred to her that her new mate and his people may leave if threatened.

Naroo listened, intensity glowed in his eyes. Tajeer glanced at his brother, then looked at their people who were gathered around the fire. There was no fear in their eyes, just determination. "What say you my brothers and sisters? Do we travel on or stay and help our new friends?"

Without being prompted, shouts of "stay, stay" rang out from the dark skins. Naroo smiled with pride and looked at Spearmaker. "My people are your people now, elder. We will stand against Elkhunter Clan with you."

Basketweaver let out a sigh of relief and told Spearmaker what Naroo had said. The light skin leader sat back and studied Naroo for a moment. A smile barely twitched on his lips. "It is good. Every day, we will send hunters to watch for the Elkhunter Clan. They are not welcome here."

8

Several weeks passed without a sign of Elkhunter's people trespassing on the Spearmaker Clan hunting grounds. The watchers sent out to look for intruders started to grow lax. They grew bored waiting to discover intruders that never appeared.

One young man from Naroo's people sat on a fallen tree trunk intently watching a squirrel dart nervously from branch to branch. He hoped the bushy tailed rodent would eventually make its way to the ground so he could have a chance to snag it.

A call of alarm from a bird in a nearby tree sent the squirrel scurrying back to its nest. The hunter moved his head slowly and looked in the direction of the ruckus the bird was making. Several shapes were moving through the trees. The watcher slowly lowered himself onto the log and slid down behind it so as not to draw attention to himself.

Three men walked carefully through the trees as they followed a game trail. Every few steps, they would pause and examine their surroundings. One of the men, a large specimen wearing a wolf skin on his head and shoulders, looked in the direction of the young hunter, stared for a moment then continued walking.

The watcher held his breath, not daring to make a sound. The intruders were far enough away so as not to pose a threat, but the young man did not relish the idea of trying to run through the snow with desperate pursuers chasing him.

When the three men climbed a ridge, they stopped, checked their surroundings again and proceeded down the hill out of sight. The young man waited for another moment or two to ensure the others weren't doubling back, then scurried back to the safety of his clan to tell them Elkhunter's men were back.

Naroo tried to calm the young man down when he returned, out of breath and shaking from his encounter with the enemy. "Slow down little brother, take a breath and speak slower so Basketweaver can understand you."

The watcher gasped a few times and recounted what he had seen and where the men were heading. Basketweaver translated the message as Spearmaker solemnly listened. The clan leader arose, grabbed a spear and announced, "It is time."

The three hunters were growing frustrated. They had only seen one deer, which bolted away before they could get close enough to use their spears. It didn't help that they hadn't eaten in almost two days. Their leader paused. "If we do not find animals, we will bring back one of Spearmaker's clan. Meat is meat." His men snorted in agreement.

One of the hunters held up his hand for quiet and pointed. Two ridges away, several deer looked to be pawing away at the snow, looking for food. Without another word, the three men checked the wind, then separated and started to make their way toward the deer in an attempt to flank them. Their strategy was to startle the deer and stampede them near one of the spearmen.

As the hunters drew closer, the deer seemed to disappear without a sound. The three men hurried over to where they had last seen the animals. Before they could react, a dozen men appeared from behind trees and surrounded them.

Spearmaker stepped forward. "You are not welcome here. Tell Elkhunter to stay on his hunting grounds."

The large man, who wore the wolf hide, stepped forward. "We hunt where we wish, old one. Our people are hungry."

Spearmaker stared at the leader. "You are Wolfkiller, son of Elkhunter. Go home to your family father. Our spears will find you if you come again."

Wolfkiller grimaced and took a step toward Spearmaker. He looked up with surprise when a tall dark skin man bearing a long spear stepped next to the older man.

"The dark skins! They sleep at your fires?" Wolfkiller snarled. "Elkhunter will not be pleased to hear this."

Spearmaker grunted an acknowledgement. "We are one clan. I am not pleased you are here. Elkhunter Clan does not hunt here. Go back or your heads will decorate our dwelling place."

Wolfkiller took a quick look around. Seeing he and his men were vastly outnumbered, Wolfkiller motioned for them to retreat. "Elkhunter will see you again, Spearmaker, and drive you away again."

Tajeer strode forth. "Your people are good at talk," he said in broken but understandable light-skin language. "My people are better with their spears. Go home, light skin!"

Wolfkiller was startled that he understood the stranger, but his ferocity returned. "I will see you again. I will wear your skin," the intruder threatened, pointing his spear at Tajeer.

Tajeer grinned. "Your wolf skins will cover the floor of my dwelling. Leave now. My spear grows thirsty for blood."

The three intruders backed away slowly, then turned and headed home. Wolfkiller did not know what would make his father more upset — that they came back empty-handed or the threats from Spearmaker and the dark skins. He did not look forward to bearing the brunt of Elkhunter's rage.

Elkhunter did not disappoint his son. The children hid and women knelt down with fear when he heard the news. He grabbed a rock and hurled it at the wall. The ricochet hit a woman in the leg. She collapsed with a scream of pain.

"When the snow leaves, we will find Spearmaker Clan. We will kill the men and take the women!" he screamed. "I am Elkhunter! My clan will hunt wherever we want. We will take the dark skins as trophies!"

In another cave, Spearmaker looked at Naroo and Tajeer. "Elkhunter will come. We will fight. Only one clan will live," he sighed resolutely.

Tajeer stared into the fire as a bold concept swirled into his brain. He spoke briefly to his brother in their tongue. Naroo gave Tajeer a surprised look, considered the idea then gestured toward the light skin leader.

"My brother and I agree. We should not wait for Elkhunter," Tajeer said to Spearmaker in light skin speech. "We should hunt them. Surprise them before they can attack us."

Spearmaker stared at them and pondered such a bold strategy.

9

Elkhunter glowered at the news. It had been almost two months since his son had returned with Spearmaker's threat to stay away from his clan's hunting grounds. Now, two pairs of scouts he had sent out to find his enemy's dwelling had not returned. The four men should have found their way home in five or six sun rises, but they had disappeared.

The family father paced the cave as his men nervously watched him. "Spearmaker would not dare to kill men from Elkhunter Clan," he snarled.

Wolfkiller shrugged. "Our men do not return, Family-Father. The dark skins show no fear. Our men's blood may be on their spears."

Elkhunter snorted in disgust, grabbed his favorite club and a spear. "All you men, follow me! We will find the hole where Spearmaker Clan hides, drag them out and kill them!"

Wolfkiller stood up. "We will follow you, Family-Father, but you leave the women and children unprotected."

Elkhunter glared at his son, grunted an acknowledgement and pointed at a boy of fourteen summers and another of thirteen summers. "You two guard the women and hunt for food while we are gone." The two youths looked dejected at being left out of a glorious adventure, but they dared not argue with Family-Father.

Noticing their reaction, Elkhunter cuffed the older boy on the head, causing him to stumble backwards. "Do not cry like babies. We will return with prizes for you." He grimaced at the younger boy, who walked with a slight limp. "Besides you will only slow us down."

The men followed Family-Father out of the cave. Each grabbed their weapon of choice, either a club, spear or both.

Most of the hunters had regained their strength and weight due to improved hunting made easier with the snow melt.

Wolfkiller led the way as they moved single file toward the last spot he had encountered Spearmaker's hunters. They had not been walking long when Wolfkiller stopped.

Something did not feel right. A scolding bird caught his attention. He brought his spear up in a defensive position and looked carefully around. The bird eventually stopped and flitted away. Seeing or hearing nothing out of place, Wolfkiller continued the trek.

A watcher high up in a tree let out his breath as the large party of hunters slowly moved out of view. He feared the pesky little bird would give him away with its incessant chirping. The spy from Spearmaker Clan made a scratch on a stick for each man he watched file under him. Naroo had selected the young man, who was known for his quickness and cleverness, for this mission. He waited several long minutes to ensure Elkhunter's warriors were out of sight when he silently slid down the tree and made his way home, making sure to take a path that would not be detected by the oncoming invaders.

Naroo patted the young man on the head when he scampered back to the clan. The youngster collapsed on the floor, panting with exhaustion. Once their spy was sure he was well away from Elkhunter's band, he ran most of the way back to their cave. He only stopped to make sure he was not being followed. From experience, the young dark skin knew he could outrun the light skins, but he respected their tracking abilities.

After gulping water from a bowl, he handed his marking stick to Naroo. The black skin leader counted the scratches and showed them to Tajeer. The two men gathered up some small stones and placed them in rows of five. Spearmaker and his men looked at the three lines plus a lone rock, indicating 16 men were approaching.

He looked puzzled and shook his head not understanding. Tajeer knelt down, pointed at the rocks, held up his open hand and counted his fingers. "This is how many men Elkhunter is bringing with him."

Spearmaker nodded that he understood. Elkhunter's party outnumbered them by one man. He was pleased with their plan to attack the invaders.

He, Naroo and Tajeer had picked out the place where they would ambush Elkhunter's men. It was a high ravine about a half day's walk from their cave. From that vantage point, they could view the nearby countryside for as far as they could see.

The clan had been preparing for this moment ever since Wolfkiller and his two men were forced to return home after being caught trespassing on their land. Spearmaker, along with several light skin and dark skin apprentices, had been busy making new spears.

Now each one of Spearmaker's men could carry three or four spears and stash them near their preselected ambush spots. Much to the men's surprise, Basketweaver thought of a clever ploy to attract the invaders' attention and lure them to the trap.

At first, Spearmaker refused to listen to an idea brought up by a mere woman. But Basketweaver convinced Tajeer. The pair seemed to have a closer bond than most mates. Tajeer told Naroo of the plan, and finally even the family father gave it his approval.

The invading hunters searched for the Spearmaker Clan for two days. Wolfkiller steered his men away from the spot where he and his two companions had been accosted earlier. They made a detour around the area, keeping a careful watch for any sign of their enemy.

That morning the band had seen a tree carved with Spearmaker's sign indicating they were entering that clan's territory. Elkhunter growled with excitement, but knew they had to approach unseen and unheard. He preferred to locate the clan's cave, then slowly approach at night and surprise the enemy when they emerged at dawn. However, the sun was starting to set, and there was no sign of Spearmaker's people.

Elkhunter begrudgingly agreed to find a campsite for the night and continue the search in the morning. It meant another night of sleeping out in the open, exposed to the elements. The large party meant they should be able to defend themselves from nighttime attack from people or animals. Sentries were posted in all directions to guard against any threat.

10

Wolfkiller snapped awake at the sound. He had fallen into a light sleep while on guard duty. Laughter? He arose from his spot and crept past several trees to find the source. It was barely dawn. The sun's light was just starting to cast rays through the forest. Wolfkiller snuck up to a large tree and slowly peered around it.

Two people meandered along the top of a ravine, stopping every now and then to pluck a plant from the ground. It was a barely adult male and a young female. They seemed to be more interested in themselves than the chore they were obviously sent out to do.

The male kept rubbing up against his companion, and the female playfully pushed him away but giggled at his clumsy efforts. Wolfkiller licked his lips at the thought of a quick kill and an easy conquest. The young male would be no match for him, and the female would be a pleasant diversion.

But he knew what it meant to find these two unaware youngsters. Spearmaker's clan must be close by, perhaps on the other side of that ravine. He broke his gaze from the playful pair and crept back to awaken his men.

Elkhunter and the other men woke with a few growls, but quickly quieted down at Wolfkiller's signal. They snatched their weapons and followed Wolfkiller to the spot where he had watched the playful couple.

The young male and female did not disappoint. They were locked in an embrace against a tree. Elkhunter's men grunted with expectation as to what their rewards would be once they dispatched the troublesome males in Spearmaker's clan.

Elkhunter took over control and gestured for his men to fan out in a parallel line, then signaled them to climb the ravine. The young couple's moans grew louder as the enemy clan moved up the hill. The advancing men could not help but be distracted by the noisy lovemaking.

The young female tapped her companion on the shoulder three times. Understanding her signal, he answered in kind. With a laugh, she pushed him away, crested the ravine and disappeared on the other side. The male shouted with feigned disappointment and followed her.

Elkhunter held up his hand to stop. He did not want his men to be discovered by a pair of careless youngsters. Not long after the pair of lovers disappeared, sounds of even more vigorous love making cascaded over the hill.

The leader motioned for his men to continue their advance. The intruders were within about twenty paces of cresting the ravine when screams rang out. A hail of spears sliced through the air. Some of Elkhunter's men fell, calling out in pain or dropping to the ground in death throes.

Spearmaker and his men charged down the ravine in a chorus of war calls and met the enemy head on. The two family-fathers spotted each other and collided with a clash of clubs.

Tajeer sprinted toward Wolfkiller and leaped at the large light skin, knocking him to the ground. Wolfkiller proved to be deceptively quick. He sprang to his feet and charged his dark skin nemesis with a raised spear. The two men circled each other, thrusting and parrying.

Wolfkiller's jabs grew more desperate when he could not breach his opponent's defenses. Instead of overreacting, Tajeer felt a strange calmness as he easily fought off the light skin's clumsy strikes. The odd sensation that he had done this before swept over him.

After another unsuccessful strike by Wolfkiller, Tajeer feinted to the left and faked a thrust. When the light skin tried to defend himself, Tajeer rolled right, stabbed Wolfkiller's chest, and sprang back. The wounded man gasped in pain and staggered backwards.

Wolfkiller swayed back and forth for a moment, grimaced and charged Tajeer at a full run. The dark skin man feinted twice to either side, causing the light skin to stab into the air. Tajeer rolled to the left and lunged again. This time his spear pierced Wolfkiller's stomach and poked out his back. The light skin warrior gasped, sank to his knees and collapsed to the ground, dead.

Spearmaker and Elkhunter traded blows with their clubs. Both raged against the other. One fought for his clan's very survival and the other for his pride and perceived right to do what he wanted. The larger Elkhunter started to drive his opponent backwards with his frenetic blows.

As Spearmaker retreated, his foot got caught in a snag, causing him to fall. With an exultant whoop, Elkhunter took a step, raised his club to deliver a killing blow when a spear sliced through his neck. Elkhunter gasped and turned around to see Naroo in position to hurl another spear when he crashed to the ground like a tree being felled.

Spearmaker stared at his dead foe, shook his head in wonder and struggled to his feet. Silence greeted him as he walked around the bloody scene of the battle, then made his way toward his warriors.

Rabbitkiller, Tajeer and the other men of Spearmaker's clan cheered when they saw their family-father approach. The light skin leader clasped Naroo's shoulder as he walked by. All of Elkhunter's men were dead.

The first volley of spears had done its job, dropping almost half their enemy. Naroo and the other men overwhelmed and killed the invaders who were left standing. The wounded enemy fighters were quickly put out of their misery.

Tajeer approached the family-father. "Four of our brave hunters sleep with their grandfathers." Spearmaker walked over to where his slain men had been laid side by side. He knelt by each one, gently placed his hand on their heads and bid them farewell.

He gestured toward the fallen enemy bodies. "Put them in a pile. Gather branches. We will burn them. Let their grandfathers find them wandering in the great darkness."

Tajeer and Rabbitkiller led the expedition to capture the remnants of Elkhunter's clan. When confronted, the two youths who were left in charge of the women and children, surrendered without a fight and begged for their lives.

The survivors were given the choice to join Spearmaker's clan or migrate elsewhere. They all opted to join. To alleviate overcrowding, Naroo and half of his people took over Elkhunter's former territory. A few of the dark skin hunters stayed with Tajeer, who refused to leave Basketweaver.

11

Searcher returned to the cluster first. Its disappointment was tempered somewhat by the greeting its cluster gave it as they swirled around the entity.

Loneliness still clung to it after the entity was abruptly ripped from the sentient known as Tajeer. The hunter male had succumbed after only forty-two seasons of life. Though he died gloriously.

Tajeer had insisted on traveling with the hunting party. His three sons tried to convince him to stay behind to teach their offspring how to make a proper spear. The dark skin had learned the skill from Spearmaker before the old clan leader had died.

However, Tajeer loved the thrill of the hunt. The younger hunters just shook their heads with amusement. Basketweaver and their two daughters clucked over him as if he were a small child, but he ignored their pleas to stay put.

"We are honored you hunt with us. We will travel fast. You must keep up," Trailfinder admonished his father. Tajeer exhaled with a derogatory huff, grabbed his spear and strode out the cave. "Keep up with me if you can, pup," he smirked.

A few hours into the hunt, the men found the trail of a small herd of woolly rhinos. One of these slow creatures would feed the clan for weeks and their fur would warm many bodies. The herd was made up of one large male, three females and two calves.

Tajeer pointed out the youngest cow — an immature adult — lagged behind the rest of the herd. She had no calf at her side and seemed oblivious to her surroundings. Trailfinder and the other hunters agreed that would be their target.

After testing the wind, the hunting party slowly crept up on the unsuspecting female. The men were in no hurry. They waited until the animals stopped to graze peacefully from time to time and made their approach. Tajeer's job was to keep an eye on the bull, which would rip out a mouthful of grass from the ground and stand guard watching the females and calves.

Tajeer moved away from the group to get a better vantage point to see the bull. When the beast turned to walk a few paces and grab another chunk of grass, Tajeer signaled his comrades. The seven other men jumped up as one and hurled their spears at the female. They then whooped, imitated other animal screams in an attempt to scare off the herd and ducked down in the grass.

The cow bellowed in pain and tried to run, but two spears had struck both legs on her left side, slowing her down. The other rhinos snorted in alarm. Not seeing an enemy, they bolted from the scene. The bull waited until the cows and calves were past him before he followed them.

Seeing the herd's retreat, the hunters caught up to the injured cow. More spears jabbed into her other two legs, impeding her progress even more. Unable to run, the wounded animal whirled to face her attackers, but the hunters easily dodged her charges and used their spears to cripple her until she slumped over.

Tajeer watched with pride as his three sons and four other men from the clan efficiently brought down the rhino. His reverie was cut short by a nearby bellow. The bull had doubled back and now was charging at a full run toward the hunting party.

Instinctively, Tajeer ran to intercept the angry rhino. We waved his hands and shouted as he scampered in the opposite direction of the slain cow. The bull took the bait and bore down on Tajeer. The old hunter only had time to throw one spear, which bounced off the bull's neck.

The animal's horn caught Tajeer in the chest. It flung his body aside and whirled to chase down the other hunters. However, Tajeer's maneuver had worked. The other hunters had time to scramble to the safety of nearby trees. The bull bellowed in anger and ran over to inspect its dying herd mate.

Trailfinder grimaced at the scene. He gripped his spear tightly as he fought the urge to leave the protection of the trees and kill the bull. Its horn still dripped with his father's blood. After a few moments of circling the young cow, the bull snorted and trotted away to rejoin the surviving members of its herd.

After making sure the bull had finally left the area, the hunters ran to where Tajeer lay. Trailfinder, his two brothers and Tajeer's old friend, Rabbitcatcher, slumped down next to the body and mourned their loss.

Searcher had to wait almost ten more solar orbits until Other joined it. This was nothing in celestial time, but it seemed like an eon to Searcher. Other was finally released when Basketweaver died one chilly winter night.

She was wrapped up in warm furs next to a fire, but her body had finally worn out. Her daughters were at her side. They stroked her hair and sang to her when she breathed her last. Even though she was a light skin, whose people had difficulty making those pleasant sounds, Basketweaver would always stop and smile when someone sang.

The two entities glowed white when they were reunited. Experiencing life again had been an exhilarating experience. They were welcomed by three entities — offspring who had died in childhood. Searcher and Other watched with a satisfaction no entity should have experienced as their progeny flourished and developed into a new race that spread throughout the world.

Other and Searcher watched over the self-aware sentients for another one hundred thousand solar revolutions. During the great ice age, when the seas dwindled to almost mere ponds of their former selves, Other guided different groups of sentients across a new land bridge that connected another set of continents.

The entities had extrapolated the sea levels would rise and cover the land bridge when the ice age finally ended. When that happened, the sentients would be cut off from each other and be left to their peculiar evolutions.

Searcher eventually grew bored with this sentient babysitting. The third planet from the sun was teeming with life. Its orbit was stable around the little yellow sun that promised to burn brightly for several billion years.

The entity was eager to blink out into the void of space and experiment with new worlds. To bring new life into existence. To feel the satisfaction of creation without having to go to the trouble of experiencing life in those frail sentient bodies.

It had sent out minor entities to find new planets that would be ripe for their assistance. From those millions of scouts, several thousand new worlds had been identified as possibly hosting life with the right intervention.

Even Other was intrigued with these reports. That entity had kept close tabs on the sentients in the planet below, but now the beings were well established and scattered across the world so that only a total extinction event would wipe them out. It was time to set off on an adventure.

Searcher and Other flashed their intention of leaving for new adventures. Guardian issued a request. It wanted to stay and protect the planet from any future threats. Its protective vibrations were strong.

The request pleased Searcher and Other. Leaving this planet guarded was an agreeable option. The two entities, which had been Sentinel, approached each other and exchanged rapid fire communication flashes.

Searcher vibrated its approval at being shed of its sentinel duties. Guardian vibrated with gratitude at being allowed to continue to serve as protector of the planet. A few thousand young entities were earmarked to stay behind and assist Guardian.

One of the entities appeared next to Guardian. Its vibration was almost twice as powerful as the other young ones. Other recognized it as one of its offspring from their sentient lives. Guardian flashed its approval.

Other drifted over to the young entity and merged with it briefly. Recognizing potential and a seed of sentience, Other delivered a spark of energy to its former daughter, endowing it with the power to interact with the promising species on the planet. The young entity emitted a brilliant white glow in appreciation. Other flashed its satisfaction and christened it Caretaker to watch over the sentients.

Searcher, Other and the remainder of their cloud swarmed together to form a massive glowing orb. The unified entity flashed a farewell to Guardian, Caretaker and their tiny cloud, then blinked away.

1

Iltani watched patiently as her father haggled with a customer. The visitor came from the east plains, which had seen a season of drought. His village was in short supply of grain. However, he came to the market leading two heifer calves.

The two men gestured at each other and pointed at the baskets of wheat Iltani's father had brought to market as well as at the freshly weaned but skinny calves. The drought had shortened the grazing period, sharply reducing the feed source for the visitor's herd.

Uselli carefully eyed the heifers. Their eyes were bright, and they tugged impatiently on their rope halters. This indicated that, even though the calves were in poor condition, they were still healthy and vigorous. The animals would bounce back quickly with a steady diet of rich, irrigated grass.

They could help expand his herd for years when they reached breeding age.

He knew the Eastern man was desperate. The wheat harvest had been bountiful for Uselli. He had plenty of grain to bargain with. "Ah, such skinny calves. I'm surprised they did not die on the trip here," Uselli smirked and shook his head in mock disappointment. "Ten baskets for both. I can't believe I'm being that generous."

The visitor threw his hands up in frustration. Haggling was always a tricky business, but he had vowed not to be cheated. "This is not even a fair trade for one of these fine beasts," he snarled.

Looking up the row of the market, the visitor pointed at another grain vendor. "Never mind. Perhaps that kind-looking fellow there will give me a fair trade. His baskets look like they are overflowing with wheat."

Uselli snorted. "Now, now my fine fellow. The trip must have put you in an ill temper. Hmm, would you take twenty-five baskets for those walking skeletons? I'm not sure they will make it back to my paddock without dying on the road."

The customer folded his arms across his chest. Now the real haggling was starting. "If you didn't notice, wheat merchant, these are heifers, worth twice what bulls would bring. Fifty baskets for the pair. My family will beat me for asking for such a low price, but I see you are a family man," he said, smiling at Iltani.

"Fifty baskets?!" Uselli erupted. "Where are the other two head for that price? Are you trying to rob me of my entire crop, Easterner? Oh what will my poor wife and children eat?"

The two men stared at each for a few moments. Neither moved nor looked away. "The gods must be smiling at you today, friend," Uselli said, cupping his face with his hands. "Forty baskets for your pitiful beasts and that is my final offer."

The visitor looked over at the baskets brimming with wheat. "That is a fair price, good merchant. That grain will help my family and our small village get through the dry season until the rains come again."

Uselli nodded with relief. "Yes, it is a fair trade, my friend. It gladdens my heart that my wheat will feed your family." He turned to look at Iltaini, who was smiling at the theatrics both men had displayed.

"Daughter, when you are finished being entertained, would you please make bullas for this trade? One for thirty baskets for our customer, and one for two heifers for your father."

The owner of the heifers snorted, "Are you forgetful, old man? The deal was forty baskets."

Uselli shrugged his shoulders. "Oh my, I meant to offer thirty, but if you insist on forty, so be it." Again, both men glared at each other then burst into laughter.

"Well played, merchant, but I am not that simple," the visitor chuckled.

"You cannot blame a poor merchant for trying," Uselli said with a wink.

The visitor shook his head. "Poor? I think not."

Uselli stood up and held out his hands. "Forgive me, my friend. I meant no insult. Iltani, mark his bulla for forty-two baskets. We are not barbarians. I wish no one to go hungry."

The other man bowed his head in gratitude. "Thank you for your generosity, kind merchant. May the gods bless you."

Uselli cleared his throat and cast a glance at Iltani. "Daughter, how are those bullas coming? I'm sure this man is anxious to get home. He has mouths to feed."

The two men watched as Iltani rolled two balls of clay and poked holes in both. She picked up four large tokens that represented ten baskets of wheat, held them up for both men's approval, punched the outside of each clay ball to make an impression then inserted them into one of the bullas. The same procedure was repeated with two smaller tokens for the extra baskets. Iltani then pressed the holes shut and placed her father's seal into the bulla.

Her second bulla was much easier. Two large tokens for the two calves were punched in the side and inserted into a hole. Iltani handed the bulla to the visitor, who squeezed the hole shut and pressed his seal into the side.

The deal was made, the goods exchanged and the handmade bulla receipts were exchanged.

Iltani crawled into bed after a successful day at the market. She dreamed of livestock and grain, playing children and the constant chatter of people bartering for a deal.

The pleasant visions melted away as another dream exploded into her unconscious mind. The experience was so lifelike, it made Iltani sit bolt upright. Her hair splayed out in all directions like she was standing in a windstorm. She scratched at her skin. It felt like tiny needles were sticking her.

The dream had seemed so real. Iltani smoothed her hair back down with her hands and shivered. The memory of the experience was still sharp.

An unfamiliar woman in glowing clothes had appeared in midair and showed Iltani a clay tablet covered with markings. The figures looked like the tokens merchants used in their bullas when completing a transaction. The glowing woman demonstrated how dozens of figures could be scratched in the clay, representing livestock, baskets of wheat, jars of wine and clothes of all types. It seemed like an endless list.

The idea to make markings on a flat surface was so simple. No constructing one of those round bullas, press a token into it to make an indentation and then fill it with tokens that may be rendered useless by this new method. Transactions between buyers and sellers would be completed so much faster as well as simplifying storage.

Despite being terrified, Iltani had managed to ask, "What do I call you?" Her own voice sounded like a whisper coming from another room. A smile formed on its beatific face.

"You are blessed with a gift above all others. I sense it when I watch you work. Share this new knowledge with your fellow artisans. All you have to do is call for Nisaba, and I will come to you in your dreams." The apparition then disappeared in a puff of mist.

Iltani tried to lie back down and go back to sleep, but she could not get the image of the glowing woman out of her head. As soon as the sun peeked through her window, Iltani snuck into the pottery lean-to behind her family's mud-brick home.

She wetted down a pile of hardened clay to make it pliable and went to work. Iltani pressed out a flattened sheet, picked up a token that had a sharpened point and started to etch the symbols Nisaba had shown her onto the surface.

Iltani was so intent on her mission, she did not hear her father call her for first meal. After the first tablet was full, she fashioned two more and continued her work.

"Daughter, I've been calling you for first meal, what are you …" Uselli stopped his scolding abruptly and watched in wonder as Iltani examined each token, then feverishly scratched the likenesses onto a tablet's surface.

When she had finished her third tablet, Iltani brushed her hair out of her eyes with a clay-caked hand, leaving a smear across her forehead. Finally noticing her father, she looked up and smiled.

"Father, a goddess spoke to me in a dream last night. She told me to make these etchings. Look, these are the symbols of all our tokens. We no longer have to make those clumsy bullas."

Uselli leaned down and picked up one of the tablets. He looked at Iltani's etched figures, then held up a token it represented. The tablet was light in his hands. Her father could see the flat surface would be easier to handle and store.

He stroked her hair in wonderment. "You say a goddess told you to do this?"

Iltani nodded. "Yes, she said her name was Nisaba. She was beautiful and on fire, Father."

Uselli admired the tablet as if it were a gold coin. "Daughter, I think this will be a wonderful thing. We can use these for transactions. The other merchants will be so envious."

Iltani laughed. "I think others will soon copy it. Nisaba said it will change our lives."

Caretaker blinked back to the small cloud of entities that watched over the third planet from the sun. It danced around Guardian in a show of joy or what passed for that exhilarating emotion in a living being.

Guardian flashed a question. Caretaker acknowledged it had made contact with one of the sentients on the planet. It signaled the sentients were ready for the next phase of their evolution, organized communication that would advance their culture.

A flash of orange from Guardian warned Caretaker about interfering with the sentients. It told Caretaker past interference on other worlds had gone awry causing whole societies to be cleansed. Caretaker vibrated a message to Guardian acknowledging it understood, but reminded the other entity that its mission was to guide the sentients toward civilization and help them grow their culture.

The two entities sent more message vibrations back and forth until both were finally satisfied with each other's motives. Both agreed to leave the sentients in peace for a few thousand solar revolutions, then revisit the culture to monitor its changes.

2

Sheshkala peeked in at his twin sister. Gemekala lay in fetal position on a bed in her darkened room. The only sounds she made were uncontrollable sobs that shook her body. He returned to his mother.

"How long has she been like this?" he whispered.

His mother shook her head. Tears streamed down and scattered into rivulets in the wrinkles on her weathered face. "She returned from the palace early this morning. The sun had barely risen. Your father found her huddled like a beggar on our doorstep."

Sheshkala reached out and hugged his mother. "She has been troubled with the antics of King Rimuc ever since she accepted the position of court scribe and was commanded to live in the palace," he said shaking his head as Gemekala's sobs echoed through the rooms of their family's home.

Asharru cupped her son's face in her hands. "You have always been able to talk with her. Please find out what happened."

He nodded, reached up and gently took his mother's hands in his. "I will try, but I've never seen her like this." Sheshkala frowned as he looked into his sister's room. "We may not like her answer, Mother, especially if it involved the king. I have heard many troubling stories about him from my friends who do business with the palace."

Asharru shuffled to a stool and sat down with a heavy sigh. "This king does not even hold court to hear grievances from our people. He is so unlike his father, King Sargon. His brother, Maniticcu, would have made a much better king."

Sheshkala knelt to her level and put a finger over his lips. "Yes, this may be true, but Rimuc won the kingship after almost killing Maniticcu in fair combat."

The old woman let out an exasperated huff. "Being stronger than another man and beating him in combat does not make him a good king."

Sheshkala knelt beside her. "You can't say this to anyone else, Mother. The king tolerates no criticism. If Rimuc is the cause for Gemekala's distress, there is nothing we can do about it."

He kissed his mother on the forehead, then rose and walked into his sister's room. "I am here, Gemekala," Sheshkala said as he pulled up a stool and sat next to her. He said nothing more to her. Every time she sobbed, he felt a stabbing pain in his heart.

The next morning, Asharru stuck her head in Gemekala's room. It took a moment for her eyes to adjust to the darkness, but she had to stifle a sob at the sight. Sheshkala had crawled into bed and lay next to his sister with his arm draped protectively over her. During the night Asharru had heard murmuring from the room, but after listening closely, she could tell it was Sheshkala singing children's lullabies.

Both siblings must have fallen asleep in the position that had comforted them since they were small children. However, it usually was Gemekala who had curled up next to her sensitive brother to soothe him after some slight, whether real or imaginary. Now, it was her brother's turn to comfort his sister from whatever torture she had suffered.

Even though they were brother and sister, the twins had always been close. Both had excelled in scribe school. Gemekala was known for her cleverness and word play, and Sheshkala was in demand for his efficiency in recording a transaction in as few words as necessary.

Sheshkala awoke to the smell of his mother's cooking. He slowly pulled himself out of bed trying not to awaken his sister, but let out a groan because his arm had gone numb from lying in one position. Gemekala woke up with a jerk, and sat straight up in bed. Her hair was matted and her eyes were swollen red from hours of crying. She stared at her brother with wide, vacant eyes.

"Are you hurt, sister? Are you in pain?" he asked, trying to sound brave, but his voice went hoarse with emotion. Gemekala just nodded and even more tears streamed down her cheeks.

"I, I need to bathe," she managed to choke out. "Is Mama near? I think I will need her help."

Sheshkala called for Asharru, who rushed to her daughter's side. He helped carry in pitchers of water for the bath, then left to give the women privacy. As soon as he stepped outside, Sheshkala almost tripped over his father, who sat cross legged on the stoop cradling a large staff. "Father, how long have you been here?"

Lu-Bau looked up with large, sad eyes. "I've been here all night. No one is going to get in to hurt her again." He paused and wiped a dirty sleeve over his eyes. "I don't care who it is. Did, did she tell you what happened?"

Sheshkala plopped down beside his father. "No, she has not said anything. But I don't think we are going to like to hear it when she does tell us. If she tells us. We may not be able to do anything about it."

His father took in a trembling breath. "Do you think the monster hurt her?"

Sheshkala stared ahead. He knew his father was referring to the king. "Possibly. Whatever happened to her took place in the palace so …" Sheshkala stopped without making an accusation, but his meaning was clear.

The three family members ate in silence. Sheshkala and his father did not ask Asharru what she had learned of Gemekala's injuries. The usually chatty older woman did not look up from her plate.

After a few more nibbles of her goat stew, Asharru let out a sob. "Oh the gods! My poor daughter has been grievously injured." She put her hands over her eyes and doubled over in pain. Her husband said nothing, but abruptly left the table, grabbed his staff and walked back outside to stand guard.

Sheshkala reached over and stroked his mother's back. "Has she eaten anything since she's been home?" Asharru could only shake her head no. He picked up an empty bowl, scooped a few ladles of stew into it and walked into his sister's room.

"Sister, you must eat something," he said softly as he sat down on the edge of her bed. "Mother made stew. It's delicious as always. Come, you need to eat to heal your body."

Gemekala choked out, "No, go away."

Sheshkala stirred the bowl, letting the odors of the seasoned meat fill the room. "I will not go away, sister. How many times did you bring me bread and honey when I was a sad little boy? It is my turn to take care of you."

After a few moments, Gemekala sat up. She shakily reached for the bowl. It was obvious she was weak from exhaustion and hunger. Sheshkala dipped a spoon into the bowl and offered it to her. She accepted a few more mouthfuls of the stew and gulped down water from a goblet.

Gemekala managed a fleeting smile. "Yes, I remember forcing you to eat. Thank you, Brother." She collapsed back into bed. Sheshkala grasped her hands and sat beside her, saying nothing.

After a few minutes, Gemekala locked eyes with her brother. Her face wrinkled in pain. "Oh, Sheshkala. Rimuc is horrible! He made all the women in court undress and dance around him as if we were whores. He, he then grabbed each one of us and did terrible things."

She let out another sob and covered her eyes with her hands. "Oh Brother, Rimuc grabbed me and took me like an animal. I tried to scream, but someone gagged me. It hurt so much, I thought he was going to kill me. When he was finished, he tossed me aside and grabbed another poor girl."

Gemekala exploded into a torrent of tears as the awful memories came flooding back to her. Sheshkala had tried to remain strong for his sister but he doubled over in pain and grief at her revelation. He could do nothing but cry and hold his sister.

No other king in recent memory had been so cruel. As Sheshkala sat next to his poor sister, a thought flashed into his mind — Maniticcu lives. Sheshkala had written several transactions for the royal brother when he purchased horses for his estate. The deposed king had praised him for his work. He was not sure what Maniticcu could do, but perhaps hope lived with the deposed young king.

3

It was mid-morning when the king finally roused himself from the stupor brought on by the previous night's drunken antics. Rimuc stumbled from his bed and roared for drink and food. Slaves came running from all directions carrying delicacies on platters and drinks in various pitchers.

"Fools! Just give me water for now," Rimuc growled. Even while he quenched his thirst by gulping directly from the water pitcher, he hungrily eyed the wine containers. "Leave the wine. I will enjoy that later."

Rimuc heaved his swollen body onto a chair and pulled himself up to the table laden with food. "Ah, sustenance after a vigorous night," he mumbled with a mouthful of food and winked at his High Counselor when the old man entered the room.

Jushur made a grand gesture of an exaggerated bow. "How is your excellency after such a busy night of entertainment?"

The King snorted with amusement. "His excellency is excellent. I must have enjoyed myself last night. I am parched and my nether regions are quite sore. My memory is a bit blurry. Tell me some of the details so I can savor them again."

The High Counselor cleared his throat. "Well, your majesty once again showed an incredible vigor. Actually, it was one of your better performances, sire. You favored every female within your reach with your attention."

Rimuc's bloodshot eyes twitched with delight. "Yes, my good Jushur. I am a majestic bull, and the women of the palace are fortunate to be in my harem. I just wish I could remember my performance more clearly. Our wine is so delicious but it addles the brain, though I think it gives me great vigor."

Jushur absent-mindedly nodded in agreement, then held up a freshly inscribed tablet close to his face. The King continued enjoying his food. He pretended not to notice the old man. The High Counselor would not dare interrupt his liege with a question. Etiquette called for the official not to speak until Rimuc granted permission.

The king took great pleasure in making other people wait for him. It was almost as fun as ordering his servants to pander to his various whims. After a couple more bites of bread slathered in honey and chugs of wine this time, Rimuc shot an exasperated look at Jushur. "Well, out with it High Counselor. What kind of business do you intend to bore me with today?"

Jushur cleared his throat. "It seems we have lost some women of the court. Three by the count so far, your highness. It seems they, ah, were not worthy of your exuberance. Two have joined their ancestors. It appears the third — the court scribe — has crawled away and probably succumbed."

This news even surprised Rimuc. "By the gods, that must have been some night!" he guffawed. "Why are the women in Agade so feeble? Do we need to raid the mountain tribes to find females worthy of holding up to my vigor?"

Rimuc stroked his beard at the thought of bringing some of those wild females into court. It could prove entertainment worthy of his greatness. "Hmm, the court scribe is gone, too? Oh well, order the School of Scribes to send me a replacement. Perhaps a male this time."

He stopped and thought for a moment. "Make sure the new scribe isn't interested in women. I don't want anyone else taking pleasure with what is rightfully mine. I don't care what the young men do with each other."

Jushur bowed. "As you wish, sire. May I give you a summation of the collection of taxes and tithes from the estates?"

The King yawned. "If you must, High Counselor. I only wish to know if the taxes are being paid on time and tithes collected as per my commands. Is the population complying as ordered?"

The High Counselor looked at his tablet one more time. He hoped his answer would placate the King. "Taxes are being collected as expected. The tithes are filling your store rooms to great abundance, sire. In fact we may need to build more granaries."

Rimuc clapped his hands. "Excellent news. So, the lords of all the cities are all complying and sending their tributes? They are bowing to my greatness?"

Only silence greeted Rimuc's question. The King saw the pained look on Jushur's face. "Well, answer me, man. Are we receiving the tributes from everyone?"

There was no way Jushur could avoid a direct question. "We have payments from all but one city, sire. Uruk is tardy according to your decree. I have sent couriers to request compensation, along with the proper penalty. I am sure it was an oversight."

Rimuc stared hard at the High Counselor. "Uruk is late? Home of my mother? My father defeated Uruk. He was too compassionate with that rat hole. What lord rules there? Who defies us?"

Jushur dreaded this moment. He felt like a traitor, giving up a name he had pledged to protect. "Sire, the lord of the city is Maniticcu."

The King pounced from his chair, sending it crashing to the floor. "My brother, the shepherd, is lord there?" he screamed. His voice rose two pitches, and his cheeks flushed in anger. "How did this happen? Why was I not notified of this traitor's treachery?"

Jushur shrugged. "It only recently came to my attention. Apparently your queen's uncle bestowed the title to your brother before he died. Not much news comes out of Uruk these days. Many trade routes diverted from there when Sargon the Great defeated King Lugal-zage-si. I am told Maniticcu has helped rebuild the city."

Rimuc picked up a goblet and hurled it against the wall. "Uruk welcomed a son of Sargon into its walls? My father never should have signed that treaty and arranged a marriage of the old king's daughter to the King in Agade! My brother stole my queen when he fled after I bested him in combat."

A growl emanated deep in the King's throat. "No matter. I never did favor that cow. Maniticcu is welcome to her. I have sired enough sons with women of my choosing to continue my royal line. Besides, while mother lives, she is still queen."

Rimuc shouted for the captain of his guards. "Uruk will pay its tribute! I owe my brother a visit. Order my war chariot and a division of spear soldiers. We march tomorrow."

4

Lu-Bau glared at the visitor. "Who are you and what do you want?" he snapped as he clutched his wooden staff in a defensive position. "You look like you come from the court. We have no business there!"

Jushur held up his hands. "No need to fear me, my brother. Yes, I am the High Counselor. I only seek the scribe, Sheshkala. I am told he has been seen here. I have a transaction and an even more important opportunity for him."

The old man stared at Jushur for a moment, then called for his son. Sheshkala frowned when he poked his head out the door. "High Counselor! Is there trouble? Our family has suffered enough from Rimuc's actions."

Jushur bowed his head. "I grieve for your loss, Sheshkala. I am here to offer you a chance at perhaps some retribution for those vile actions." The son and father exchanged surprised glances, but said nothing.

The High Counselor noticed. "It seems I have assumed the worst, but perhaps it is not as tragic as I feared. It would be most joyous if that were true. Several young women have died from the brutality that night. Say no more to me. My ignorance cannot be passed on if I am asked."

Sheshkala nodded his appreciation. Lu-Bau stepped aside and invited Jushur into the house. As was customary, Asharru served the guest wine and offered food. Jushur graciously partook of both. All dined in silence and waited for the High Counselor to speak.

"My visit today is twofold," Jushur said after taking one last sip of wine. "I come to offer Sheshkala a commission. It is not palace business, but more of a, ah, personal undertaking for me."

Sheshkala leaned forward. "I am honored to be asked, High Counselor, but why me? There are many talented scribes in Agade. What service is it you require?"

Jushur's eyes narrowed as he studied the young man. The intensity and intelligence reflected in the young man's dark eyes were exactly what the High Counselor had hoped to find.

"The commission would be a message, actually a warning, for Maniticcu, who is lord in Uruk. The King is preparing to march on the city to demand payment for overdue taxes and tribute. Most likely retribution is on his mind."

"Of course I will gladly accept that commission. Wait, you said your offer was twofold. Is there more?"

A wide smile greeted Sheshkala. "I thought perhaps there would be a personal reason you would like to contact the lord of Uruk," Jushur said. "He might be most interested in hearing the goings on in the palace and the people who have been hurt."

Asharru tried to stifle a sob. The High Counselor noted she glanced toward a darkened room just off the kitchen where they were sitting. "All members of your family may have an interest in your visit to Uruk. I am told Maniticcu is much changed but still is of honorable character."

Jushur pulled out a small sack of coins from his robe and tossed it on the table. He also handed Sheshkala a small tablet that bore his personal seal and a short inscription: "My Lord, I entreat you to hear this scribe's story."

"Now scribe, listen carefully. The king is preparing to march to Uruk tomorrow with a company of spearmen." Sheshkala grabbed his tools and started to reach for a tablet to inscribe the message, but was stopped with a wave from Jushur.

"No, do not record this. If Rimuc's men capture you and find a message about the king's intention, it will mean death for all of us. Hopefully my words will be too obtuse for them to understand."

Sheshkala stared for a moment at the visitor, then put his tools down. He now realized the gravity of his mission.

The High Counselor continued with his instructions. "Rimuc and his men will reach Uruk in three days if they travel at the fastest pace. Knowing the king, it likely will take him at least four days. He likes his breaks and comforts. A man on horse can reach Uruk in a half day."

Sheshkala reached across the table and clasped hands with the High Counselor. "I gladly accept your offer. However, I will need to secure a horse for the trip. My family does not own such an animal."

Jushur winked. "No need to worry, young scribe. I have sent word to Stable Number Three on the north outskirts to have a horse ready and saddled for you in the morning. Tell them you're on business for the High Counselor. Sometimes holding such a title has its benefits, though not many these days," he said glancing toward the darkened room.

The High Counselor groaned as he lifted himself off the bench. "I am getting too old for this business. I pray to the gods I live long enough to see a change. I dare not say more." He thanked Asharru and Lu-Bau for their hospitality.

Jushur gazed at Sheshkala one last time. "May your trip be safe and fruitful, young scribe," he said, then shuffled out the door.

Maniticcu was curious about the stranger who had arrived at the gates of Uruk on a horse heaving with exhaustion and lathered in sweat. The scribe from Agade forgot the proper decorum, demanding an immediate audience with the lord of the city. He claimed to be on a mission from Maniticcu's old friend, Jushur.

Although he could not read, the lord recognized the High Counselor's seal on the small tablet. "Have a seat young man and take some water," Maniticcu said, then called for his personal scribe to read the tablets to him.

An elderly figure, who looked to be more skeleton than man, tottered out and eased himself down on the bench beside the lord — an unusual action for a subordinate to take. "Hmm, the craftsmanship of this tablet is exceptional," he croaked in admiration while examining the large tablet. "Is this your work or are you a mere messenger?"

Sheshkala was still dizzy from the arduous journey. His face and hair were streaked with dust from the road. "My work?" he asked, a bit confused by the unexpected question. "No, master, it came from the High Counselor at Agade."

The old scribe shook his head and chuckled. "Master, eh? It is good to see manners and etiquette have not died with the rise of Rimuc the Beast. You have been taught well, young man.

"I'm surprised Jushur still can write. He must have had a reason to have sent you scurrying here," the scribe said, then glanced at the small tablet. "Yes, yes, must be a very good reason."

A loud cough made both scribes jump. "I am pleased the craftsmanship meets with your approval, Namtar, but get on with the reading before you walk with your ancestors," Maniticcu growled, but the twinkle in his eyes gave away his humor at the old man's ramblings.

"Yes, yes, the impatience of the young. It would not hurt you to learn the etiquette displayed by our visitor if I may say so, my lord." An impatient wave by Maniticcu told Namtar he had better do as asked.

"Let's see here. It entreats us to listen to our visitor's words. So, young man, what message is so important that you almost killed a horse getting here?"

Sheshkala drew in a trembling breath. "The King marches with spearmen to Uruk to personally collect the taxes and tribute he claims he is owed."

Maniticcu's expression changed. His eyes glowed with hatred. "So, my brother marches here to collect taxes and tributes that are not due for another three years. It is a pity it does not say when they left Agade or how many march with the fat jackass."

Sheshkala bowed and asked permission to address his hosts again. "Yes, yes, boy. Speak for the gods' sake," Maniticcu said, not hiding his impatience. "I am no king, speak when you need to."

The young man winced a bit. He had no experience associating with royalty. "I waited until Rimuc, I mean the King, left with the soldiers. They departed Agade mid-morning. I counted sixty spearmen, Lord."

Maniticcu sat back and let out a guffaw. "So, my brother thinks he can threaten Uruk with sixty men. Well done, young man. We are in your debt. I think we can greet the King properly as well as give the bloated ox what he wants."

Namtar picked up the small tablet and read it to Maniticcu. The lord gestured to Sheshkala. "Tell us your story, young scribe. We owe you that and much more."

Sheshkala took a deep breath and swallowed some refreshing water. He started slowly describing Rimuc's savage antics at the palace, then his words spilled out like a cascading mountain stream as he described the brutalization his sister suffered, as well as the deaths of the other poor girls.

The young scribe tried unsuccessfully to stifle a sob when he finished. Tears streamed down his cheeks. "I, I beg your pardon for my reaction, Lord." The emotionally and physically exhausted young man hung his head, covering his face with his hands. A hand clasped his shoulder.

"There, there young scribe, it is a terrible thing your family has endured," Namtar said in a much stronger voice than

Sheshkala had heard earlier. "It seems the people of Agade suffer needlessly."

Another hand patted his other shoulder. "I am ashamed to call the fatted bull my brother," Maniticcu snarled. "One day, he may pay the price for his actions. We must wait for the right time. Now, take some rest, bathe and eat. For now we give the king what he wants and see if that is enough to placate him."

5

Rimuc was not in a good mood. The sun was hot, and he was always thirsty. The journey to Uruk was taking much longer than had been predicted. Of course starting mid-morning every day after he had enjoyed a luscious breakfast and then stopping four to five times a day to rest in the shade of a grove made the march slow going.

It was in the middle of the third day, and his captain reported they had at least a day and a half to go until they reached the city where his exiled brother was lord. Rimuc looked forward to plundering the once rich capital, taking what he desired and humiliating Maniticcu once again.

This was Rimuc's first venture outside Agade's gates since he had gained the kingship after beating his brother in bloody hand-to-hand combat seven years ago. It was fortunate he was bigger and stronger than Maniticcu at the time. He practically had to kill his older sibling before being declared the victor.

The King did not understand the thrill his father, Sargon the Great, took in leading columns of troops on these tedious marches only to have the lords of the enemy cities sue for peace before hardly any blood was spilled.

Rimuc surveyed the company of spearmen that followed him. His High Counselor assured him sixty soldiers would be enough, along with his presence, to make the gates of Uruk swing open and people prostrate themselves when he approached. He looked forward to marching through the streets like a victorious warrior, just like Sargon had done fifty years ago.

His reverie was cut short when one of the forward scouts approached at a gallop. "Your majesty, a supply caravan from Uruk approaches carrying its tribute of wheat, wine and other products for delivery in Agade. They should reach us in about an hour."

A disgusted snort exploded from the King as he stepped down from his chariot. "We have not marched all this way just to act as a security contingent for a supply train. The tribute is late. A penalty needs to be adjudicated."

The scout bowed. "Yes sire, the caravan's leader informed me Uruk has increased its tribute by ten percent to account for the penalty."

Rimuc called for his tent to be raised, then turned back to the scout. "The lord of Uruk does not decide what the penalty will be. That is my decision. We will take possession of the tribute, then march into the city to take what we desire."

This time the scout dropped to one knee. "Begging the King's indulgence, the men of Uruk travel with one hundred spearmen on foot and twenty archers."

For once the great blusterer was struck dumb. Rimuc stood with his mouth open. The numbers advantage from the approaching caravan was clear to even him. He finally gained his tongue and addressed the captain of his spearmen. "The gall of Uruk to march with such a force. They would not dare to attack the King!"

The captain shook his head. "Most likely not, sire. I recommend my men take defensive positions to guard you from attack." He turned to the scout. "Tell me how they march. In war formation or single file? What is their mood?"

Caught off guard by the captain's questions, the scout coughed and spit out the water he had just sipped from his pouch. "The Uruk men are in single file, sir. They sing as they march. Even the leader was singing. I was greeted with courtesy."

Rimuc walked a few paces away, gesturing for the captain to follow. "That is a good sign, is it not, captain?" he asked in a whisper. He did not want the scout to detect his fear.

The captain saluted. "Yes, sire, it would seem so. I still want to station our men in a defensive position." Trying to feign bravado, Rimuc waved for the captain to carry out the plan and slunk into his tent on shaky legs. He had not expected to be challenged in a show of force.

It was not long when Rimuc and his men could hear the faint strains of singing in the distance. The voices grew stronger as the supply caravan gradually came into view approaching Rimuc's encampment at a respectable clip.

The King's captain rode out to greet the caravan when it was three spear throws away. Rimuc nervously peered through the flap in his tent and watched his officer speak with a man mounted on a great black stallion. The two men looked to be haggling until an agreement must have been reached that was equitable to both.

"Well, captain, what was determined by that parlay?" Rimuc demanded when the officer returned to the tent. The captain bowed and said the Uruk leader had agreed to meet the King half way. Each leader would be escorted by ten men to discuss the transfer of goods.

Rimuc started to object when a horn sounded from the caravan's ranks. Both men peered out the tent to see the men of Uruk organize into combat formation, spears at the ready. "Sire, I humbly advise you to take the Uruk lord's offer."

The King's face reddened with anger. "Who is that bastard who dares to demand terms with me?" The captain started to say something but was cut off with a shout. "Yes, I realize those vermin outnumber us for now. They had better show the proper respect or I will burn Uruk to the ground and take all its people as slaves!"

Even from the distance where the caravan had halted, Maniticcu heard an angry bellow from the tent. A smile creased his lips. "It appears we have the attention of the King," he said to his men. "At ease men, the great toad does not move fast." Laughter rippled through the ranks of the Uruk men.

Eventually, the flap of the tent opened as a rotund man lumbered out and was immediately surrounded by ten men. "By the gods, the King is as wide as a pair of oxen," Maniticcu said under his breath. He turned to his ten-man contingent and signaled for them to follow him.

Rimuc frowned as the Uruk men approached. None of them looked to be fearful in his presence. A halt was called when the two groups reached within ten paces of each other.

After a few moments of silence while the two groups glared suspiciously at each other, the Uruk leader took a step forward and bowed. "We are honored to greet the King. We come bearing the tribute as your couriers have requested even though the treaty calls for another three years reprieve. Never let it be said Uruk does not comply."

Rimuc stared at the other man. That voice was so familiar. The man's face bore scars that criss crossed his face, and his left eye drooped a bit. An impressive braided beard ran down the middle of his chest, and his long dark hair cascaded down his back.

"We march to collect what is owed Agade," Rimuc snarled. "What man dares to deliver terms to the King? I decide what terms are acceptable."

The Lord of Uruk smirked. "I see you have not changed, brother. Well, at least your nature has not changed."

Rimuc sucked in his breath. "Maniticcu! It is you?! How dare you challenge me as to what tribute is owed!"

Maniticcu crossed his arms. "Uruk has a treaty that no tribute be required of it for 60 years after Sargon became king. You swore to uphold all treaties when you assumed the kingship. It was witnessed by all the lords of the great cities. It appears Agade is well fed and not starving. Our tribute stands as delivered."

The King charged forward, coming nose to nose with his sibling. "I see, brother, that you bear the scars of our last meeting. You always were slow to learn."

Rimuc's reaction did not not surprise Maniticcu. The Lord of Uruk leaned in and whispered in the King's ear. "I am ready if you care to challenge me, brother. This time it will be decided by the men of Agade and Uruk. I await your decision."

At some unseen signal, the Uruk men snapped to attention and lowered their spears in combat-ready position. Rimuc took half a step back. The veins in his neck popped out. "You dare disrespect me," the King hissed. "This is not over, brother! You will see me again. I will finish the fight next time."

Maniticcu smiled again, which made Rimuc even angrier. "I look forward to our next meeting, brother," he called out loudly so both contingents could hear. "In the meantime, the tribute from Uruk is yours. Enjoy the march back to Agade. I hope you have brought enough water for the return trip."

Rimuc sputtered in fury. He and his men had counted on filling their bellies and their water casks during their stay in Uruk. Now, his damnable brother had forced him to accept a less-than-desirable tribute, and he faced an even more unpleasant march home. Saying anything contradictory would only make him lose respect of anyone within earshot.

The King snarled, whirled around and stomped back to his tent. Maniticcu signaled for his men to turn about face and march away. To add to the insult, Rimuc had to listen to the Uruk men sing a victory ballad as they departed.

6

Rimuc was still fuming over his encounter with his estranged brother the next morning. Revenge for the insult of what he considered insufficient tribute still boiled in his heart. "Captain, bring me the scout from yesterday," he shouted. The scout appeared almost immediately after his command. "Tell me, where do the fields of Uruk begin?"

The scout bowed. "The first field lies less than a half day's march from here, sire. It's a fine estate with many servants to work the fields. I was offered water for myself and my horse when I passed."

A smile broke out on Rimuc's broad face — the first sign of pleasure since he had undertaken this mission. "Captain, what do the scouts tell us? Has my bastard brother returned to Uruk?" The captain saluted and affirmed the road was clear of Maniticcu and his men.

"Excellent!" the King shouted. "Leave a small group to guard the caravan. We march to pay a visit to this estate. I will take possession of what I'm owed."

Kurum's jaw dropped when he saw a war chariot charging toward him and a handful of other field workers through the wheat field. The standard of the King glinted in the sun. A company of spearmen ran in formation behind Rimuc.

The poor man stood frozen with fright and barely jumped out of the way of the snorting horses when the chariot pulled up. "Bow before your king," Rimuc bellowed. Kurum and the other men fell to their knees. "Forgive your servants, sire. Your visit is a surprise."

Rimuc guffawed. "Yes, I imagine our presence was not anticipated. Tell me, peasant, who is the foreman of this estate?" Kurum raised his head and tapped his chest. "I, I am, sire. How may I be of assistance?"

The King gestured toward his panting men who had just caught up with him. They stood in tight formation behind the chariot. "See, captain, there is a citizen of Uruk who is capable of showing proper respect." The captain gave a slight nod of approval.

"Well, my good man, call all your female servants and have them line up for me to inspect," Rimuc ordered. Kurum gestured to a young boy and sent him running to fetch the women.

"Gather your field hands and have them assist the captain and his men in emptying your granaries. I am commandeering your crop and anything else that strikes my fancy. My rightful tribute will be paid!"

Kurum held out his clasped hand. "Mercy, sire, I beg of you not to take our stores. This is the grain that will feed our families and animals through the dry spell."

A frowning Rimuc stepped out of his chariot. "You did not beg permission to speak, peasant. You people of Uruk need to be taught the proper respect when addressing your king!" Poor Kurum dropped to his hands and knees, his eyes focused on the ground. Rimuc pulled out his sword, pointed it skyward with both hands and swung it down on Kurum's neck, cleaving his head from its body.

"At last! The first blood on my war sword," the King crowed as he admired his dripping weapon. "Now I understand the thrill of battle." Strange sounds caught his attention. Kurum's men lay nearby crying and wailing. A few had vomited from the murder they had just witnessed.

"I will spare you peasants if you immediately show the captain and my men your granaries," Rimuc yelled. "Gather your flocks as well. We will need to eat tonight. Now move!" The field hands struggled to their feet and staggered toward the buildings of the estate under guard of the King's men.

A few hours later, a small caravan of donkeys laden with grain, sheep carcasses and refilled water skins stood ready. Rimuc smiled with approval at the confiscated goods, but now his attention was focused on the people lined up before him.

"My, my, I had hoped for better specimens than this," he grumbled while inspecting the rag-tag mixture of men and women of all ages. "We have scullery slaves at the palace more appealing than this lot."

The king paused in front of a young woman holding a baby of about six months of age. "Give the pup to the hag next to you. Let me see you, girl." The mother shook with fear and sobbed as she clutched her child.

Seeing Rimuc's grimace, the old woman reached out and pulled the baby away from its mother. "There, there, dear, I'll take care of the little one. You know I will." The baby started howling at being separated.

The King gestured for the old woman to take the baby away from the group. He then pulled the young woman out of the line and ordered her to stand still. Rimuc continued on, selecting six more women and four young boys. Three other older women were ordered to join the one holding the baby.

"Not what I was hoping for, but it's the best this lot has to offer," he said to the captain, who was standing at his side. "Add them to the caravan. They may make acceptable slaves for the palace." Rimuc turned to the captain. "Kill the remaining men, but leave the old women. They will make good witnesses of what has transpired this day." The women shrieked in terror as they watched Rimuc's spearman dispatch their men folk.

"Burn the fields and the buildings. Uruk will understand what happens when it refuses a command from Agade." The King smiled as he watched the flames race across the fields. "So this is what it feels like to be a conqueror," he chortled. "It suits me."

Maniticcu stretched out in the spacious bathing pool in the former palace of Uruk. It was one of the few luxuries he allowed himself to enjoy. A goblet of wine dangled from his hand. He was still basking from his triumphant meeting with that fat jackass of a brother.

The lord of Uruk had forced the king to take what was offered and return to Agade with his tail between his legs. The feeling did not make up for the physical and mental scars Rimuc had inflicted on him years earlier, but Maniticcu gleaned some satisfaction for the opportunity to confront the beast of Agade.

A knock on the door jolted him from his pleasant daydream. Maniticcu called for whoever it was bothering him to enter. An ashen-faced Namtar trudged in followed by Sheshkala, who looked more somber than normal. "Yes, what is it that you trouble me with? What has happened? It looks like you have just lost your mothers."

Namtar started to speak, but his voice cracked with emotion. His eyes brimmed with tears. "Pardon, my lord. The scouts have returned from searching for the source of smoke that was spotted yesterday. The king did not return home as we expected, but raided an estate."

The old scribe's knees started to buckle. Sheshkala grabbed Namtar and guided him to a bench. Maniticcu climbed out of the pool, rushed over and knelt by Namtar's side. "Tell me, old friend. What happened?" he asked softly.

Namtar was seized with a fit of coughing. He doubled over and shook his head as grief flooded over him. "The King killed Kurum, Namtar's brother, and his men slew seven other men," Sheshkala said. "Some young women and boys were seized. The granaries were emptied, livestock slaughtered, and the fields and buildings were set on fire. Four old women and a baby were spared. They have been brought to the palace."

Maniticcu sat back, a stunned look on his face. He reached out and gripped the old man's knee. "I am so sorry, Namtar. Rimuc is a monster, but I did not know he was capable of such atrocities."

Namtar clasped Maniticcu's hands in his. "My brother loved working the fields and tending the sheep. His family thrived and were so happy. Now, my lord, they are gone."

Still dripping from his bath, Maniticcu stood up and screamed with fury. "Enough! This is the land of the civilized kings! Rimuc must be stopped."

The scribe motioned to Sheshkala that he needed help to rise from the bench. "My lord, you cannot march on Agade. It is fortified and protected by hundreds of spearmen and archers."

Maniticcu stood silent for a few moments. "It will not take an army to defeat Rimuc. One man should be enough."

7

The King in Agade, as he was called by his subjects, strutted about the palace like a conquering hero who had returned from a successful campaign. "You should have been there, old man," Rimuc laughed when Jushur entered his quarters. "My coward of a brother, who hides under the protection of Uruk, now understands I always get what I demand."

Jushur had heard of the slaughter of the peasants and looting of their property. He struggled to maintain a neutral expression. "Yes, sire, your triumph is the talk of the city. However, you have received word from Uruk," the scribe said holding up a tablet. "Maniticcu expresses his outrage at your actions and is calling for compensation for the stolen goods and return of the people."

Rimuc guffawed so hard he almost toppled over. "Does he now? The nerve of that bastard to challenge me! He says he learned what expressing outrage means. Yet he sends his demands written on tablets. My brother has the soul of a scribe. He's not fit to rule anywhere."

A cough interrupted the King's oration. Seeing the old scribe's furrowed brows, Rimuc chortled. "Do not be insulted, Jushur. You have to agree with me that scribes do not have the souls of warriors. You and your fellows fulfill a vital function, but you are not leaders."

Rimuc slapped his giant belly with both hands. "Yes, indeed, the gods have favored me." He turned to Jushur, who had regained his composure. "Send this message to that illegitimate lord in Uruk: Request denied. Further challenges of this nature will be seen as an insult and the people of Uruk will be dealt with as traitors." The King clapped his hands, pleased at his eloquence. "How does that sound, old scribe?"

Jushur bowed. "Very scholarly, sire. I shall send a tablet with a messenger right away to Uruk."

More boisterous laughter echoed through the palace. "Scholarly? Excellent! Is there nothing I can not do?"

After Rimuc had enjoyed his moment of brilliance, he called for the captain of his guards. "Tell me, what do our spies say of the activities in Uruk? Are they preparing for war?"

The captain bowed. "No, sire. By all accounts, no soldiers or bowmen are being mustered. The gates are open to travelers. I am told there is a pall about the place. It is said the lord has cut his beard in mourning and refuses to leave the palace. It seems they bow to your authority."

Rimuc snorted with derision. "The rats in Uruk have learned their lesson. They won't be a hindrance to the celebration of my seventh anniversary of winning the throne. Invite all the lords under my protection except that ungrateful bastard of a brother."

The King rubbed his hands together as if he were a child getting ready to open a present. "Jushur! I have another edict. Request each attending lord to bring me five comely slave girls. That shall be their anniversary tribute to me. In three weeks we shall have a celebration worthy of a king!"

A soft, exasperated sigh escaped from Jushur's lips. "Is that all, sire?" He waited patiently for an answer while Rimuc drained a large cup of wine. The King did not bother wiping his mouth as some of the red liquid trickled through his beard, dripping onto his protruding stomach.

"No, wait. Uruk indeed will be at the feast!" Rimuc exploded in laughter. "In fact the feast will be supplied by Uruk. Serve the lamb and goat we harvested from those ungrateful wretches and bake breads and other cakes from the granaries we seized. And make sure the Uruk whores serve my guests the food and wine. I will offer them to my guests for their amusement. I am sure I will be bored with them by then."

The scribe bowed. He fought to control his churning stomach. "As you wish, sire. The edicts will be recorded and released." Without asking for permission to leave, Jushur paced out of the room. He stopped momentarily to listen if Rimuc objected. Hearing nothing, Jushur stumbled away to find a place to vomit.

After snatching a dirty serving bowl from one of the servants, Jushur thought he had found a private corner for him to expel the contents of his stomach. It comforted him to kneel on the floor and press his head against the cool wall.

"Take this and clean yourself, old friend," a sympathetic but familiar voice said as someone behind him dropped a wet cloth in his lap. Jushur's head was still spinning from the exertion. "Thank you," he gasped, too dizzy to look up. "It must have been something I ate."

This time the voice whispered in his ear. "More likely it was something you heard. Some terrible announcement you have to convey." A whiff of perfume wafted into his nostrils. He recognized the scent. With a jolt, the scribe remembered who it was — the queen matriarch — the mother of Rimuc and Maniticcu!

Jushur struggled to rise, but his feet were too wobbly to respond. "Forgive me, my lady. I meant no disrespect to the sanctity of the palace. The sickness came upon me so quickly."

A small hand stroked the back of Jushur's neck. "Do not fear, old friend," Shatu-Murrim smiled down at the scribe. Even though she was in her sixties, old for women of their land, the queen matriarch was still beautiful. Her long dark hair now was streaked with white, but her smooth skin looked like that of a woman half her age. Beautiful blue earrings jangled when she spoke. A large multi-coiled gold necklace glinted in the afternoon light.

"I am ashamed of Rimuc's actions," Shatu-Murrim said. "They are unbecoming of a son of Sargon. I loved both my sons when they were babies. However, only one is fit to be king, and it is not the one who wears the crown."

Finally being able to focus, the scribe looked up and saw a sympathetic face gazing down at him. He dared not respond. This could be a trap to make sure he was loyal to Rimuc.

Shatu-Murrim patted his knee. "It is best you keep silent. No one can know what transpires here." She leaned so close to his face that he could feel and smell her sweet breath on his cheek. "I am confident you can get word to the lord in Uruk. Send a simple message. Tell my son he has many friends in Agade and in the palace."

She started to leave, but paused. "Please add this to the message: 'A window that can be used for escape also may be used to enter.' " The queen matriarch smiled one more time, then glided gracefully away, leaving Jushur to recover. He finally struggled to his feet and headed to his study. The scribe would be up half the night writing those messages.

Gemekala stared intently at her brother as he told his family about his trip to Uruk and meeting the deposed king. "Maniticcu has a plan to overthrow the beast," Sheshkala said, casting a quick glance at his sister. "I do not know what it is. I left for home shortly after Rimuc and his men looted the estate. You are all sworn to secrecy."

Asharru shrugged and shook her head. "What can we say if we know nothing?" Sheshkala laughed. It had been a long time since he felt a release of emotion. "Yes, Mother, but Rimuc can not hear about it."

A soft voice whispered something. If they did not know better, Gemekala's family could have mistaken it for a breeze dancing through the room. They did not dare insist that

Gemekala repeat herself. The young woman only recently had left her room after being brutalized by Rimuc.

"It is true, brother? Maniticcu is coming?" she asked in a much stronger tone this time. Sheshkala nodded. "Yes, sister. It is wonderful to see you."

Gemekala glanced at him briefly, but her eyes drifted away and stared into space. A shadow seemed to cross her face as it took on a look of fierce determination. "Brother, can you tell me how many lords have been invited to the King's feast?"

He sat back and counted on his fingers. "All the lords of the great cities have been ordered to attend. Without Uruk that makes nine. Why?"

Gemekala stood up from her bench. "I have a tablet to write. Brother, I will require your assistance to make eight copies when I'm finished." Sheshkala nodded, "Of course, sister." Without another word, she walked into the clay workshop where she toiled through the night, only stopping when she curled up on the floor after collapsing with exhaustion.

8

Maniticcu listened carefully to the message from his mother as it was read to him. His lips pursed into a sly grin as he remembered a certain window in the corner of the palace he used to squeeze through as a boy and shimmy down a date palm when escaping to explore the outside world.

"It is good news the queen supports you, my lord," the general of Uruk's unofficial army said. "However, we can not fit an invading force through a window or even get close enough to the palace to attempt to do so."

The lord held up three fingers. "No, General, I will attempt to carry out my original plan. Find me three of your best fighters who come from the hill country. I need shepherds."

Maniticcu laughed when he saw the astonished look on the general's face. "An invading force will draw much more attention. We require another plan."

Before the general could object again, a large flock of sheep surged through the street outside the palace. One shepherd walked in front and five others trailed behind in case stragglers tried to make an escape.

"My good men, halt if you please," Maniticcu called out as he approached the five shepherds. One of the men stopped, put two fingers in his mouth and let loose with two shrill whistles. The entire flock stopped. Confused bleats echoed off the walls of the buildings.

One of the shepherds walked over to meet Maniticcu. "What is your business? We can't keep these animals still long or they will scatter through the city." Maniticcu started to reply but was uncharacteristically cut off by the general.

"Hold your tongue, woolgatherer! You are addressing the Lord of Uruk. Show some respect!"

Maniticcu frowned at his officer's outburst and was about to chastise him, when he spotted movement out of the corner of his eye. "My Lord, forgive your ignorant servants. It's been three years since we have traveled to Uruk for market. We did not recognize you." All five men had dropped to their knees on the street and looked like they were preparing to be beaten.

"Rise, good men, I perceive no insult," Maniticcu said, gesturing for them to get to their feet. "I propose a transaction with you. It is an unusual request."

The large shepherd broke into an almost toothless smile. "Very good, Lord. How many sheep do you require? We will offer a fair price."

Maniticcu approached the shepherds and spoke with them in a hushed voice. "Beg your pardon, my Lord. You want what?" the large shepherd blurted out. He received a nod and smile as confirmation. "Very good, Lord. When we are finished at market, we will come to the palace before we return." The shepherd turned, then whistled once, signaling the flock to continue on its journey.

"Keep a tight look out, men! We don't want thieves bothering our citizens during the king's celebration now do we?" the captain of the palace guards called out to the sentries who were watching the masses of people stream into Agade. He suspiciously eyed four men strolling together. They wore shepherds' garb, but something about them drew his attention.

"You men there, stop," the captain ordered. He sniffed in disgust when he approached the group. "My gods, don't you shepherds ever bathe? You smell like you've been rolling in sheep shit. Where are your sheep?"

A young man with a close-cropped beard bowed to the officer. "Forgive us, sir. These are the only clothes we have. We heard about the celebration. We come to buy sheep to grow our flocks. The wolves have been fierce this year. Took many lambs. We do not have enough to sell at market." Two of his companions voiced their agreement.

The sergeant took a step back and coughed. "I can tell from your accents you are hill folk. No one but shepherds would put up with that stench." All had spoken except the tallest one of the group who kept his eyes trained on the ground.

"I didn't hear you speak up, man," the sergeant growled as he inspected the man. The shepherd shook his head and made grunting sounds.

"Forgive poor Enmul, sir," the first shepherd said. "The fool made a pass at an innkeeper's wife two years ago. The innkeeper almost killed him with a blow to the head from a pitcher. He's been mute ever since. Hears a little but not much."

Enmul nodded and started gesturing and babbling incoherently. His face and scraggly beard were caked with road dust.

"Oh dear, he's trying to tell you the story of how he was injured," the first shepherd said.

The sergeant waved for Enmul to stop. "Enough! Serves the fool right. You may pass. I hope you brought enough coin for a bath and new clothes. Not many people will be as patient with you as I have been. On your way!"

The first shepherd bowed. "Thank you for your kindness, sir." The four visitors continued on, blending into the throng and strolled through the giant gate of Agade.

"On your way, drunks. Your stench is making me ill. Find somewhere else to take a piss," a guard outside the palace of

Agade barked at four men who stumbled up to him. The second guard looked on in amusement. "More outlanders enjoying cheap wine, I see. Be gone fellows or he will crack your heads with his spear shaft."

One of the drunks chortled and gestured at the guards. "Look at these sorry excuses for soldiers. They must be very important to be watching trees outside the palace walls." His companions erupted in laughter. One of the men started to shuffle into the date palm grove. "I will explode if I don't piss now. Here, let me water this tree."

The first guard growled and started to raise the butt of his spear when one of the other drunks brought him to his knees with a fierce fist jab to the ribs. Before the second guard could respond, two of the other men grabbed him, forcing him to the ground. Both guards were quickly dragged into the darkness among the trees.

"Who do you swear loyalty to? The beast Rimuc or Maniticcu, the rightful king?" one of the attackers whispered as he pressed a knife into the first guard's neck.

The guard grimaced but frowned. "You dogs will be flayed alive for amusement by the King. How dare you attack his majesty's guards. You will not escape Agade ..." His voice was cut off abruptly when the knife plunged into his neck, ending his life.

"Now you. Who do you swear allegiance to?" one of the other attackers hissed at the second guard who lay pinned to the ground, a knife also at his throat. The guard's eyes widened with terror as he whimpered. "Have mercy on me, I beg you. I only serve the King because my father owes a debt to the palace. I owe him no loyalty, I swear."

One of the attackers patted the guard on the head. "Good answer. We let you live for now. Remove your clothes. We need to borrow them."

The guard complied and watched as his dead counterpart was stripped of his garments. Two of the attackers changed into the guards' clothes and assumed positions outside the palace walls. He was taken to a tree and ordered to sit with his back to the trunk. His hands and feet were bound and a gag placed over his mouth.

"You will live if you do not speak or move," the tallest attacker said as he knelt by the captive. "If my man returns, you will be set free and your father's debt forgiven. I, Maniticcu, son of Sargon, swear."

The young man stared in wonder as he watched the Lord of Uruk and his companion scramble up an old date palm tree and maneuver themselves near a window on the second floor of the palace.

9

Sisuthros watched the dancing girls with feigned interest. He and the other lords of the great cities were attending Rimuc's anniversary celebration only because the tyrant's invitation was a thinly veiled threat.

The Lord of Kish glanced around the room, nodding occasionally when he made eye contact with some of his counterparts. Sisuthros finally spotted who he was looking for — the Lord of Lagash.

He strolled over and casually greeted Yahurum. "It is good to see you, cousin, though the circumstances are a bit strained if I may say so." Yahurum lifted his goblet in greeting but only grunted. The corners of his mouth curled down slightly.

Sisuthros watched the festivities for a bit, then leaned toward his cousin. "Before departing for this celebration, I received a most worrisome message in a tablet concerning abuses by a certain lord."

Yahurum let loose with a choking cough, almost spitting out his wine. "What? I received a similar message. It troubled me greatly when my scribe read it to me. I did not know what to make of it."

The frown on the Lord of Lagash's face grew more pronounced. "Killing unarmed peasants, looting their property, raping girls. That is not the way a lord is supposed to act. Our ancestors, the first great kings, declared that we are to be stewards of the people."

Sisuthros took a sip from his goblet. "If we only knew who this lord was, then he could be replaced by another." Yahurum shook his head and only managed a disgusted snort as a loud belly laugh cascaded through the crowd.

"I take my leave, cousin," Sisuthros said, bowing. "I am curious to see if the other lords received a similar message." Yahurum nodded, then looked around the vast hall. "I see the Lord of Kullah is at the feast table. I will speak with him about it. Besides, I am hungry."

The Uruk slave girl was hurrying by a window in the palace when she heard the song of a familiar bird. She walked for a few paces, then stopped and listened. This was a bird she had often heard in the fields on the estate outside Uruk. The bird did not belong in the city.

She tiptoed to the window, tentatively looked out and stifled a scream of delight. Looking back at her was the Lord of Uruk. His finger was pressed tightly against his lips, indicating silence. "My Lord! Is that really you?" she whispered, not believing her eyes.

Maniticcu waved. "Yes, girl. It thrills my heart to see you alive. I need help to make the jump to the window. The branch does not go as far as I thought. I did not come all this way to die in a date grove." The girl stared at him for a moment longer, then disappeared.

The Lord of Uruk leaned back against the trunk. He exhaled in frustration. The success of his mission to regain his crown now rested with a frightened girl. Maniticcu did not have long to swim in his dark thoughts.

He jumped when a voice gushed, "Oh the gods, it is him!" Five heads peered out of the window. The women of Uruk had not believed the girl when she ran to them babbling about their lord in a tree. One of the women held up a rope and tossed one end to Maniticcu.

"Who has the other end? Is it tied to something solid?" he called. A familiar face looked out and waved. It was the daughter of Kurum, the foreman killed by Rimuc.

She held up the other end of the rope. "We have it, Lord." Five pairs of hands raised in the air. All held onto the rope. "Jump, sire. We will pull you through." Maniticcu looked down at the Uruk soldier who followed him up the tree.

"They are women of Uruk, Lord," the soldier said. "You can trust them. This may be your only chance."

Maniticcu tied his end of the rope around his waist and tightly clutched the slack. The Lord of Uruk saw five pairs of determined eyes looking back at him. He took a deep breath and jumped.

10

Sisuthros was growing disgusted as he watched the king's outlandish and lewd behavior. He noticed the other lords of the land were talking amongst themselves and paying little attention to Rimuc who was howling with pleasure during the festivities.

The din in the hall was constant with the buzz of conversation combined with blaring horns and drums that seemed to beat ceaselessly. Rimuc looked to be in his element. His booming laughter only added to the din. The King had taken part in many celebrations since ascending the throne, but his anniversary event was topping them all.

Tables of food from all over the land lined the perimeter of the great hall. The dancing girls performed nonstop. Whenever a dancer Rimuc took an interest in swirled near, he would grab her and take whatever pleasure that amused him with the young woman.

Every now and then the King would call for one of the lords to join him in the debauchery. Only one guest, a young lord freshly appointed by Rimuc, accepted the call to partake in the outlandish activities.

Conversations changed to startled gasps as the other lords and their entourages noticed strangers standing behind the king. One of the dancing girls halted and stared. She soon was joined by her companions. The musicians and drummers stopped in mid song and beat.

Rimuc was the last one to sense the change in the atmosphere of the hall. He had just snatched another dancer who was struggling in his grasp. "What has happened you fools? Carry on! This is a celebration," he shouted. A startled Rimuc shoved the girl away when someone spoke behind him.

"Rimuc, you have disgraced the crown of Sargon. I challenge you to combat." The king whirled around and stared with disbelief. Maniticcu and another man stood behind him with knives drawn.

Struggling to his feet, Rimuc pointed at his brother and screamed. "You came to murder me! That is not fair combat! I have already defeated you, brother. You are lucky I spared you. Now begone before I have you arrested and beheaded."

Maniticcu shook his head and tossed away the knife. "I do not need this to fight you. Come, we will decide who is fit to wear the crown of our father."

Rimuc screamed in indignation. "Guards, seize these men! Their deaths will be the final amusement of my celebration."

The captain of the guard and some of his men started to move toward the two intruders but were stopped when Shatu-Murrim blocked their way. "Guards, you are not to interfere!" the matriarch queen ordered. She turned and walked toward her sons. "No, Maniticcu's challenge is honorable. Rimuc, you have disgraced the crown of Sargon. Prove you are worthy of it."

For once Rimuc was speechless. He stood with his mouth open. "Mother!? You defy me, too? Is no one loyal to the King?" he screamed in fury.

Sisuthros strode toward the front of the crowd. "As the Lord of Kish, birthplace of the great kings of the land, I find this challenge honorable."

He was joined by Yahurum. "I, too, declare this challenge honorable," the Lord of Lagash announced in his deep baritone voice. One by one, all the lords, except the young one who lay in drunken stupor at Rimuc's feet, called out in agreement.

"Ahh! Traitors, all of you!" Rimuc yelled. Without warning, he flung the wine goblet he had been holding at his brother and rushed his foe like a bull charging into battle.

Maniticcu easily ducked the flying goblet, flung his robe off and waited for the onslaught.

Just as the King reached him, Maniticcu dodged to the side, kicked out a leg and tripped Rimuc, who fell with a crash. With great effort, Rimuc stumbled to his feet. He already was sweating from the wine and exertion of his previous activities.

"You have gone soft, great fat one," Maniticcu snarled. "I am no slave girl who cannot escape you."

The King pointed at his brother. "Fight like a man, you dog," he huffed.

Maniticcu shook his head in disgust. "This is combat, you coward. Not like slaughtering a defenseless field laborer."

With a roar, Rimuc rushed forward in an attempt to grab his opponent, but he was only greeted with a fist to his temple. The King slumped to one knee with a groan. The next hit slammed full force in his ribs, knocking him to the ground.

Maniticcu leaped on top of his brother, putting him in a choke hold. Rimuc gagged and rolled onto his back, hoping to squash his brother. Even though Maniticcu could hardly breathe from the great weight, he squeezed with all his strength, fueled by the memories of the beating he had suffered at the hands of Rimuc seven years ago.

The Lord of Uruk gave one violent effort to kick out from underneath Rimuc and was rewarded when his gasping brother rolled to one side. Rimuc started flailing his arms wildly. The King's face turned a deep red and his eyes bulged from the pressure on his throat.

Maniticcu could feel Rimuc weakening. This only strengthened his resolve. A voice from far away seeped through his rage, catching his attention.

"Please Maniticcu, do not kill your brother," Shatu-Murrim implored as she knelt beside her two struggling sons. "Rimuc, do you yield? He will kill you!"

The king could barely focus as the air was being squeezed out of him. He heard "yield" and responded by slapping the floor — the signal for surrender.

"Maniticcu, release him now!" the matriarch queen implored her first born. The Lord of Uruk growled with disappointment, but released his hold. He rolled away and rose to his feet. Rimuc lay in a heap, gasping and choking for air.

Shatu-Murrim took Maniticcu's arm and led him to the edge of the crowd. "Maniticcu has defeated Rimuc in fair combat and claims the crown of Sargon," she said. "I give my blessing. What say you, my lords?"

Sisuthros approached and bowed to Maniticcu. "Hail to the King of the land. Long may he and his sons and sons of his sons, reign!" Yahurum, the other lords and everyone in the great hall joined in, shouting "aye."

Maniticcu's companion stood guard over the defeated Rimuc, who remained on the floor. His hands covered his face. "Sire, what do we do with him? Is he to be executed?" the Uruk soldier asked as he looked in disgust at the whimpering man.

The new king squeezed his mother's hands. "No, he spared me the first time we fought. I now spare him, but cast him into exile."

Maniticcu walked over and knelt by Rimuc. "You are free to go, brother, but you are forbidden to reside in any of the great cities of the land. If you return to Agade, I will pay one thousand shekels for your head. I understand one of your old friends owns a house of whores in the outlying city of Bit Bunkakki. Perhaps you can be king there."

Under guard, Rimuc was ushered out of the great hall, never to be seen again.

11

Maniticcu smiled as he listened to the tale of The Great Fatted Bull read to him by his new head scribe. "I am pleased with my mother's role in the tale. I would like to hear it again."

Sheshkala bowed, found the entry on the freshly created tablet and read it a second time for the King. "His mother says, 'The Fatted King is not a lordly one. As for me, I know that I don't place great trust in him.' "

All in the room praised the story, except one young man. Naram-Suen sat quietly. His mouth dipped in a frown.

"What troubles you, my son?" Maniticcu asked.

"It is a good tale, Father," the heir to the throne said, "however, I am worried future kings will be troubled. This story tells how a lord can be deposed. They may not know the tale of the good King Maniticcu taking back his rightful crown."

Naram-Suen was a serious thinker who had read the works of the great philosophers of their people. "I mean no disrespect, Father, but the day may come when the seed of Sargon no longer rules in the land. Your father gained the crown after battling the old king in Uruk. Perhaps a son of Kish or a son of Lagash or even another in Uruk may claim the kingship some day."

The High Counselor agreed. "Naram-Suen is wise," Jushur said. "The scribe who wrote this is to be congratulated, but I cannot advise the tale to be copied for all to read."

Sheshkala asked permission to speak. Maniticcu chuckled. "Once again, scribe, you do not need to seek permission to speak in court."

He blushed a bit. "Thank you, sire. It has only been six months since you asked me to serve you. I am still learning proper court etiquette." The king waved for Sheshkala to continue.

"Perhaps the learned Jushur, an honored student of the Great School of Scribes, would care to look at the tablet," Sheshkala said as he handed the tablet to the High Counselor. "I would like his opinion on its craftsmanship."

Jushur chuckled. "You flatter me, young man. I heard you read the tale. You give me an easy task." His grin slowly melted away as he studied the tablet. He ran his fingers from right to left trying to decipher the characters as was tradition with scribes in the land.

The High Counselor put the tablet down on his lap and cast a puzzled look at Sheshkala. "I can not read this. I do not understand how this can be. This tablet makes no sense. The words are incorrect. I only recognized the names Lu-mah and Nu-mah."

Jushur scratched his chin as he pondered the problem and looked at Sheshkala. "Did you write this?" The scribe shook his head no. "Do you know who created this? He must be very clever."

Sheshkala tried unsuccessfully to stifle a chuckle. "Yes, the scribe is very clever indeed, High Counselor."

The king leaned forward. "How is this possible? Sheshkala read from the tablet, but you cannot."

Jushur shook his head in disbelief as he studied the tablet. "It does not make sense," he mumbled. "What is the secret?"

Sheshkala walked over to Jushur and showed him a series of supposedly insignificant characters at the bottom. "Apply these characters to the text. The scribe who created this calls it a code."

Once again, the High Counselor studied the tablet. His lips moved as he painstakingly read it. "This is magic, indeed. Ah, wait. Now I understand. Lu-mah is a bad lord and Nu-mah is the good lord who avenges a wrong."

Jushur laughed. "Sire, it is your story. But, it is hidden in characters that make no sense until the secret of the code is revealed. Very clever indeed, young man."

Sheshkala bowed. "I cannot take credit, High Counselor."

An arm reached over Jushur's shoulder and picked up the tablet. "I wish to look at it. May I?" Naram-Suen asked. Jushur jumped a bit but nodded in approval. "Of course, prince. You have been trained in scribe writing. I am eager to hear your opinion."

The High Counselor watched with amusement as a scowling Naram-Suen carefully inspected the tablet. He knew the prince considered himself to be an accomplished scholar and indeed he was, but sometimes the royal heir's opinion of his abilities did not match reality. However, the young man meant well and had a good heart.

After more studying and expelling an exasperated "humpf," Naram-Suen handed the tablet back. "My compliments to the creator. I have never seen anything like it before. Please show me how to read the code."

Sheshkala sat next to the prince and pointed out which characters should be substituted in the text. After the lesson, the prince looked up. A huge smile lit up his face. "It is as if a cloud has lifted and revealed the tale. This is very clever. Very few people will be able to read this, father. Your story will be remembered, but it will remain hidden from those who would misuse it."

Maniticcu reached over and ruffled his son's long black hair. "That pleases me greatly." The king turned to Sheshkala. "Who is this scribe? He should be properly rewarded."

Sheshkala looked as if he had been stabbed. The color drained from his face. "Forgive me, my king. The scribe lives in fear of retribution and begged me not reveal a name. I was told presenting this tablet to the court would be honor enough."

Jushur studied the scribe's face. Before Maniticcu could respond, he stood up. "Forgive an old man, sire. My body stiffens when I sit too long," he said hoping the diversion would work. "Well, well, it seems to me if this scribe wishes to remain in the shadows, perhaps that is best."

The High Counselor and king locked eyes for a moment. Neither spoke. Jushur's eyes flicked at Sheshkala who sat very still. The scribe stared at the floor not daring to look at the three men, lest he be forced to reveal his precious secret.

Jushur shuffled over to Sheshkala. He stood behind him, patting him on the shoulder. "Forgive my manners, young man. How does your family fare? The last time I visited, you were mourning a tragedy. I hope they are all well."

Sheshkala looked up, startled at the question but took comfort in Jushur's kindly smile. "My family is well, thank you High Counselor. We are no longer in mourning. The wounds are healing slowly."

Once again, Maniticcu's eyes met Jushur's. Something in the old man's gaze told the king not to insist on an answer. "Very well, scribe. If you do see the writer again, please pass along my thanks." Naram-Suen started to object, but was cut off by a wave from his father. "This can be discussed later."

Later that day, when Sheshkala shared the evening meal with his family, Gemekala timidly asked him if the tablet had been read to the King. "Yes, he was very happy with the accounting of his story and even more pleased with the secrecy that protects it."

He paused to take a sip of wine. "Old Jushur and even the prince thought it was clever. They said if the scribe who created it wishes to remain unknown, then they will honor *his* wishes."

For the first time in months, Sheshkala saw his sister smile.

Guardian flashed white, indicating approval of the events with the sentients it and Caretaker monitored. Communication between the higher life forms appeared to have thwarted more unnecessary violence and bloodshed among them, Guardian messaged its counterpart.

Caretaker experienced an unfamiliar vibration. It was a feeling the entity vaguely remembered from a past organic life — pride. The sentients on the third planet from the sun appeared to be making progress toward civilization.

While the two entities were discussing the future of the promising sentients on the planet, a shock wave of energy stung their entire cloud. Guardian was momentarily frozen, unable to respond with a defensive reaction.

A familiar vibration emanated from a new giant glowing orb that hung in space before them. The orb flickered then dissipated revealing Other and a strange metallic object. Other flashed an iridescent blue, greeting Caretaker and Guardian as if it were a mother uniting with her long-lost children.

Caretaker danced around Other sending vibrations of welcome. However, Guardian hovered near the alien. It was mistrustful of something so unfamiliar. The entity attempted to taste the object but was zapped almost into nothingness by a powerful jolt of energy.

Other rendered assistance to Guardian by merging with it, momentarily restoring its energy. It sent vibrations to Caretaker and Guardian explaining that the alien object contained highly evolved life forms that would study, possibly manipulate and take some of the planet's sentients for settlement elsewhere.

Guardian and Caretaker both flashed red with objections. Other called for a merging with the two entities. The story unfolded in nanoseconds. Caretaker and Guardian learned the alien craft contained a species that had evolved from the original family of Searcher and Other.

Searcher had found the intelligent life forms when it was looking for potential planets for habitation. After tasting the alien sentients, Searcher discovered the familiar vibrations of the old family. The organisms were the descendants of the ship it had spared during a cleansing.

It took several solar revolutions, but communication was finally established between the entities and the new sentients. Both sides agreed to work together to seed other worlds with higher life forms. And now they were here to harvest some of the third planet's inhabitants and scatter them in distant galaxies.

Guardian objected with a flash of red. A cataclysmic event in the past made it distrustful of these aliens. Their ancestors had sent that first automated ship that tried to destroy the third and fourth planets as well as their family cloud.

The entity merged briefly with Caretaker to communicate its misgivings, but its partner would not defy Other. Still glowing red with displeasure at the turn of events, it told Caretaker it could no longer protect the planet due to the alien intrusion.

Caretaker flashed yellow with sadness. Guardian bade farewell, then blinked away leaving Caretaker and their small cloud to monitor the planet by themselves. As Other communicated more orders to Caretaker, the alien craft entered the planet's atmosphere in search of the native sentients.

IV

THE ARCHITECTS OF OMNIPOTENCE

1

The flying ship circled slowly over the continents of the fertile world it was surveying. Panels on the bottom of the ship reflected either white or blue to confuse any onlookers and to keep the barbaric sentients on the planet from panicking. There would be plenty of time later for first contact when the visitors deemed the time was right.

After ten days of collecting sentient specimens while darting over mountains, searching through lush valleys and skimming over the vast oceans between the continents, it was time to examine their findings. The craft set down in a mountain meadow inhabited only by lower life organisms.

High Commander Gyntaf waited patiently while Head Scientist Ail plugged its research into the control monitor. Ail snorted with relief as the first image appeared on the giant wall vid.

"As well you know, High Commander, we have collected thirty-nine sentients from various locales on this planet. It is curious. All share 99.99 percent of the same DNA. They are basically the same species despite their various skin colors, facial structures and body shapes. We have not run thorough reproduction tests, but the blood analyses indicate every specimen could breed and reproduce fully fertile progeny with each other."

Gyntaf said nothing as it watched hundreds of images flash over the screen, showing sentients of all ages and races at play, eating, hunting, performing reproductive acts in a variety of odd ways and giving birth.

"These are the sentients the vibration beings requested to populate their new worlds? Their reproductive practices are hasty, physical acts. I find it odd that it takes two beings with their peculiar physical anomalies to produce offspring. It is not as efficient as our species. Each one of us can produce offspring."

The head scientist agreed. "Yes, High Commander. The sentients are not the only species that require contributions from two individuals to reproduce. A vast majority of the lower organisms here also practice this method."

Gyntaf blew out a derisive whuff through its nose slits. "That is what happens when evolution is not monitored carefully — inefficiency. Apparently Searcher and Other value this species for its survival instincts and adaptability. Unfortunately, these characteristics are connected to a genetic combative tendency. I see you needed to apply extra restraints to the sentients with those protruding sex organs."

Ail confirmed with a grunt. "Even some of the sentients with the internal sex organs — I call them birthlings — can be quite violent. Their howls are most awful. After sedating the beasts, I have managed to collect valuable genetic samples."

The High Commander swiveled its platform around to inspect the lineup of experts who stood nearby ready to give their reports. Gyntaf called on the geology expert. "Does this planet have anything to offer us?"

Daearegwr stepped up to the control bank that swept in a semicircle halfway around the command center and slipped in a wafer-shaped module. "Yes, High Commander, the planet is rich in many precious metals. However, it will be most difficult to obtain them with the small crews the High Ones allow us to travel with."

Gyntaf gestured to another expert. "This is one of richest planets in food stuff I have ever researched," gushed Nutrition Specialist Maethgyt. The local sentients are able to consume plants and life forms — very unusual. All the tests I have run indicate many of the native plants will be nutritious, with a few genetic modifications of course, to our species."

The Chief Hydrologist concurred with Maethgyt. "We will be able to consume the fresh water of this world after it is run through a simple purification system. Our species could live here indefinitely if need be."

Head Scientist Ail stepped forward, seeking permission to speak, which was granted. "We possibly could live on this planet but only at high elevations. The oxygen content is much too rich for our species close to their sea levels. We would choke to death. That is why I recommended landing at this location. We may leave the craft and explore without oxygen masks for short periods."

Gyntaf swiveled back and watched images from all over the planet dance on the vid screen. "It seems this planet offers riches as well as challenges. We will need assistance from those clumsy sentients to harvest minerals. How difficult will it be to coerce them to work?"

Ail emitted a strange mewling noise of amusement. "It seems the sentients of all these races do not understand each other. They all speak different languages."

The High Commander swung its long angular neck around and glared at Ail. "How can this be? Those beings have to have a common mother language if they originated from the same ancestors. We have to translate almost forty languages to communicate with them?"

The Head Scientist held up its long arms in frustration. "I extrapolate that these sentients may speak hundreds or even thousands of languages. This may explain the different stages of cultural evolution among the races."

Gyntaf blew out an even louder whuff to show its annoyance. "The High Ones have presented us with a difficult challenge."

"Tell the crew they have three solar risings to explore the terrain." The High Commander turned and addressed the assembled experts: "That should give you accomplished scientists the time to come up with solutions on how to control these barbarians."

As the experts were shuffling out of the command center, Gyntaf beckoned Ail and Maethgyt to come closer for a personal conference. "Have any of your sentient specimens died from your tests?" the High Commander asked. Ail confirmed a few had succumbed. "If they are still fresh, I wish to sample one. It has been too long since I have dined on flesh."

Maethgyt looked at Ail. "If the Head Scientist would be so kind as to offer me a sample, I will prepare a meal for you, High Commander." Ail agreed but looked the other way, a bit sickened at the thought of eating a fellow sentient.

"Nonsense," Gyntaf said, gesturing toward its two subordinates. "There should be plenty for the three of us to dine on. We will make it a celebratory feast. If we have to transport and work with these beasts, then we should be able to enjoy some simple pleasures from them."

After being dismissed, the two scientists were well away from earshot of Gyntaf when Maethgyt stumbled against the wall of the ship, making gurgling and gagging sounds. Ail bent over, hiccuping violently and trying desperately not to expel its last meal.

"I will visit the medical officer before I deliver the meal," Maethgyt said. "We will need an elixir for our stomachs so we don't embarrass ourselves in front of the High Commander." Ail gasped a "yes," but continued hiccuping.

Gyntaf pulled up a pop-up screen and swayed back and forth on its platform, snorting in amusement as it watched the two science officers retch in the hallway. "Weaklings," the leader murmured to itself. "We will have to do many unpleasant things to these so-called sentients before they are useful to us."

2

Ail stood in the command center of the ship waiting to be recognized while Gyntaf stared intently at a small screen. The High Commander knew the Head Scientist was there; it just wanted Ail to appreciate who was in charge of this mission.

Without warning, Gyntaf swung around on its platform and pointed one of its four tentacled fingers at Ail. "There have been three solar risings. What plan have you and your counterparts created to deal with the beasts?"

The Head Scientist had become accustomed to Gyntaf's theatrical tactics to keep the crew subdued. "My colleagues and I have a plan that should bring a vast majority of the sentients under our control."

Despite itself, Gyntaf bobbed its head up and down with excitement and gestured for Ail to continue.

"We intensely studied twenty of the dominant cultures and found they all have a commonality — the belief in deities. We believe this practice of worshiping unseen forces was fostered early in their genetic history by the High Ones. It is our theory that we can use this trait to our advantage."

Gyntaf contorted its long neck in an upward arc as it considered the plan. "Deity? Belief in something they cannot touch or see. Such primitives we have had foisted on us. How can we use this practice to our advantage?"

Ail swelled with pride as it inserted an info cube into the command console. "We will provide them with deities they can see, touch and best of all, fear. We can produce these deities from the population itself. My colleagues and I can train, reprogram and genetically manipulate a selected few sentients to do our bidding. They will be able to interact and manipulate their populations."

The High Commander expelled a whuff of pleasure. "Use their own species against them? How deliciously devious of you and your cohorts." Gyntaf gazed into space for a moment, then focused again on Ail. "How do we control these deities without keeping them caged?"

Ail tried not to show its pleasure at anticipating Gyntaf's question. "We will educate these deities as to our abilities and the power of our technology. They will know we are the source of their power and can eliminate them at our whim. Forgive me, High Commander, but it will be a partnership similar to what the High Ones have imposed on us."

Gyntaf narrowed its large saucer-like eyes into slits at the mention of the High Ones — those mysterious energy entities of Sentinel's cluster that could cast all members of their race into nonexistence on a whim. The High Ones spared one small group from Family during a cleansing of their original home planet, letting it evolve into a species of exceptional intellectual achievement.

"Interesting, slightly interfering with the evolution of a species in an effort to control it," Gyntaf said. "Has this ever been done before on the other worlds?"

Ail thrummed its long fingers on its chest. "We do not believe so, High Commander. Every first contact we have on record has always gone according to plan. The terrorized population surrenders and complies with our wishes."

Gyntaf bobbed its head again, excited at the potential of this plan. It then did something out of character that even surprised the stoic Ail. It praised an underling. "A brilliant plan! Most impressive, Head Scientist. Convey my congratulations to your colleagues. I will nominate all of you to be used as blueprint breeders. Your genetics should be spread throughout our kind to enhance our species."

The Head Scientist stared in wonder at its leader. Gyntaf was offering a rare honor to Ail and its colleagues that usually was bestowed on heroes. "My sincere thanks, High Commander."

Gyntaf flicked a nonchalant wave. "Of course the honor is commensurate with carrying out the plan and bringing the sentient populations under control. I assume it will take many solar orbits before our altered deities will be released?"

Ail bowed its head in the affirmative. "Yes, High Commander. It will depend on how young we start with each sentient. We will not release our deities until we are satisfied that they are ready."

With another of its famous whuffs, Gyntaf whirled back around to the command console. "Get to work then, Head Scientist. We need to build you and your colleagues a research facility to carry out this aggressive plan. I would like to see Home World again before I dry up and whither away into nonexistence."

3

Cronus frowned at the news. "Zenicetes still lives? How is that possible?! We sent him to the front lines on the battle field. An Aeolian archer or spear man was sure to bring him down."

Melampos shrugged. "He is a true son of yours, Sire. He fights with an energy, even joy, which frightens the enemy." The general frowned as he studied the report on his scroll. "The Aeolian king swore his men would kill his half-breed grandson. He was not happy to give his daughter to you when his people sued for peace."

The Dorian king paced back and forth in the great hall. "I never should have allowed his mother to raise him away from the palace. Now, I have another son to worry about. I've exiled all my royal children to my fortress on Mount Olympus. My counselors warned me Poseidon would cause me the most grief, but they were wrong."

Cronus slumped his chair, worried about this new threat to his leadership. "How old is this cub of my blood?" he growled. One of his scribes hastily searched through a satchel of scrolls and sighed with relief when he found what he was looking for. "It appears your youngest son is sixteen, sire."

"What?!" the King yelled, slamming down his goblet so hard that wine exploded out of it like a volcano. "That's a mere child! Grown warriors can't even cut down a green boy?"

Melampos cleared his throat. "Pardon, Sire, but Zenicetes stands about a head taller than most men. He already has a full beard and a mane of red hair, not unlike yours. The young man is most imposing. He also is accompanied by a troop of fifty very loyal young men he calls his brothers."

Cronus could not help but chuckle with pride. "Of course he is imposing. That seed springs from a mighty tree!" His eyes narrowed. "He has followers already? As my son, I am sure he dreams of deposing me and claiming the kingship. That's what I did. I expect no less of my offspring. Now, give me a plan how to remove this threat. I want to sleep peacefully for a change."

An old man stood up and waited to be recognized. Cronus waved for his eldest counselor to speak. "Sire, I have been told Zenicetes has an insatiable appetite for women."

The king furrowed his brow but let loose with a great belly laugh. "I would expect no less from a royal son. Go on, continue."

The counselor bowed. "Perhaps the lad would respond to an invitation to a wedding feast — his wedding feast. We have received many offers from minor kings offering their daughters to your sons in hopes of forming alliances before you overthrow them in battle. Appeal to his ego and his appetites, Sire. This young lion may be an easy snare after he has satiated himself with wine, food and a woman."

Cronus stared at the old man in disbelief, then roared his approval. "What a deliciously deceptive plan! At sixteen I would have run for three straight days to be so honored. Is there a suitable bride? We need a prize that will make him come in from the wild."

General Melampos conferred with the old counselor for a moment, then turned to the king. "Sire, one of the Achaean kings has offered his daughter. I have seen her. She is a tall, dark-haired beauty. One that surely will catch your son's eye. Any young man would kill his brother to bed that one."

Rising from his chair, Cronus nodded to Melampos and to the counselor. "Excellent plan." He called for a scribe, who came running and sat down on a stool. "Make the arrangements. We will accept the Achaean king's offer. Send word to Zenicetes that by royal command he is to be wed during the next full moon. A refusal will be seen as treason. If he accepts, we will capture him. If he refuses, I will have him killed."

A chuckle escaped the counselor. "It appears, Sire, that you have added your own inescapable ingredient to our 'deliciously deceptive' plan, as you described it." Cronus nodded and lifted his goblet to salute the old man.

Zenicetes' eyes grew as wide as saucers as one of his men read aloud the scroll that was delivered by none other than Melampos, the general of Cronus' armies. "I am ordered to appear at court to be married to some Achaean princess I have never met? Am I but a pawn to my father?"

Melampos gestured toward the prince. "This marriage is your reward for your victory in battle. You are the first son he has bestowed with such an honor."

One of Zenicetes' followers smirked. "We have heard Cronus has imprisoned his sons, even his daughters. How do we know the king can be trusted?"

The general's eyes narrowed into slits as he took two steps forward. His hand gripped his sword's handle. Even though his weapon was sheathed, his intention was obvious to all in the tent. Melampos' words came out slow but strong.

"This is not an invitation, pup. The king's orders are to be heeded. Otherwise Zenicetes will be declared an enemy and treated as such. His other sons and daughters are under guard for their own protection." A heavy silence filled the tent as both parties weighed their options. It was broken when a smiling Zenicetes rose from his seat and walked toward the general.

"Marriage and a banquet feast sound much more enjoyable than being under guard for my own protection. Can you at least tell me, General, if this Achaean princess is pleasant to look at?"

Melampos took his hand off his sword and offered it to Zenicetes. "I have seen the princess myself. I swear she is a beauty — dark-haired and tall. Not as tall as you, Prince, but in my opinion an excellent match."

The Prince and the General grasped each other's arms. "Please send my regards to the King, and tell him I am humbled by his generous request, which I most gladly will accept," Zenicetes said.

He turned to the two companions who had accompanied him to the meeting with Melampos and his two men. "What a grand occasion this will be!" the young prince crowed. "On the same day I will meet my father and my bride." He looked back at the general. "Perhaps the King is getting ready to announce his successor. I will try my best to convince him that I am worthy."

Melampos shook his head. "Who knows the king's mind? I am not privy to those plans, Prince. The King was most impressed by your victory over your grandfather's army and wants to reward you appropriately."

Zenicetes beamed with pride. This was the first time anyone in the King's court had addressed him as Prince. He took it as a sign of acceptance.

After bidding the Prince farewell, Melampos was amazed at how well the meeting had gone. He had been impressed with Zenicetes but was surprised that the young man had been so easily swayed by compliments and his own ambitions. *Oh to be young and so full of blind confidence. Cronus will be most pleased,* Melampos thought as he walked away.

The wedding feast had been glorious. Zenicetes could not have been more impressed with Metis, his bride. Melampos had not exaggerated about her beauty. King Cronus seemed genuinely happy to see him. Father and son sat next to each other at a large table laden with meats, cheeses, fruits and of course wine pitchers that never seemed to go empty.

Long-winded speeches were delivered by lords from across the land, always followed by never ending toasts to King Cronus and the new royal couple. It was well into the night when a chant arose from the raucous crowd: "To bed, to bed!"

A cheer erupted when Zenicetes stumbled to his feet. Even though drunk, the Prince had the wherewithal to ask for the King's permission to leave. Cronus applauded the couple and granted the request to depart, which brought an even louder roar from the banquet goers.

Zenicetes held out his hand to Metis. He almost fell over two times, but his bride ably caught the prince and helped maneuver him to the large private room that featured a huge bed on a platform full of soft lambskin blankets.

The couple had barely shed their clothes and collapsed giggling on the bed, when the door crashed open. Several dozen of Cronus' men charged toward the newlyweds. Thinking this was part of the festivities, Zenicetes sat up and tried to order the interlopers away but collapsed from dizziness caused by the copious amount of wine he had consumed.

Someone screamed, perhaps it was Metis. Then Zenicetes faintly heard shouts of anger and calls to arms as his men charged in after the intruders and tried to rush to his side.

A crack of thunder, followed by a blinding light, brought the combatants to their knees before any of them could draw blood. Another loud crack echoed through the palace knocking everyone but Metis unconscious.

At the first sign of the attack, she had hidden underneath a layer of the lambskins. She peaked out and watched in terror as monsters appeared from a heavy mist and gathered around Zenicetes.

"Yes, yes, this is the specimen we want," Ail gurgled as it ran a quick scan over Zenicetes limp body. The operation was going much more smoothly than the alien scientist had predicted. Ail had expected the tall, young sentient to put up a fight. Whatever beverage the youngster had consumed apparently had drugged him into unconsciousness. A curious, but positive turn.

One of the alien retraction team members gestured toward the pile of blankets where Metis was hiding. "Head Scientist, one of the sentients is still alert."

Ail snorted. "Leave it. The birthling is of no concern to us." The alien swung its long neck around and glimpsed terror-glazed eyes staring back at it. "Yes, leave it. The story of our specimen's abduction may become legend and only help when we return it with our improvements."

Metis watched helplessly as Zenicetes' body was placed on a stretcher by the monsters, then fainted when another ear-splitting explosion cascaded through the palace.

The minuscule entity flashed orange with excitement as it conveyed the message to Caretaker. Apparently, the alien vessels turned off their vibration shields once they were well within the planet's atmosphere. It seemed the world's magnetic fields interfered with their technology. The scout entity had followed one of those curious metal ships to the surface and discovered it not only could touch the vessel but enter it without being detected.

Caretaker emitted a vibrant blue, indicating pleasure. This information was most welcome. The alien crafts were vulnerable to entity influence. That information must be used wisely. If its cloud attacked the aliens, they would have to act in concert before the enemy could take action to defend themselves.

The only solace Caretaker experienced was the fact the aliens were not exterminating the sentients. At the moment, the intruders seemed intent on studying some of the intelligent species. Caretaker watched with trepidation, however, as thousands of the self-aware beings were collected and gathered into ships to be taken away.

The entity normally would have fought this action, but Other had explained those sentients were to be used to colonize other worlds that would support life. No more letting life evolve into a clumsy mess when these life forms, with their fierce survival instincts but malleable minds, were acceptable candidates.

Caretaker was curious why the aliens were concentrating so much time and effort on only seven sentients. It was such an insignificant number. Caretaker emitted a call for a gathering of its small cloud of entities. It transmitted the information from the scout, then ordered all activities by the aliens to be closely monitored. Caretaker especially wanted to know what the aliens were planning to do with those seven sentients.

4

Zenicetes tried to open his eyes, but they felt heavy and refused to move. His body ached with such a dull throbbing pain that he could not lift his head. He tried to remember what had happened.

His last memories were of the grand wedding feast. The young man had been feted by none other than King Cronus and married to an Achaean princess. Everything after that was a blurred, confused dream. Zenicetes remembered the feel of the lambskin blankets when he collapsed on the bed, the sounds of men rushing into the room, then an ear-splitting explosion. Everything went black after that.

Was he dead? No, he could feel pain. Perhaps he was dying. Zenicetes groaned as he tried to move, but managed to finally open his eyes. Two dark-skinned men stood nearby watching him with amusement.

Look, our 'little' brother has finally awakened. One of the men smiled and walked towards him. Zenicetes twitched in terror. He had heard the voice in his head, not with his ears.

What kind of magic was this? Were they gods? He tried to calm his breathing, but his heart pounded so hard it felt like it was trying to explode from his chest. Another thought made his body stiffen with fright. If these were gods, then he may be their sacrifice.

The wedding feast was a trap, Zenicetes thought. *Cronus must have offered me as a sacrifice to eliminate another threat to his crown. I was so foolish to have accepted his invitation.*

Amenemsou, you have frightened the giant, another voice echoed in his head. *He has not been conditioned as we have. He still thinks as a barbarian.*

The closest man nodded. *You are correct. Zenicetes, we are gods or are becoming gods. Do not fear. No harm is going to come to you. Our masters have chosen you to become a god as well.*

With great effort, Zenicetes turned his head to look at Amenemsou. He tried to speak, but no words came out. The man, who looked like one of the traders from the southern lands, pointed to his head. *Say it with your mind, barbarian.*

Zenicetes frowned. This was twice now he had been called that insult. *I am not a barbarian, you dark-skinned son of a thief.* The thought escaped from his mind before he could control it. The two strange men burst out laughing.

Another voice echoed in his head. *Well done, you son of a goat herder. You are learning.* The man farthest away was nodding his head. His lips curled in a smirk. Zenicetes stared at him. He had never seen a person with such a flat face and dark reddish skin tone.

Four new figures seemed to appear out of nowhere, hovered momentarily over Zenicetes bed, then gently landed on the floor. A handsome dark-skinned young man with long, flowing black hair smiled down at him.

Greetings, brother. You are the last chosen one among the great races to join us. Amenemsou tells me you are still in pain. We have all experienced the great discomfort of being bestowed the gifts. It will pass soon enough, and your body will flow with a power you have never felt before.

Zenicetes allowed his eyes to drift away to peer at the other three men. He focused first on the man nearest the "speaker." His appearance was not unlike his people, but a great, curly black beard flowed down his face. The man's black hair rubbed against his shoulders, but it was not as long as the speaker's.

The prince stared in wonder at the other two men. One of them had eyes that were crinkled half shut as if stung by the sun. The other man's eyes were more oval and turned down at the corners, but he had the most unusual facial hair. A long mustache dripped down his face and half a beard dangled from his chin.

A loud guffaw made Zenicetes jump. *Look, our young warrior seems to be startled by our brothers from the eastern peoples. He may be the size of a tree, but he shrinks at the sight of a new face.* The long-bearded man shook his head with amusement.

Amenemsou, the first man who communicated with Zenicetes, leaned over him. *Gods from the stars have chosen us to be gods among our peoples. They have put magic in our bodies to help us live a thousand lifetimes! They are teaching us some of their knowledge, which we will then teach others.*

He straightened up, took a step backward and again pointed to his head. *This is how we can talk with each other. We do not understand each others' words, but mind speak is the same for all of us.*

Zenicetes' mind was exploding with questions, but his eyes grew heavy from exhaustion. The first man reached out and patted his shoulder. *You will learn everything in due time, barbarian. Now rest. The masters have placed a lot of magic in your body.*

The young prince frowned and grunted in frustration. *I am not a bar ...* He then collapsed into a deep sleep as disturbing dreams invaded his mind.

The smell of food finally roused Zenicetes from his heavy slumber. His stomach gurgled with hunger. When his eyes fluttered open, he saw the six men sitting at a long table laden with meats and fruit. He stretched his muscles and was greeted only with stiffness. The pain was gone.

Look, the young warrior awakens. Come join us, barbarian. It has been weeks since you have eaten solid food. The voice must have come from the man with the long beard who grinned wickedly at him. The other five men looked up and greeted him.

Zenicetes swung his feet over the bed and tried to stand. His weak legs almost collapsed under him, but he caught himself. The long-haired handsome man started to rise to help, but was stopped by the others. *Did you foretell that we all would be beset with battles and attacks from within and without?* Long-beard asked. *Our new brother will have to learn to react fast and defend himself for centuries. No time to coddle him now.*

The long-haired man nodded and sat back down. The other diners returned to their meals. Zenicetes stretched his legs a few more times until he could feel the tingle of blood flowing through them. He stood up again and even though a bit wobbly, the young man managed to shuffle to the table. Once there, he couldn't shove the food into his mouth fast enough.

Zenicetes finally stopped eating to reach for a mug. He almost spit the contents out. *This is just water? Where is the wine? If we are to be gods, surely they must serve us wine.* The other men just shook their heads.

Long-beard tossed a bunch of grapes to Zenicetes. *This is as close to wine as we can get, barbarian. The masters can do wondrous things, but it escapes them how to make a good batch of wine. Their attempts taste like horse piss!* The other men nodded in agreement.

Zenicetes stood up and pounded the table with his fist. *I am not a barbarian, you desert dweller. My name is Zenicetes and you will address me so.* Long-beard chuckled. *It is about time you introduced yourself. It is an honor to meet you,*

Zenicetes. I was given the birth name, Enmerkar, but I have chosen Anu as my god name.

One by one, the other men stood and introduced themselves:

I was born Govinda but have chosen Krishna as my god name.

I am Ninigi and will keep my name.

My family name Huangdi shall be my god name.

I was given the name, Quetzelchel, at birth but choose the god name Quetzalcoatl.

Amenemsou is too lowly of a name for a god so I will be called Amun.

The newest member to join the party of gods sat back in wonder. *Why did some of you choose different names? Becoming a god will bring honor to birth names and families.*

Amun nodded. *Perhaps, yes. But, we now will have many enemies. Even though we are becoming gods, we will not be able to protect our blood kin from all danger.*

Krishna smiled as he reached for a piece of fruit. *It also is important, my friend, to choose a name that our people can say in reverence. In prayers if need be. It must flow from the tongue and into their hearts.*

Anu erupted with one of his famous guffaws. *It also will be a good thing to have a name that strikes terror in the hearts of our enemies.*

Zenicetes was silent for a few moments. *How do you choose a name?*

Quetzalcoatl sat back and shook his head. *It will come to you in a dream, little brother. Many new ideas come to us in dreams. Perhaps from the masters. Perhaps not.* The others stared at Krishna. *Even I do not know how this happens. It is indeed a mystery.*

The next morning, Zenicetes was silent during first meal even though Anu greeted him with a lusty: *Good morning, barbarian!* He consumed several mouthfuls before stopping.

Krishna looked at him expectantly as a half smile flickered on his face. *It seems little brother has something to say.*

Nodding, the young man took a deep breath. *What does it mean when you dream of two names?* The other gods-in-training stopped eating and waited. *I awoke with two names in my mind. A voice told me my native people will call me Zeus, and a strange northern people will call me Odin.*

Anu walked over to Zeus/Odin and slapped him on the back so hard it caused him to cough. *Well, little brother, so you are the god of two peoples we were told about. The masters must have great faith in you. You are a barbarian no longer!*

5

Caretaker flashed orange with concern at the latest report from its scouts. All the gods, except Krishna, who had been released by the aliens with genetic upgrades aided by tech-driven weapons and flyers, were abusing the natural-born sentients. Those seven individuals were now more than mere sentients, they were enhanced beings.

If they were not using the fellow sentients for slaves to mine precious minerals for the aliens, they were forcing them to labor for their own pride or using them as pawns in war games. Caretaker watched with curiosity as these males mated with hundreds or even thousands of females, producing myriad offspring.

Several of the enhanced beings handpicked sons and daughters to assist them, also turning them into superior specimens. One of enhanced sentients, a large individual with fiery red hair, freed his brothers and sisters after killing his father, then rewarded his siblings with extra abilities.

This red-haired enhanced being and another of its kind with a flowing black beard and long black hair loved to amuse themselves by watching their people go to war. Tribes of the same people, who lived in different communities, often were inspired to challenge each other for superiority, property and land.

After growing bored with watching the sentients who worshipped them slaughter each other, two of the enhancements decided to use their followers in a chess match to see which culture would prevail. Once again, fearing the aliens and enhanced sentients were doing more and more harm to the natural-born sentients, Caretaker emitted millions of distress vibrations in the hope of contacting the wandering Guardian.

Anu smirked at his drinking partner as they gazed at the vid screen the aliens had provided that covered the entire wall of his mountain palace. *So, you maintain that your paltry city states with their warring peoples will be able to work together to face my followers who are united under one ruler — a descendant of mine. Nonsense!* Even in mind speak, his dismissive tone was obvious.

He raised his cup and took a long drink. *I will admit superiority to your people in one thing. They are masters at making wine. This is delicious. I have tried for centuries to educate my people how to replicate this. Perhaps it is the soil.*

Zeus reclined in his chair and squinted in annoyance at his pompous friend. But who could blame him? After all, they were gods. There was little they could not do to their people or the land.

Perhaps your people just lack an adequate teacher. After all, the masters taught us many things — science, mathematics, the art of war, astrology — but they did not know much about agriculture or how to produce nutritious food from the land. He watched with amusement as Anu's face shifted to a frown.

Anu leaned forward and waved a hand at the screen. The image of an army of thousands filled the screen. Horsemen, archers, chariots and spear men marched with impressive precision.

Possibly, but I have the numbers advantage, my friend. Anu's smile returned. And, superior forces always triumph over well-meaning but inferior numbers. *I would hate to see the needless bloodshed of almost one thousand fine warriors wasted for an inevitable outcome.*

Zeus snorted and waved his hand. *Nothing is inevitable, brother god. It appears my men have chosen terrain that will negate those superior numbers. Our metal weapons and shields will be most annoying to your warriors' antiquated armaments.*

Anu zoomed out on his video screen. Indeed, Zeus' pesky followers had found a narrow mountain pass to defend. *"A good tactic I must admit,"* he muttered aloud and in mind speak. *"It may slow my warriors down, but they eventually will sweep your people aside like bothersome leaves."*

Raising a goblet, Zeus proposed a wager. *If my people repel yours, not even for a day or two but make them withdraw, I have a prize I wish to win.*

The other god shrugged. *Won't the outcome of the battle be enough? You can have anything you wish now, my friend.* Zeus did not answer but just stared at his friend. *Fine! What is the wager?* Anu asked, raising his hands in frustration.

Your king's eldest daughter, Zeus said, licking his lips. *She looks like the princess my father promised me all those years ago. The masters snatched me away before I got to enjoy her.*

Anu erupted with laughter. *You have laid with dozens of your women, perhaps hundreds! But, you require one more? Your appetite is amazing. If I agree, then you must fulfill my wish if your men lose the battle.*

Zeus nodded. Agreed. *What is it the mighty Anu with his vast lands and millions of followers desires?*

The other man's eyes glinted with a feral desire. The heads of all your fallen soldiers. I want them to adorn my walls.

Even Zeus, who had seen murder, rape and mayhem of every stripe that humans could do to each other, was surprised. *You have as much appetite for blood as I do for women, Anu. Let it be so.*

The two gods shook hands, toasted each other, then sat back to watch how the battle played out.

Caretaker was about to intervene in the upcoming battle when something curious happened. The entity did not approve of the sentients killing each other over resources, when the land could adequately provide for all. However, the smaller forces not only held their own but slaughtered members of the large army by the hundreds.

Even Guardian would have been impressed, but the entity was still exploring the galaxy. Since the drama over a battle among the sentients did not threaten the planet, Caretaker did not contact Other or Searcher.

Time and time again the stalwart defenders held and forced the attackers back. The larger force only gained the upper hand when a traitor showed the invaders another route to approach the defenders from the rear. Seven days later, the defenders finally fell when attacked by the front and rear.

The entity was impressed with the courage of the small force, which mostly was made up of warriors from a city called Sparta. Through hundreds of tastings, Caretaker sensed the people of the invaded land were not defeated but biding their time. For once, Caretaker followed the example of the sentients and waited.

Anu rubbed his hands in glee as he watched Zeus' sentients get swarmed over and wiped out. *Defeated by treachery and not by honorable combat,* Zeus growled in mind speak.

Quit whining, brother! Anu crowed. *A conquest is a conquest no matter how the game is played. My followers are gathering the heads as we speak. I told the king my request in a dream. He is very pliable.*

Zeus sighed with resignation, sat back in his chair and took a deep drink out of his goblet. He had noticed the defenders' main force retreat before the betrayal had occurred. His brother, Poseidon, reported their defending forces were forming an impressive naval fleet under the leadership of a brilliant admiral. Perhaps all was not lost.

Well, the battle is lost but perchance not the war, Zeus said. *Would you care to double the bet?*

Anu stared at his god brother, then doubled over as laughter exploded from him in great gusts. *My army marches through your lands by the thousands. You are disappointed your reign as a god may be diminished as your people succumb to my kind and our beliefs. If I am generous, I will let you sit by my side and toss you a wench to slake that disgusting desire of yours.*

Zeus felt the anger in him rise slowly, not unlike a boiling cauldron. He carefully put down his goblet and glared at Anu. *The war is not over until I tell my people to surrender. All of their kings are sons of my sons' sons. When they do triumph, I will return for retribution, 'brother.'* He got up from his chair and headed out the hall toward his flyer. The god needed to return to his fortress on Mt. Olympus. He had messages to send to his kings.

Anu shook his head in wonderment and called out after his departing brother god. "I look forward to you slinking back to me to beg for a seat on my council. Perhaps I will make you god of shepherds."

Even though Zeus did understand the words, he knew it was an insult. He kept on walking and already was planning his revenge on the boisterous Anu.

6

Caretaker watched with interest as Zeus visited each of his kings. The enhanced being used a sonic transmitter to put everyone in the general vicinity into a deep sleep. Zeus usually then sat down at the edge of the bed and touched the temples of the sleeping man.

Thus, each king awoke the next morning with the same dream message: The enemy approaches from the east. Set aside your differences with your fellow kings and work together. Only a united front with your superior weapons and knowledge of the terrain will win the war. The future of your people depends on this cooperation.

Despite his good intentions, the red-haired god apparently could not help himself. Oftentimes, after delivering his message, Zeus would take liberties with whatever female or females slept with the kings. If he found other nearby females who appealed to him, he mated with them as well.

As far as Caretaker could ascertain, the overly virile male was not injuring the females, except for the occasional offspring that resulted from the commingling. Most times the females were either unaware of the interaction or assumed their king had taken them during the night.

Reproduction was necessary to the future of the sentient species. The morality or lack of morality as to how the male availed himself on the females was not in the lexicon of Caretaker's vibrations, so it was a moot point.

The brother of the red-haired god also lent a hand in this surreptitious dream messaging. Poseidon was a master of the sea, so he spent hours imparting naval warfare tactics to the admiral of a fleet which guarded access from the east.

Results of the interactions between the enhanced beings with their lesser sentients was fascinating to watch. Caretaker and its subordinate entities danced from one battle zone to another when the sentients finally clashed several lunar cycles later.

The unified armies of the red-haired enhanced being picked the terrain and time they wished to engage the invaders. This time the defenders' numbers and better weaponry were keys to driving out the invaders. All the cities which had been occupied were freed.

Victory on land also was reflected by the dominance of the defenders' ships. Now blessed with superior tactical skill, the admiral led his fleet to an almost complete destruction of the invading navy. After heavy losses on land and at sea, the defeated invaders returned to their homeland.

Zeus strode into the palace escorted by a large wagon which seemed to follow him as if by magic. He stopped in front of another man, then tapped an indentation on his wrist bracelet. The wagon buzzed forward a few feet and stopped. Pressing another button, Zeus smirked as a gate on the wagon opened and dumped out its contents — 1,000 severed heads.

I thought I'd add these to your collection, Anu. These are the heads of various captains of your army and navy. You may display them as you will to remind you of the defeat at the hands of an outnumbered army.

Zeus held up his hands in mock humility. *Oh, don't offer me a reward, dear brother god. Victory is the only flavor I wish to savor today.* He burst out in a hearty, derisive laugh, turned and started to walk away.

"Stop, you defiler!" Anu screamed, forgetting to mind speak, as he leaped from his marble throne and marched toward Zeus. *How dare you dishonor my men! We had no agreement to do this.*

Zeus turned and faced the angry god. *You disgrace my people by hanging their heads the same way as animal trophies on your walls. Do not talk to me about dishonor!*

Anu pointed at the mounted heads of Zeus' warriors that lined a great hallway. *We had a wager for those heads! You agreed to it! You know as well as I that we can do what we want with the lower specimens. The masters have decreed it.*

Snorting with disgust, Zeus shook his head. *Call it a gift then. I care not what you do with them.* He started to walk away when he heard a sword slide out of a scabbard behind him. Instinctively, he whirled and pulled out his sword just in time to ward off a strike from the enraged Anu.

The sound of the collision of alien metal on metal roiled down the hallway and exploded out of the palace. Echoes of this strike and the hundreds of others that followed as the two gods clashed frightened everyone within thousands of miles. Never before had people heard such fierce and continuous thunder.

Anu fought with fury. His blows came fast, but they were predictable. Zeus was in his element once again. The thrill of the battle filled him with excitement as he danced and parried Anu's efforts.

Hour upon hour, the two men fought to a draw. Neither drew the other's blood. Finally, an exhausted, sweat-soaked Anu backed up, panting. *Enough of this barbarism!* He raised his arm with the alien bracelet and pointed it at Zeus.

The red-haired god moved in a blur before his opponent could act. Zeus hurled his sword at Anu and watched in desperate relief as it sliced into his throat. Anu staggered backwards in shock, then sank to his knees.

Knowing he did not have much time with the regenerative powers the masters had engineered them with, Zeus rushed forward, yanked the sword out, clasped it firmly with both hands and swung it with all his strength. The only sound that followed was the slight gurgling of blood that spurted out of Anu's body and the thud, thud, thud of his head bouncing on the marble floor.

An exhausted Zeus was relieved at winning the fight but did not comprehend what he had accomplished. He readied himself to withstand an attack by Anu's people seeking revenge, but no one came. Anu had never deified any of his sons or daughters, fearing that one of them would try to usurp his power.

With the fight over, Zeus sunk to his knees. The thrill of victory quickly subsided as he realized he had just killed a fellow deity. Zeus had broken the code he and the other gods had sworn to each other — to never harm one another.

A great sadness washed over him. Zeus and Anu had had their disagreements over the past hundred years or so, but they had been more alike than the other gods. With a heavy sigh, Zeus picked up Anu's head, walked over to his foe's throne and set it down facing outward, looking down the great hall of which the dead god had been so fond.

Before he could take another step, Zeus watched in wonder as dozens of small orbs filled the room and danced about. They flew over to Anu's body, then examined the severed head.

Zeus found himself trembling. *Is it the masters?* he thought. Had they found out already that one of their gods had killed a counterpart?

The lights neither coalesced into a living form nor appeared threatening. Several swooped around him. One even seemed to enter his body and come out the other side, but Zeus felt nothing. After a few moments, the lights flashed a variety of colors, then disappeared with a crack.

Zeus suddenly felt very alone. He had killed hundreds of foes in self defense and sometimes for pleasure, but he never felt such remorse. The masters had given him his powers, but what would they do now?

He leaned against a wall and slid down to a sitting position. Who could he tell? Would the other gods take it as a threat and attack him? Which of the other brother gods could he confide in?

Quetzalcoatl was across the great ocean and ruled an entire continent by himself. The deity was too interested in ceremonies held to honor him to be bothered by Anu's death.

Amun might be the most upset. He and Anu were close. Their people traded with each other. This god commanded an army of thousands. His minions were ruled by his progeny and would do as Amun commanded.

Huangdi may not be too bothered over Anu's demise. Even though he ruled over millions east of Anu's sphere of influence, the two gods distrusted each other. Their peoples often clashed.

Ninigi was content to watch over his curious island and its homogenous people. His main threat would be from Huangdi if that god chose to challenge him.

Then there was Krishna. The wise one who had the gift of foresight. Krishna's people were protected by impassable and dangerous land barriers. He seemed to fear no one.

Zeus held up his bracelet. Lights on it flashed as he punched some keys. Krishna's familiar voice soon answered through the translation emitter. "My brother, what has happened? I had a terrible waking dream. I only awoke after the most horrendous thunder."

The red-haired god took a deep breath. "Anu is dead. He challenged me, and I killed him in a fair battle. I take no pride in it nor had I planned it."

Only silence greeted his statement. "Dead? Oh, this is not good, my brother. Have you heard from the masters?"

Zeus sighed. "Not that I am aware. They have not been in contact. At least I do not believe so. Strange lights appeared after Anu died, but they did not harm me."

Krishna's tone changed. "Lights you say? Did they dance and change colors?"

Zeus's eyes widened. "Yes. Have you seen them? What are they?"

"I do not know," Krishna said. "I do not believe they are from the masters. I tried to communicate with them, but I was unsuccessful. However, your news is most distressful. It seems we are not indestructible after all. Good luck, my brother. I do not know what fate awaits you."

Zeus took a deep breath and got to his feet. "Will you tell me if you hear of a threat against me?"

The answer came back immediately. "I promise, my brother. On my honor."

Zeus pressed a button, disconnecting the connection. He strode down the hall one last time. He got into his flyer and returned to Mt. Olympus to prepare for whatever fate had in store for him.

7

Ail let out a surprised whuff as it studied the control panel. "This can't be. There must be something wrong with the signal transmission," the alien muttered as its long, tentacled fingers danced over the control panel. "Systems Control, this is Head Scientist Ail. I am requesting an upload check on transmission antenna number one. Is it functioning within acceptable parameters?"

Barely a minute had passed when Ail's comm speaker buzzed. "This is Systems Control. Antenna number one is operating as it should. Reboot and systems check show no issues. Transmission from specimen number one appears to have ceased. Is that what your instruments show?"

Ail snorted and wagged its long neck. "Confirmed, Systems Control. Head Scientist out."

A derisive gurgle interrupted Ail's troubled thoughts. "Do you have something to report, Head Scientist? Is there an issue with one of our possessions on that dreary planet?" Gyntaf had been monitoring the communication between its two subordinates but wanted to hear the news personally.

"It appears specimen number one is deceased as you already have determined, High Commander," Ail answered. The scientist did not bother looking at its superior. It already knew Gyntaf was bobbing its head with excitement.

The High Commander was enjoying this moment of discomfort for the arrogant scientist. "All of its body apparatuses have confirmed this?"

Ail slowly turned in its chair to face the commander. "Brain function gone. Heartbeat stopped. Lung function stopped. All other bio systems are offline. Specimen number one is dead."

Gyntaf swung around and tapped a key on the large control screen on its desk. "Yes, this is most disturbing, Head Scientist. Most disturbing, indeed. One of your superior specimens has killed another. How unusual for this species!"

An even louder gurgle spewed from the commander's nose slits. "How many solar revolutions has it been since we released our agents on the planet?"

The scientist did not need to consult the records. "It has been 2,896 solar orbits." Ail bowed its head. "Congratulations. You have won the wagering board, High Commander."

Gyntaf relished the moment. "Not surprising for this violent species, Head Scientist. You were too optimistic to bet 4,000 orbits. I am impressed those barbarians showed enough restraint to last this long before setting upon each other like wild carnivores."

Once again, Ail bowed its long neck in supplication. "What do you require as your trophy for winning the wager, High Commander?"

The alien leader tapped another key on its console, watched its screen intently, and then erupted in a loud, delighted whuff. "Records Operation just downloaded a very entertaining battle between two of our specimens. For some reason Number One attacked Number Seven after that precocious giant delivered a load of severed heads in some kind of tribute after one of their war games. The two fought, and Seven exterminated One in quite an impressive, violent move."

Gyntaf leaned back. "Yes, impressively violent. Number Seven will be my reward. We need to make an example of the creature so our other enhanced specimens will keep their place. We can't have our orders challenged. Head Nutritionist will turn that specimen into a delicious banquet. I will share this meal with my first-level officers of course."

Ail tried not to reveal both its stomachs were churning at the thought of eating another one of the planet's sentients, much less one of their prized specimens. "In all due respect, High Commander, but another death will throw our order out of balance."

Gyntaf snorted and swung its elongated neck back and forth. "You worry too much, Head Scientist. One of Number Seven's spawn will be able to become the chief deity, and we can choose one of Number Six's progeny to take over for Number One. Perhaps it will expand that family line of pyramid-building skills to another land.

"This will only solidify our control. Hopefully we will get another 2,000 solar orbits out of the new order before one of our specimens kills one of its kind again."

The commander dismissed Ail and broadcast a command to the Head Engineer. "Prepare the ship for a planetary expedition and arm the weapons. Our specimen may not come willingly."

Caretaker's cloud gathered around it as the scouts reported increased energy levels coming from the alien mother ship. Apparently, it was getting ready to move — but where? Perhaps the aliens had grown bored with their experiment and were finally leaving the planet, handing control back to entity cloud as it should be.

However, the vessel maneuvered toward the planet and started to slowly enter the atmosphere. Its vibration shields flashed with ominous power fluctuations to prevent interference from the entities. The cloud prepared to follow the ship to the surface and wait for the moment when the shields were powered down so it could maneuver in the planet's gravity.

However, the mass of entities was interrupted by a giant white orb that appeared in its midst. Guardian had returned. Caretaker quickly merged with its prodigal partner and, in less than a nanosecond, brought the powerful entity up to speed.

Guardian flashed orange, then delivered a message vibration to the cloud. During its travels the entity had found Sentinel and Other. The original two entities had decreed the cloud that guarded the planet was allowed to regain control if it deemed the aliens were interfering with the inhabitants' cultural progress. Many worlds had been successfully seeded with the sentients' descendants, making the presence of the aliens now an unnecessary annoyance.

Curious as to the motives of the aliens, Guardian followed the ship into the atmosphere, masking its vibration signature by blending with the vessel's engine emissions.

"Are you sure your weapon is going to work?" Zeus asked a handsome blond-haired man as he stared dubiously at the giant needle aimed at the sky. The god sat back and pondered his fate in the outpost Apollo had secretly built in an unassuming mountain range.

Krishna had alerted Zeus that the masters were heading for his Mount Olympus palace. Even though the aliens ordered their puppet deities not to interfere, Krishna circumvented the command by just passing along a message.

Not long after Krishna's warning, the aliens contacted Zeus. The masters said they were disappointed with his actions that resulted in the termination of Anu or Number One as they called him. The aliens told him to prepare for a meeting.

Zeus sighed. "Perhaps I should be the warrior I was bred to be and go meet my fate. You may be picked as my successor, Apollo. That would greatly please me."

"This weapon is your only hope, Father," Apollo responded as he fiddled with a keypad located at the base of a giant needle that pointed at the sky. "I fear they will terminate you. Who knows who they will pick as your successor?"

Apollo shrugged and steadied the readouts on the screen. "No one knows the minds of the masters. They may decide to cleanse all of us. I believe that is the term I've read from their communications. Besides, I would have to live in constant suspicion of my siblings if I became King of the Gods. I am satisfied with the order as it is now. We work well with each other, not against each other."

A gush of laughter exploded from Zeus. "Well said and much appreciated, my son. Are you sure the masters are not aware of your contraption? We do not understand all their science, only that which they deemed necessary to teach us."

The younger god turned and smiled at his father. "For the past two hundred years, I have slowly drained reserve power supplies to this high-energy transmitter based on specifications I downloaded from the masters' ship and have created a cloaking shield which hides this outpost. It only took another hundred years to build the weapon from the equipment they gave us to maintain our technology."

Zeus smiled as he gripped Apollo's shoulder. "I am so grateful the masters agreed to give you some of their tech implants." His mood quickly changed, though. "What happens if the weapon does not function or is unable to bring down their ship?"

Apollo momentarily stopped studying the screen. "If the weapon does not destroy their ship, then I assume the masters will fire on our location and kill us. At least we will die as warriors and not as the experimental animals they think we are."

The King of the Gods narrowed his eyes and nodded. "We have lived a thousand lifetimes and have enjoyed our time here." He crossed his arms while glancing at the large monitor on the wall. "Where is the ship now?"

After a flurry of typing, Apollo looked at his father. "They are in the stratosphere now. Most likely they will reach us in five minutes."

Zeus let out a long exhale. "Make sure you have a good target before you fire, son. If we have one shot, make sure you hit them."

Four minutes later, Zeus' bracelet chimed. The masters were calling. "Number Seven, you are required to transport to our ship with your flyer immediately at the coordinates we transmitted. We do not see your ship's signature yet. Comply."

Zeus swallowed and spoke into his comm bracelet. "Understood. However, the flyer seems to have some technical malfunction. The engines won't fire due to a power fluctuation. My apologies, Masters."

After a short pause, the expressionless voice returned. "What is the cause of the fluctuation? We cannot find your location with our bio sensors. Move to a different location so we can identify you."

Apollo stole a quick glance at his father. "The cloaking shield is working. They cannot track us. I need the ship to be closer to target it."

Zeus raised his bracelet practically to his mouth and purposely mumbled. "Your transmission is garbled. I did not understand your message. Yes, we are having an unknown fluctuation. The signal is weak. Where do you want me to move?"

The voice from the bracelet returned. "Stay where you are, Number Seven. We are lowering altitude to enhance the signal." Both gods stared at the wall monitor and saw a tiny silver dot in the sky slowly grow larger as it descended.

Apollo held up one hand with all the fingers extended as he intently studied his screen. He poised his other hand over a green button on the weapon's console.

Slowly, he lowered his fingers one by one. Four, three, two … then jerked back in surprise as if hit by an unseen blow. Both gods were stunned by a blinding white flash, followed by thunder that cascaded down the mountains.

"Good shot, son!" Zeus shouted as he jumped up and down pummeling Apollo on the back. By the heavens, that was an explosion."

The younger god shook his head in wonder. "That wasn't me, father. I did not fire. I needed two more seconds to target it. The ship just blew up on its own."

Zeus threw up his hands in triumph. "I don't care how it happened …" His celebration was cut short by alarms going off in the outpost. An automated voice cut in through the intercom system: "Power sources are offline, repeat, power sources are offline. Emergency doors have been opened. Power supplies down to twenty percent, nineteen percent, eighteen percent …"

The two gods stared at each other in shock. "What is happening?" Zeus yelled, then clutched his heart and writhed in agony, falling to the floor. "Father!" Apollo screamed. He started to rush to Zeus's aid, but doubled over in pain as all his organs curled up as if they were on fire. He too collapsed, gasping.

The intercom voice continued: "Power loss in five, four, three, two, one. Emergency lights activated." Then, silence.

Guardian blinked back to Caretaker and the cloud. "It is done," Guardian flashed. "The aliens have been cleansed." Caretaker and the cloud exploded in a shower of bright blue, then set about destroying all the satellites in orbit that the aliens had released. Once again, the planet was theirs.

8

The old man waited patiently by the mountain village's well while the platoon of soldiers slaked their thirst and filled their water bags. Most of the other villagers had slunk away, not wanting to draw the ire of the soldiers, but the elder with the great white beard splattered with flecks of red watched impassively.

When the platoon had finished, some of the soldiers searched for shade and others lounged around the well chatting, oblivious of the old man. An officer finally spotted the peasant and eyed him for a few moments. Even though the old man was a bit stooped, the Roman captain could see he had been tall and well-muscled at one time.

"Where's your manners, lads? Can't you see an elder waits for water? Move aside and let him draw what he needs." The lounging soldiers glanced at the old man expecting to see fear in his eyes, but his eyes twinkled with amusement.

"Many thanks, Captain. I appreciate the consideration," the elder said in perfect Latin as he shuffled over to the well. "I will only be a moment, my needs are few." He started to shakily lower the bucket into the well, when an arm patted him on the shoulder.

The captain took over the crank and smoothly lowered the bucket and raised it in an efficient motion. "There you go, Uncle," he said as he lifted the pail and poured the cool, fresh water into the elder's jar. "You speak our language perfectly. I detected no accent. Have you visited Rome?"

He was answered by a soft laugh. "Thank you for kindness. Yes, I visited there many years ago before you were born. At that time I was assessing the growth of the Roman culture. I seem to have a talent for language."

The officer's eyes glinted suspiciously as his demeanor changed. His hand gripped the hilt of his sheathed sword. "Were you spying on our empire? Which king were you commanded by?"

This time the old man tilted his head back and let loose with a hearty laugh. "No, Captain. I was under no orders and certainly not beholden to any king, although I knew a great many in our land. I was merely studying what looked to be a potential empire."

The captain relaxed as he studied his companion. He removed his hand from the hilt. "Potential empire?" he smirked and shook his head at the peasant's audacity. "Rome has been powerful for centuries now. We will conquer the world with the help of Jupiter and Mars."

"Ah, Jupiter is it?" the old man snorted. "My people worshipped him as Zeus, his chosen name." He pointed a crooked finger at the Roman. "It is not right that you changed the names of the gods. They were created with those. I am pleased you call Apollo by his rightful name. He would be most pleased."

It was the captain's turn to laugh. "So you know the gods' will, eh? We are the conquerors, Uncle. The names need to be what we can pronounce in our language. Zeus sounds like a sneeze. Besides, I don't think the gods care as long as they are worshipped. We build temples to them to curry their favor. No ill will has befallen us."

The two men stood nose to nose for a moment until the old man shrugged. "It is true. You are the conquerors, for now," he winked, picking up his full jug of water in a surprisingly smooth effort.

"Were you a soldier, Uncle? You have the demeanor and physique of one who has seen many campaigns."

The old man nodded. "Yes, Captain, I have seen a myriad of campaigns by many kings. As a young man, I was a soldier in my father's army until a most peculiar event interrupted my wedding banquet."

He chuckled again. "I am so old, I have forgotten how many years have passed. I have been blessed with a most interesting life. Why, I have even seen the gods!"

Nodding to the captain, the old man turned and started to walk away but stopped when the Roman called out. "Uncle, could I have the honor of knowing your name?"

He looked back and smiled. "Zenicetes was my birth name. Born to a king and princess, but I was not destined to be a king of men. That was long ago. I am just a humble peasant now. Good day, Roman."

The captain chuckled. "You are one more thing, Uncle. A great storyteller."

Zenicetes waved and continued on his way.

V

1

Guardian and Caretaker flashed vibrations of concern as they followed the latest activity of the sentients on the sun's third planet in that distant spiral arm of the galaxy. Caretaker transmitted its assessment of the need for interference with the sentients. It had been about one hundred solar revolutions since the advanced culture from the planet's eastern continent had discovered the western continents where the more primitive members of their race lived.

Instead of a peaceful greeting, the more advanced race was killing and pillaging its way through the continents. Whole cultures were decimated by the warriors in their armor and advanced weapons. Women were used for entertainment, and men and children were enslaved to do the bidding of the intruders.

Caretaker proposed it was time for it and Guardian to return to the planet in sentient forms to assist the less-advanced cultures, which had co-existed for thousands of solar revolutions.

Guardian considered its partner's request, but it had doubts. The two entities had interacted with the sentients before. However, their mission had always been to advance their culture, improving the lives of those interesting yet frustrating two-legged organisms that flirted with intelligence.

After every visit, there had been a burst of culture and advancement only to have another group of primitives eventually overrun and destroy almost everything the advanced sentients had achieved.

Guardian saw the advanced race was spreading its culture throughout the world despite the savage methods it was using. Interfering may only wipe out one more advanced culture, sending the sentients spinning back into another dark age.

Besides, the expansion of the advanced sentients would abate sooner or later and then the two groups would finally assimilate. The death and mistreatment of the less advanced sentients would be a painful but necessary sacrifice to the superior race that would evolve from all this strife.

Caretaker considered Guardian's position, then flashed its disagreement with its partner's assessment. Caretaker issued a rare ultimatum — either bond with a sentient and assist with the rescue of less advanced beings or stay away and do not interfere.

Guardian flashed yellow with surprise. It requested time to reconsider the situation before Caretaker and its cohorts would act. Caretaker considered the proposal and transmitted a vibration of agreement.

After three nanoseconds of contemplation, Guardian offered a compromise in a message vibration — to explore and taste the leaders of both groups to determine if there are individuals worthy of their bonding efforts.

Caretaker signaled an agreement. It presented ten thousand reliable entity tasters to help with the mission. The entities would take action only if a consensus was reached after the tasting. Guardian vibrated an agreement.

Two solar days later, the entities met and formed a conversation cluster. Various elements of the cluster glowed red, then orange, which shifted to green, and finally transformed to blue. The cluster dispersed. An agreement had been reached.

The tasting had revealed many individuals in the less advanced sentient group possessing high levels of vibrations. Their energies just needed to be encouraged. One individual in particular had the potential to be a forceful leader. All that was needed was a message this sentient could receive and pass on to the others.

Now it was time to wait and watch for the opportune time for the entities to deliver their message.

2

Growling Bear sat seething in his cramped jail cell. Even though he and forty-six of his fellow caciques — or medicine men as the Spanish invaders called them — had just been whipped, Growling Bear was boiling with hatred. Blood ran down his back from the open wounds as a result of the lash, but this was nothing compared with his feelings as he stared at the body of his cousin hanging limply across the aisle.

Sun Brother had been so distraught and in so much pain, he tied his belt around his neck, fastened it to a ceiling rafter and stepped off a stool. His gentle relative, who lived in a nearby pueblo, slowly choked to death. Growling Bear chanted the death song to help Sun Brother walk in peace to the spirit world.

Growling Bear's cousin had chosen to die at his own hand rather than be publicly hanged with the three other Pueblo men the Spanish had drawn lots to face the executioner. Sun Brother's sin, according to the Spanish, was healing his people with native remedies while he sang to them.

The people he healed claimed they could feel a warm vibration surge through their bodies while Sun Brother sang. Of course, this offended the Spanish, who curiously worshipped a great healer who accomplished similar feats. But, how dare a heathen emulate the One without confessing his sins and being baptized!

To add insult to this egregious death, the Spaniards laughed while they cut the body down and dragged it out to be burned with the three other men who were swinging from the hastily built gallows. Heathens were burned. Only good Christians were allowed to be buried and receive rites.

The Pueblo men had been dragged from their homes and marched to Santa Fe. The Spanish charged the natives with sorcery and plotting against them. Growling Bear and a few other of the caciques had been holding council on how to respond to the growing aggression by the invaders, who thought nothing of kidnapping their women and forcing the Pueblo people to work as slaves while "encouraging" them to abandon the religion of their ancestors and convert to worshiping this foreign God.

A few days later, Growling Bear told the sister of Sun Brother what had happened when she and her son visited the jail to bring food to the incarcerated men. "Do not weep for Sun Brother, he is with his grandfathers," he told the slain man's sister as she crouched on the floor in grief.

Growling Bear gestured for the young man to come close. "Run and tell the leaders of the nearest pueblos what has happened here. More may die if we remain here with these Spanish." The youth nodded and brushed tears away on his sleeve. Sun Brother was training him in the arts of being a healer. His uncle had been a patient and kind teacher.

The Spanish governor was preparing to take his siesta after enjoying a fine meal of lamb stew, when he was rudely interrupted by a breathless aide. "All apologies, Señor, but guards at the gates say it is an emergency."

Governor Trevino swung his feet from his bed onto the floor. "What is it this time? Has another horse escaped its corral? Can it not wait?"

The nervous lieutenant only shook his head and stared at the floor, not daring to meet his commander's eyes. "No, no,

Señor. Native men, almost a hundred, are the gate demanding the surviving caciques be released or they will make war."

Trevino stumbled to his window, where he could see the gate. Indeed a crowd of natives swarmed near the entrance. They carried clubs, spears and were laden with bows and arrows. It was obvious this was not a hunting party.

"Santa Maria, we do not have the men to ward off an attack," Trevino gasped. "What else do the natives demand?"

The lieutenant shook his head. "Nothing else, Señor. They just want their caciques returned."

Trevino pulled on his boots, stomped out the door and shouted for the captain of the guard. After a quick conference, the captain nodded in agreement with his superior's decision. "Open the cells and release the medicine men," the captain yelled. "Battle formation," he ordered. "I want all our rifles trained on the natives in case they decide to attack."

However, the exchange went peacefully. No shots were fired or arrows unleashed. The warriors welcomed their comrades back. One of the prisoners locked eyes with Trevino as he stumbled out into the sunlight. The look of hatred was obvious, but the native man said nothing as he left with the others.

≻≻≻≻≻

Determined not to be captured again, Growling Bear made his way to Taos Pueblo. There he could be among people sympathetic to his cause while he rested and recuperated from his wounds.

A week or so after arriving, Growling Bear was meditating in the estufa -- meeting place -- in the pueblo. His heart was heavy. So far, his people had been unable to stop the invaders from encroaching on their land and forcing their ways upon them.

As Growling Bear allowed his mind to open up, a loud lighting-like crack startled him. Growling Bear's hair stood on end, and his skin felt like scorpions were crawling on it. A bright light filled the room. He sat mesmerized by the three people who stood before him. They looked to be of the Pueblo people, but fire blazed from their bodies.

One of them approached Growling Bear. "I am Caudi and my companions are Tilini and Tleume. We have heard the cries of your people. You have been chosen to lead your people against the invaders."

Growling Bear sat frozen in place. He had experienced visions during sleep but never was blessed with a waking dream. His ears did not hear the message, but his mind understood what the being was saying.

Caudi floated in the air above Growling Bear. "The Pueblo people must fight as one family. Many strands make a strong rope." The plan seemed simple when Caudi laid it out for Growling Bear. Uniting the pueblos was the only way his people could drive out the invaders.

Caudi stared intently at Growling Bear. "When you have unified the Pueblos, then make peace with the Apache and Navajo. Show them your scars and tell them of Sun Brother's sacrifice."

"The Navajo and Apache?! We have been at war with them since the time of our grandfathers' grandfathers." Ashamed of his outburst, Growling Bear slumped to the floor in contrition. His temper and outspokenness had gotten him into trouble before, but now he had the gall to challenge a being of the light.

The fire emanating from Caudi grew larger and turned a dark orange. However, the being who called itself Tilini floated close to Growling Bear. Instead of being burned by the fire or reprimanded, Growling Bear thought he heard a soft chuckle.

"Ah, brave warrior, that is why we have chosen you. The people will listen to one, such as yourself, who will show no fear when you tell your story. It may take many full moons until you have gathered the warriors you need."

Growling Bear sat back up but bowed his head in respect. The third being approached. "When you have the Pueblo, Apache and Navajo people united, take cords of maguey fiber and tie five knots in them," Tleume ordered. "Find your swiftest youths and have them deliver the ropes to your allies. Tell them to untie a knot each day. The day of the attack will be when the last knot is untied."

Caudi's light had returned to its initial white color. "Be wary of one close to you who does not share the belief in your mission. Unpleasant action may need to be taken."

The three beings rose together toward the ceiling. Once again lightning shot forth with a loud snap. Growling Bear hunched over with his hands over his ears. The room felt like the air had been sucked out of it. When he looked up, the beings were gone.

3

Growling Bear's family sat in rapt attention as he told them of his waking vision. Only one, his daughter's husband, expressed doubt as to what he had seen. "It is the work of diablo!" exclaimed Nicolas, the son-in-law. "Father, we must consult a priest to drive these demons from the pueblo."

Nicolas was of the Pueblo people, but he had converted to Christianity and been baptized with his family. He had chosen a Spanish name and refused to be called by the Pueblo name his grandfather had given him.

Even though he and Singing Water had been bonded in a Pueblo ceremony officiated by Growling Bear, Nicolas kept insisting the pair exchange vows in one of the mission churches. He also wanted Singing Water to be baptized and take a Christian name.

This angered Growling Bear, who refused to give his blessing. The young couple lived in the pueblo with Growling Bear's family and to her credit, so far, Singing Water honored her father.

"If Singing Water approves, you can be released from the bond and go back to your family," said Growling Bear. He glowered at Nicolas, who stared in fear at the floor. "You are free to return to your Spanish. They have brought nothing but death and sadness to our people."

Nicolas took a deep breath. Despite his fervor for the new religion, he loved Singing Water. Being forced to leave her would break his heart. "I will not speak of this again, Father. I wish to remain with Singing Water."

Growling Bear winced every time Nicolas called him "Father." It always sounded insincere. Besides, the Spanish called their religious men, Father, and said it with great piety.

"You may stay only if Singing Water wishes it."

Growling Bear's daughter smiled, "I do, Father. Thank you."

Growling Bear returned to his meal, but dark thoughts troubled him. He did not trust Nicolas. The youth would be privy to his plans as he prepared to contact the other Pueblos as well as the Apaches and Navajo.

As Growing Bear pondered this troubling situation, he remembered the last words Caudi, the light being, had told him: "Be wary of one close to you ..."

A dark plan formed in Growling Bear's mind. He sat quietly for a while letting the tension in the room abate. "Forgive me, Nicolas. I may have misjudged you. I do not trust any Christian after being whipped like an animal. But, you did not carry the lash."

Nicolas looked like a great weight had lifted from him. "Thank you, Father. I regret that you were injured." Growling Bear choked back what he wanted to say, but nodded as if accepting the youth's clumsy attempt at contrition. Growling Bear noticed Nicolas did not say it was wrong what the Spanish had done to him. This only cemented his plans.

"It has been too long since I have hunted," Growling Bear said casually. "I need to think of more pleasant things. Nicolas would you care to accompany an old man to make sure he doesn't get lost chasing rabbits? I hear the people admire your hunting prowess."

Nicolas looked up, stunned at the unexpected invitation. "Yes, of course, Father," he actually said it with more conviction this time. "But you are not an old man. It would be an honor to learn from you."

Singing Water smiled with relief at the apparent truce her father was proposing with her husband. Growling Bear's heart sank a bit at his daughter's reaction. He feared this may be the last time she would be happy with him.

Growling Bear gestured toward the door and returned to his meal. "Good, let us leave at first light when the animals come out to forage."

The two men walked in silence in the early dawn. It did not take long for Nicolas to draw his bow on a rabbit crouched underneath a juniper tree. The missile found its mark. Growling Bear gave the young man a nod of approval and kept walking.

Nicolas stopped and held up the rabbit. "Do you not want to thank the rabbit's spirit for presenting us with food?"

Growling Bear shook his head and kept walking. "No, it was a Christian arrow that killed the rabbit. Say a prayer if you wish." Nicholas frowned at the suggestion but said nothing. Hunting was not a priority to Growling Bear this day. He had a specific location in mind.

When another rabbit flushed after a bit, Growling Bear drew on it, but winced in pain when he pulled back his bow string. His arrow missed badly. His back had not fully healed from the injuries he received at the hands of the Spanish.

"It appears it is up to you to fill our stew pots tonight," Growling Bear shook his head in feigned regret. "My back still weeps in pain." Nicolas smiled as he held up his bow. "I will hunt for both of us."

An hour later, Nicolas had bagged three more rabbits. The two men were near one of the giant buttes that dotted the landscape. Growling Bear stopped and looked up at the rock formation that poked into the sky. "My grandfather died up there. When I was a young man, I would climb to the top and talk to his spirit. It has been many harvests since we have spoken."

Growling Bear looked at Nicolas. "You may return to the village if you wish. I do not know if your Christ will speak to you there. You are welcome to come, but do not interfere with my prayers." Without waiting for a response, Growling Bear started climbing the butte, using the path and footholds only the Pueblo people could see.

Nicolas shuffled his feet, not knowing what to do. If he returned without Growling Bear, the women and the cacique's sons would be concerned. His accomplishment of bringing home a meal would be foreshadowed by his lack of respect for seeing that his elder had returned safely.

The young man had not climbed this particular butte, which made him even more hesitant. He looked toward the top.

"It is closer to heaven up there, perhaps God will hear me better," he whispered to himself. He bundled his rabbits together, hung them from a nearby pinyon branch and scrambled after Growling Bear.

Nicolas could hardly keep up with the man who was more than twenty harvests his elder. For being injured, Growling Bear snaked up the side of the butte grabbing barely detectable depressions like a cat stalking its prey.

Growling Bear reached the top of the butte after about a half hour's traverse. Below him, Nicolas panted heavily as he struggled with the last few hand holds. The older man sat at the edge and waited. Soon, Nicolas's hand poked over the top grasping for the last hold that would help pull him up and over a ledge.

With a grunt, the young man peered over the edge, locking eyes with his wife's father. "Do you value this Spanish god more than your people, even your wife?" Growling Bear asked Nicholas, who was panting from exhaustion.

The young man's eyes grew wide with fear. "The priests tell me that it must be so."

Growling Bear's eyes narrowed. "Tell me again, how the Christian prayer starts."

To his credit, Nicolas did not beg. "In the name of the Father …" With that, Growling Bear stuck out his foot and gave Nicolas a push. The young man disappeared from sight. Only the clattering of rocks told Growling Bear that his murderous plan had worked.

Growling Bear stayed on the summit meditating for almost two hours. At last he saw a vision of his grandfather. The old healer looked sad, but a familiar voice spoke in the cacique's mind. "You have done what is necessary. Now, you can proceed with the plan to free your people."

With a heavy sigh, Growling Bear slowly climbed down the butte. His heart was heavy. This was the first and hopefully the last time he would have to take the life of one of his people. Growling Bear stopped, knelt by Nicholas' body and sang the death song. "I do not know if your grandfathers will welcome you, but you treated my daughter well."

Singing Water screamed with sorrow when she heard the news. She pulled her hair and pounded her chest. Growling Bear did not lie to her. "He told me his Spanish religion was more important to him than you or the Pueblo people. He would have told the Spanish of my plan to unite the people and drive the invaders away."

The women of the pueblo surrounded Singing Water and gently ushered her to a room where she could mourn her husband properly. Growling Bear frowned as he watched his daughter depart. He feared she would never grace him with a smile again.

4

Bidziil listened intently to the Tewa man's story. The visitor had been granted his request to meet with the council only because news of the cacique's capture and subsequent release had been talked about over his people's fires.

Also, the Navajo leader's curiosity had been aroused by the courage it took for an enemy of his people to boldly approach them. Now, Growling Bear's story of the three beings in the estufa amazed him.

However, one of the leaders was not convinced. "This Tewa man wants us to fight his people's battles," Hashkeh Naabah snarled. "We have kept the Spanish away from our women and lands. It is not our fault your warriors cannot defend your people."

Growling Bear sat motionless as he listened to the translator, a young woman, repeat what was being said. He asked her to tell him the name of the man who had spoken.

"He is Hashkeh Naabah. It means Angry Warrior," she said in Spanish, the language all the peoples in the area had been forced to learn.

Growling Bear smiled. "A good name. My people have started calling me Angry Bear." She translated his response. Even Hashkeh Naabah relaxed and nodded in appreciation.

The cacique then asked about the other Navajo leader. "He is Bidziil," the translator replied. "In Navajo, it means He is Strong."

Growling Bear stood straight up in one smooth motion from his cross-legged position. A fairly impressive feat for a man of more than forty harvests. He removed his shirt and turned his back to the council so all could see his healing scars.

"My Navajo brothers, this is what happens to our people who oppose the Spanish. It darkens my heart that what Hashkeh Naabah said about defending my people is true. What will happen when more Spanish arrive or are born and desire more land and slaves? When they thirst for more than the Pueblo people can provide?"

Growling Bear faced the council and let the translator catch up. "Their guns will kill many warriors and destroy your villages. Your arrows will fall harmlessly off their armor." He stopped and paused for effect. "Their religion will make your grandchildren forget the ways of their grandfathers. The grandmothers will weep."

A familiar voice then spoke to him. "I am here, Growling Bear. Hold out your hands, and I will reveal myself."

Growling Bear stretched out his arms. "Behold Tilini!" He smiled at the now familiar popping sound, which was followed by the scorpion-stinging sensation on the council members' skin. The Navajo leaders all jumped and started rubbing their bodies at the irritation.

A light exploded into the room revealing Tilini. As before, fire shot out of all the figure's appendages. "Growling Bear tells the truth. We have chosen him to be the messenger and the leader who will drive the Spanish invaders from your land. Do what he says or become slaves to the Spanish." With another loud crack, Tilini was gone.

The Navajo council sat in stunned silence. "The being of the light spoke in Navajo. But, I did not hear it." Bidziil said softly tapping his temple. "The being came at his command!" Even the brave Hashkeh Naabah was wide eyed with newfound respect.

Growling Bear was surprised at what the Navajo leader had said. He understood much of the Navajo tongue but did not want to reveal that to his hosts. *Interesting, the beings must be able to speak in any language,* Growling Bear thought to himself. *Of course they can. They are beings of the light.*

Bidziil stood up and faced Growling Bear. "You speak the truth. The Navajo people will follow you. From this day forward, your Navajo name will be Shilah."

Before the translator could say anything, Growling Bear smiled. "Brother. I am honored by the name you have given me," he said in perfect Navajo.

Bidziil smiled. "You are a man of many layers, Shilah, and wise as well. How may we assist you?" Growling Bear told the council about the knotted cord.

"We will follow you into battle, Shilah. I pledge our warriors to you," Hashkeh Naabah said. "How many of the Pueblo people will fight with you?"

Growling Bear returned to his sitting position and started counting with his fingers. "Of course the Tewa, Northern Tiwa, Towa and Tano. I do not trust the Southern Tiwa or Piro. Too many of their daughters have married Spanish and produced mestizo grandchildren."

Hashkeh Naabah thought for a moment. "We may need more warriors, Shilah."

Growling Bear agreed. "I will travel to meet with the Zuni, Hopi and Apache. The Spanish have attacked some of their villages and taken their women. It will be difficult I fear. I do not know their words."

Bidziil waved into the air. "I will travel with you, Shilah. I speak Hopi. If the light being speaks to them, they will follow." He then turned and gazed at Hashkeh Naabah.

"Do not call them Zuni. That is a Spanish word," the war chief explained. "They are the A'shiwi people. I won an A'shiwi wife in a battle five harvests ago. I understand some of their words. I will travel with you to speak with them."

Growling Bear stared off in space, nodded and smiled as if he had just finished a conversation. The other men sat patiently and watched. At last, he turned his eyes to his companions.

"Tilini says it is wise to honor our brothers of the land with their words," he said, confirming their suspicions that he had been communicating with one of the spirit beings. "However, he says the invaders have given us a gift that we may use against them."

Hashkeh Naabah leaned forward. "Horses?" he asked eagerly.

"No, but that day will come," Growling Bear said. "The Spanish tongue. Many of us have been forced to learn their strange talk. We can use their words to speak to all the people. Perhaps even the Apache will join us if we can speak to them."

Hashkeh Naabah nodded. "I know the Tinneh, or Apache as you call them, have fought the Spanish ever since the invaders arrived. They may welcome an invitation to go to war."

Growling Bear smiled as he stared into the distance for another moment. "Forgive me, brothers. Tilini told me the Navajo would be important in uniting all the peoples." The Navajo leaders nodded, then invited Growling Bear to eat and rest before continuing his journey.

The young men sat perfectly still, watching in reverence as Growling Bear gave them their instructions. The fifty-some runners had been given the same thing — cords of maguey fiber with five knots tied in them.

It had taken Growling Bear five years to accomplish his mission. He had contacted 45 pueblos, the farthest being 50 miles east of the Rio Grande. His journey also had taken him to the A'shiwi 120 miles away and the Hopi 200 miles from the river.

No other Pueblo man had traveled so far and contacted so many people of the land without being harmed. Growling Bear had personally picked these young men for their bravery and running skills.

"You will not be harmed when you show the Pueblo men and warriors of the Hopi and Apache the cords. Tell them to wait for the full moon, then untie one knot at the end of each day. We will attack when the last knot is untied."

Each young man clutched their ropes as if they were sacred relics. Growling Bear blessed each runner, then watched them scatter in different directions as they raced off on their dangerous missions.

5

Eagle Watcher sat hunched over in his Santa Fe jail cell. He and another youth had the misfortune of being captured by the Spanish after Pueblo sympathizers betrayed them. Eagle Watcher's right arm hung loosely after being broken by the Spanish torturers. The pain was excruciating. It throbbed with every breath he took.

Across the aisle, Runs With Deer lay on the floor of his cell. Both eyes were swollen shut from the beatings. Blood pooled from his back. The lashings had been so severe, the Pueblo youth of only fifteen harvests had passed out. Only the unsteady rise and fall of his chest was proof he was still alive.

A door swung open and clanged against a wall, followed by the sound of boots on the floor. Without looking, Eagle Watcher guessed four men were approaching. The group stopped briefly to check on Runs With Deer. One of the men laughed. It was a threatening sound, like a dog's bark.

The men then walked over to Eagle Watcher's cell. "This one's still conscious," one of the Spanish men said. "Your friend over there looks to be near death. No use to us. Should we send him to his ancestors or are you ready to talk?"

Eagle Watcher turned his head slowly. Four bearded men stood glaring at him. Even through his pain-glazed eyes, he could see their hatred. He could almost smell it on them. He tried to think clearly, but his mind was foggy from the pain that wracked his body.

One of the men held up a cord with five knots in it. "What is the meaning of this rope, Indian?" snarled the Spanish man who had been instrumental in the beatings and whippings of the two youths.

Tears ran down Eagle Watcher's cheeks. He just wanted the pain to go away. "Attack in five days after the full moon," he rasped.

The expression on the men's faces changed from rage to shock. "Attack? Where? By who?" the head torturer demanded.

The youth of sixteen harvests bent over. A different pain, one that stung his soul, filled his being — guilt. He had just betrayed his people. If he was going to be a traitor, he wanted his words to sting these terrible men.

"Many Pueblos will rise up and burn your churches and kill your priests," Eagle Watcher said with surprising strength. "We will kill your people in their rancheros. We will attack the city and drive you from our land."

Another Spanish man shoved the torturer aside. He wore no armor but was attired in those strange clothes the invaders wore when not at war. His beard was trimmed shorter, and he smelled like he bathed in spring flowers.

"The Pueblos will attack? As one force? Why, there aren't enough men to mount a serious threat."

Eagle Watcher shook his head slowly. The more worried these Spanish sounded the better it felt. It almost took the pain away. Almost.

"We do not fight alone, Spaniard. The A'shiwi, Hopi, Navajo and Apaches will join us." A moment of clarity surged through Eagle Watcher's brain. "Where are the other runners? I see only Runs With Deer and myself."

The Spaniard gasped and glanced at his companions. "You Indians are working together with the other tribes?" He stopped as the realization set in. "Even the Apache join you?" The Spanish had been unable to make inroads in Apache territory. The fierce warriors had so far kept them at bay.

"Other runners? How many other runners?" the trim-bearded man demanded. However, his voice revealed his true feelings — fear.

Eagle Watcher shook his head. "I do not know, Man Who Smells Like Flowers." Several of the other Spaniards coughed trying to mask their unexpected surge of amusement. The Pueblo youth held up his good hand, palm out, extending all five fingers. "Many times more than this," he said, then gasped as another wave of pain shot through his body.

The Spaniard's eyes widened and the color left his already pale complexion. "Tell me, Indian," he shouted. "Forty, fifty, sixty?"

Eagle Watcher slumped back down. He felt dizzy and sick. "I do not know your words, diablo," he mumbled, then collapsed unconscious on the floor.

Governor Trevino, the man who smelled like flowers, whirled around to face his companion. "If this is true, we will be attacked by hundreds of warriors. Send armed parties to the rancheros and get those people back to the fort. We might have a chance to outlast them. We do not have enough men to face them in open battle."

Two of the Spaniards walked quickly from the room to carry out the governor's orders. The torturer gestured at the two Pueblo youths. "Sir, what do you want done with these two Indians?" Trevino swiped his hand across his throat and hurried out of the room to oversee preparations for the coming attack.

Eagle Watcher vaguely heard the door to his cell open and felt the vibration of boots as they walked over to him. He felt his head being raised, then something was slipped around his neck.

A quick tug caused a white light to explode through his brain. For a brief moment, Eagle Watcher saw Tilini smiling at him. "It is time to go home, young warrior. Follow me." Then his pain was gone.

Growling Bear shook his head at the sad news. Two Pueblo youths had been captured by the Spanish. When he asked their names, the messenger paused, then told him.

The cacique put his hands to his face in sorrow. His sister's son, Eagle Watcher, was one of the two prisoners. Growling Bear had been fond of the young man who loved to sit on the buttes and watch the magnificent winged predators. Growling Bear had named him when he was a young boy.

He knew all too well what fate befell the two young men. They would be tortured to near death until they gave away their plans. Growling Bear looked at his war council. "Tell as many as you can. We attack a day early. No mercy for the invaders. They have no honor."

6

Governor Trevino sat slumped in a chair in his palace as he read report after report of the natives' attack on his people. Their settlements had been destroyed, priests killed, churches burned to the ground. The governor had sent out armed parties to escort survivors back to Santa Fe.

Now, one thousand more civilians had crowded into the fort in Santa Fe, which was defended by fewer than two hundred soldiers. Water and food were running out. His men estimated several thousand native warriors had surrounded Santa Fe.

Curiously, the natives hadn't mounted an attack. They seemed content to starve the Spanish out or pick them off one by one if they dared to venture out on foraging trips.

The native people were using the tried and true tactic of the siege. If the attackers had access to food and water, this strategy almost always worked. Sooner or later, the defenders would run out of supplies and be forced to surrender or worse yet — overrun. Trevino's men calculated the fort could hold out for only two more weeks before their stocks ran out.

Friar Estefan had just begun his predawn prayers when his door burst open. Flower Gatherer rushed in. Her eyes were wide with terror. "Forgive me, Friar, but warriors are coming to kill you and burn the church. Warriors from all the pueblos are attacking at once. You must leave now!"

The young friar gasped in shock, hurriedly gathered a few of his belongings and followed the native girl out the side door. She grabbed his sleeve and pulled him to the safety of some nearby pinyon trees.

Just as they ducked down, the pair heard yelling and war shouts coming from the mission church. Not long afterwards, flames could be seen licking up the sides, and moments later, the roof exploded in a giant blaze.

"Why?" Estefan mumbled. Flower Gatherer put her hand over his mouth and shook her head vigorously. They watched the horrific scene for another few minutes, then she gestured for the friar to follow her in a zigzag pattern through the trees and rested again in a thick grove not far from one of the buttes that rose like giant monoliths throughout the landscape.

"Why are the Pueblo people attacking the churches?" Estefan whispered after waiting in silence for what seemed like an interminable amount of time.

Flower Gatherer held up her hand. She peered into the early dawn light, listening intently. After determining they were not being followed, she turned towards the priest.

"Growling Bear has gathered warriors from the people of the land — the Pueblos, Hopi, A'shiwi, Navajo and Apache — to drive the Spanish away. The rancheros take our people as slaves, and many priests beat us if we do not swear allegiance to your God. You Spanish have destroyed our kivas, our places of worship."

She paused and looked fondly at the young friar. Even though he shaved his head, his eyes still shone with youthful exuberance. "You are different, Friar Estefan. You do not beat us or yell insults at us. You sing to the children and talk to us as equals. I did not want you to join your God, yet."

Estefan reached out and grasped Flower Gatherer's hand. He wiped tears from his eyes with the sleeve of his cowl. "Thank you, my friend. It has troubled my spirit how your people have been treated."

The girl of fourteen harvests or so, rose from her spot and gestured for him to follow. "Are you taking me back to my people?" he asked.

She shook her head and looked back at him over her shoulder. "No, Friar. There are too many warriors between us and your people. You would be killed. I am taking you to the only one who may listen to you. Use your words wisely and speak the truth. He is a wise man, who has many powers."

Estefan stopped. "Who is it?" he asked, trying to mask his trembling voice.

Flower Gatherer stopped. Her solemn eyes met his. "Growling Bear."

The attack was going pretty much as Growling Bear had foreseen. The priests in the churches and many of the colonists were taken completely by surprise. They were killed where they were found, whether worshipping, eating or sleeping.

The native people were as merciless as the Spanish had been when they attacked their pueblos and destroyed the kivas. No mercy was given for age or sex. Now, what was left of the Spanish were huddled together in Santa Fe or Isleta, about seventy miles to the south.

Growling Bear knew an outright attack would lead to the needless slaughter of his people from the superior weapons of the Spanish. But, the white men had dwindling resources. He knew the Spanish would not attack and risk the annihilation of their people.

The Spanish would only come out in force for one reason — escape. Growling Bear was patient. His people had plenty of food and water. The native warriors even started drawing lots for when the Spanish would attempt their retreat.

Cords with various numbers of knots depicting how many days the Spanish could last were passed out among their people.

Much to Growling Bear's surprise, the Spanish soldiers came rushing out in a defensive maneuver only eleven days after the siege began. Growling Bear had picked a cord with thirteen knots in it. His people would have held out for one full moon, maybe two.

The native warriors retreated from the soldiers, but not without taking many enemy lives. While this battle was going on, another wave of Spanish broke out and made their escape, defended by the remainder of the garrison. The soldiers only retreated when they received word their fellow Spanish had escaped.

Instead of a counterattack, Growling Bear ordered the warriors only to follow the fleeing colonists. His people stayed out of range of their weapons and disappeared into the brush when the Spanish charged at them on their horses.

But the native people made sure the Spanish knew they were there — following, watching — perhaps lying in wait, ready to attack if the white men let their guard down. This uncertainty and fear did exactly what Growling Bear had hoped — the Spanish fled south as quickly as they could.

Growling Bear's warriors did not attack when the Santa Fe refugees joined with their fellows in Isleta and continued south. The warriors shadowed the escapees all the way to the Mexican border. They stopped and watched with pride as the Spanish kept trudging along. The intent was not to slaughter all the Spanish but to intimidate them.

Growling Bear wanted the Spanish to know the people of the land would defend themselves. The cacique knew an all-out slaughter of innocents would only draw a terrible retribution of revenge from the intruders.

Growling Bear sent a handful of scouts to trail the Spanish as they trekked south. The scouts returned after three days and reported the defeated caravan did not change course.

It took several weeks for the Spanish to tally their losses from the unified attacks. Governor Trevino reported to his superiors in a voice heavy with shame. "Señors, four hundred of our people were killed by the natives during their offensive. We believe twenty-one priests were among those murdered."

One of his fellow governors leaned forward. "How many of our people were spared?"

Trevino checked his tally sheet. "Two thousand, señor. We were able to escort them to safety."

The questioner tapped his fingers thoughtfully on the desk, where he and three counterparts sat behind. "By the grace of God, perhaps? Or, from the reports I have read, you were spared by the native people?"

Trevino looked up and frowned. "Yes, señor, perhaps. The natives followed us to the border, but did not attack during our march."

The other man leaned back, crossing his arms over his chest. "It seems the natives acted with honor once they achieved their goal — removing our people from the land."

7

Growling Bear glowered across the fire at the two visitors. A girl from an outlying pueblo had dared to save one of the friars he had ordered killed. In truth, he admired Flower Gatherer's courage in bringing the young Spaniard to a meeting where the elders guaranteed their guests' safety.

The girl had risked her life to save this Christian. The least Growling Bear could do was to hear her story and test the character of the friar who sat before him. He stared into Estefan's eyes, trying to read his spirit. Was it poisonous or was there honor and truth to be found there?

Friar Estefan knew his life depended on the verdict of Growling Bear. He could not quell his fright at being the center of attention of the leader of the Pueblo revolt. On their journey to the meeting, other Pueblo people had told Flower Gatherer all the Spanish had either been killed or driven from their land.

Growling Bear turned toward Flower Gatherer. "Why have you brought this Christian before me? My orders were to kill or drive all the Spanish from our lands. This man is the last one of his kind left alive among our people."

Flower Gatherer shifted uncomfortably where she sat. She had never sat at council before, let alone been asked to speak. But, saving Friar Estefan was important. It was the right thing to do. A voice in her head told her to say what she was thinking.

"Thank you, Growling Bear, for agreeing to hear me, a mere girl of fourteen harvests. Friar Estefan is not like the other priests who have beat and punished our people. He speaks to us as equals and has shown great kindness to our pueblo. He has cared for our sick. He invites us to hear him and does not order us. He listens to our stories and sings to the children."

Growling Bear held up his hand for silence. He stared again at the young friar, who looked back at him with a calmness that impressed him. Perhaps the Spaniard did not understand his life was at stake.

"Does this priest understand our language or do I have to speak in the hideous tongue his people have forced us to learn?"

Friar Estefan drew in a deep breath. He understood perfectly what he said next could mean life or death. He thought a quick prayer for calmness and clarity of thought.

"Growling Bear and Honored Council, I thank you for agreeing to honor Flower Gatherer's request and to hear my words," he said in the Tewa language. Friar Estefan's Franciscan teachers had instilled in him the importance of learning other people's languages. One old instructor was adamant that non-Christians would be much more likely to convert if they understood the message in their own words.

"It has troubled my heart how my Christian brothers have treated your people. I have always lived my life as my mother taught me as a small child. It is from the Bible, but the words should be true to everyone: Treat others as you would treat yourself. I say these words to you in truth. If you find me worthy of life, I promise to deliver your message back to the Spanish authorities."

Friar Estefan stopped and drew a deep breath. "Yes, I am afraid of death. Yes, I believe I will join my Christ after I die. But, I believe my life's journey is not over yet."

Growling Bear stared into the fire for a moment, then looked at the Spaniard. He was supposed to hate this enemy, but the young friar reminded him of Sun Brother, his gentle cousin who had been tortured and killed.

As he studied the young man, a tiny figure that looked like Tilini, the light being, appeared to be dancing on the friar's shoulder. Growling Bear needed no further convincing.

"I find no poison in the Spaniard's words. It takes great courage to say you are frightened in front of an enemy. We know there are many evil men among the Spanish, but now we know there is one good man who walks with them."

He stopped and looked at the other Pueblo men gathered at council. None of them spoke against the Spaniard.

"Let us return this man of Christ back to his people," Growling Bear said. "Perhaps he can teach his brothers to act as he has toward our people. I am not an innocent child to believe the Spanish will not return, maybe many times. It will be a good thing to have this man among his people when they invade again."

Letting out a trembling breath, Friar Estefan started to make the sign of the cross but stopped himself when he saw Growling Bear's mouth twitch into a frown. "Forgive me, honored elders. I will pray when I am alone. Thank you for listening to my words and for granting me my life."

Growling Bear resumed his stoic expression. "I will send ten warriors with you to make sure you reach your people safely. You will be treated with respect on your journey. Christian, when you return to the Spanish, tell them the people of the land will fight for our homes if they invade again."

Friar Estefan nodded that he understood. Without another word, the cacique gestured for the friar and Flower Gatherer to leave.

Diego de Vargas leaned forward in his chair as he listened to Friar Estefan's amazing story of how he was rescued, had his life spared by the leader of the Pueblo revolt, was escorted by native warriors and finally handed over to a patrol of Spanish soldiers.

The friar's account was backed up by the garrison's captain, who had interviewed his soldiers after Friar Estefan was released to their custody. The friar had been in good spirits and was relatively healthy considering his two-week journey to find Spanish authorities.

At first the Chief Judge thought the friar might be a traitor who traded his life for information about the Spanish. But, after hearing the account from a sincere-sounding Estefan and reading the captain's letter, Diego determined the friar must be telling the truth.

"You say there are no Spanish left alive in New Mexico?" he asked.

Friar Estefan shrugged. "I do not know that for certain, señor, but I saw no living Spanish on my journey south. If there are survivors, they live at the behest of the Pueblo people."

Diego's head snapped up at Friar Estefan's reference to "Pueblo people." Natives was the nicest word the Spanish called them. The most common slurs were heathens or savages. Other friars and priests often referred to them as "godless pagans."

"Pueblo people, eh, Friar? Yes, it is obvious Governor Trevino and his soldiers greatly underestimated these Pueblo people." He leaned down and rummaged through a desk drawer, finally pulling out another parchment. After quickly scanning it, he nodded at the friar.

"They coordinated an attack with former enemies, killed hundreds of our people in the initial onslaught, lay siege to Santa Fe and drove several thousand survivors to the border without taking more lives. Indeed, the natives or Pueblo people, whatever we call them, should never be taken lightly again."

Friar Estefan shifted uncomfortably in his chair. By Diego's tone, he knew what the Chief Judge meant. The Pueblo people would be treated as dangerous adversaries in future invasion plans of New Mexico.

The friar was torn between his loyalty to Spain and his respect for the native people who had saved his life and treated him well. Further incursions by the Spanish into New Mexico would likely be bloody affairs. The Pueblo people would not stand a chance against well-armed Spanish soldiers.

Diego did not concern himself with what would happen to the Pueblo people. What he saw was a golden opportunity for a bright young man, such as himself, to climb the social and economic ladder.

8

The old man groaned as he attempted to sit up from his cot to get a better look at his visitors, but the effort was too much. A woman knelt toward him and lifted his head. She offered him a cool drink of water from one of the beautifully crafted bowls his people were known for.

"Thank you, my child," Growling Bear rasped. "I hear my grandfather talk to me in my dreams. He tells me he is waiting for me. The hunting is good, and the crops are bountiful where he dwells. The rivers are full and flow over the land."

The young woman eased his head back down. His breathing sounded better, but it was still shallow. "Do you remember us, Great Leader?" she asked gently.

Growling Bear squinted at the two people, but his vision was blurry. "Great Leader? You honor me. It has been many harvests since I have heard those words. Come closer, my eyes are failing me. Your voice is familiar, child."

The woman gestured for her companion to join her. When the man approached, Growling Bear gasped, which triggered a coughing fit. "A Spaniard? Have you come to punish me for my 'crimes' against your people? You might be too late to torture an old man." Even in his feeble state, the defiant tone was still obvious.

"No, great cacique, I come in peace. You and Flower Gatherer saved my life twelve years ago. I am Father Estefan, now. You knew me as Friar Estefan."

Growling Bear stared at the speaker, trying to understand his words. A smile slowly flickered across his face as his memory cleared momentarily. "A young girl saved a Spaniard's life after we drove the invaders from our land the first time, I believe."

Flower Gatherer nodded and took the old man's hands in hers. "Yes, Great Leader. I am Flower Gatherer, the girl who begged you to save this Spaniard."

With a shaky hand, Growling Bear reached up and touched her cheek. "You have grown into a beautiful woman, child. I am pleased. Our people no longer call me Great Leader. Our freedom did not last long, I'm afraid. Distrust spread among the people during the drought even after we defeated the invaders two more times."

A tear slowly made its way down his face, following the craggy lines in his cheek. Flower Gatherer brought his hands to her face.

"Our people fought off the Spanish for twelve years, Great Leader. Yes, they have returned, but they no longer beat or take our people as slaves. They let us speak our tongues and sing to our grandfathers and grandmothers. Yes, many of our people flock to their Christ, but there is peace."

Growling Bear gestured for Flower Gatherer to come closer so he could whisper in her ear. "I weep not for our people, child. They will flourish somehow. Caudi, Tilini and Tleume no longer speak to me. The people stopped following me when I could no longer summon them. They abandoned me after we drove the Spanish away."

The old man closed his eyes for a moment, fighting to draw breath. His eyes fluttered open again as he focused on Father Estefan. "Ah, you must be the priest who came with the Spanish when they overran our people at last. I am told this man of your Christ called for mercy."

Father Estefan simply nodded. He felt no hatred toward the old man, only sorrow at seeing him so close to death. "Yes, cacique. The new governor, Diego de Vargas, asked me to help broker peace to save the lives of both our peoples."

Growling Bear let out a husky bark. His visitors looked momentarily alarmed, then realized it was a laugh. The old man's eyes sparkled with clarity as he gazed at a vision only he could see on the priest's shoulder.

"Tilini dances again!" He turned his head and looked deeply into Father Estefan's eyes. "My heart is happy that I saved this Spaniard." Growling Bear drew in one more trembling breath, then joined his grandfather.

Guardian flashed displeasure at Caretaker. "We agreed not to involve ourselves with the native sentients after they drove the invaders away. It was only a matter of time until the well-armed organisms would return and be victorious."

Caretaker emitted a casual signal of disregard. "I did not interfere. The body was too weak to retain its energy. One last dance put the emissary at ease. He deserved to say goodbye. See, his energy joins us now."

The new light being flickered uncertainly. "Caudi and Tilini?"

Guardian flashed a soft blue vibration. It felt something like amusement. "Welcome home. We are proud of your accomplishments with the sentients. Caretaker will guide you to the cluster. Your organic memories will soon fade."

The energy being reflected on its reactions. Pride? Amusement? More of those interesting emotions it vaguely remembered.

VI

1

Caretaker glowed orange with concern as it considered Guardian's report. "It seems the great cultural experiment of these sentients in that new nation you helped foster will soon be challenged," Guardian impassively vibrated to its partner.

"Your nurturing of this latest sentient experiment has been commendable, but our higher organisms appear to be repeating the mistakes of their ancestors by squabbling over property. The sentients' efforts to defeat a war-like empire and establish a new culture was most impressive. However, this unique union has existed for less than one hundred solar orbits, and its culture may be at an impasse. A great storm is brewing."

Caretaker flared red. "The property the sentients are quarreling over are other sentients. I have been patient with the new nation, waiting for more than three hundred solar orbits for their society to mature and free their fellow enslaved sentients. It is disappointing only a portion of their culture has become enlightened."

Guardian circled its counterpart in sympathy. "Enlightened societies have short life spans. This species always replaces them with single-minded leaders such as kings, dictators or a dominant class of deity worshippers. The original philosophy of this society was noble, but the sentients who constructed it are flawed."

A faint blue glow slowly emanated from Caretaker and grew brighter as the entity formed a new plan. "Once again your wisdom has offered inspiration," the entity messaged its partner. "We need to find and foster leaders who will guide their nation through the great cataclysm that is on the horizon."

Guardian paused for almost a full second, considering the options. "I will assist in the plan. If we fail, the society will evolve as all others have done so. If we succeed, then this experiment will continue until the next upheaval challenges it."

The two entities vibrated in agreement, then called in their family cloud. Caretaker relayed the message to thousands of minor entities: "A tasting of the sentients in the new nation is required. Leaders of great intelligence and courage are needed."

2

The tea tray shook in the maid's trembling hands, almost spilling its contents as she sat it on the parlor room table. "For goodness sake, Lucy! Whatever is the matter? If you are ill, you know you may rest," Harriet said, looking on with concern.

Lucy shook her head, but couldn't stop the tears from streaming down her face. "N-n-no ma'am, I'm not sick. Thank you."

Harriet stood up and took Lucy's hands in hers. It was a stark contrast. The smooth, small hands of an educated white woman held the black hands of her seventeen-year-old servant that were already heavily calloused and scarred. "For heaven's sake child, tell me what is troubling you. This is not your former life. You are free here. You may speak your mind. Here, sit and join me. I insist!"

Still shaking, Lucy sat down in one of the parlor room chairs. It felt wrong for her to be sitting in what she called the fancy room. She stopped crying when Harriet handed her a cup of tea. "Oh no, Miss Harriet. You shouldn't have done that!" Harriet waved away any further protests and sat patiently while the young woman composed herself.

Lucy gingerly lifted the porcelain tea cup to her lips. The hot liquid felt good and seemed to calm her nerves. She set the cup carefully down on its saucer and took a deep breath.

"I'm so sorry to trouble you, ma'am, but Mr. Dawes, the butcher, told me that slaver bounty hunters were in town looking to round up runaways. He said they have the right to take us back. Even white folks up here can't stop 'em." She shivered in fright at the thought of being forced to go back to that cruel life.

Harriet frowned but said nothing for a few moments. "Lucy, you have my word that Mr. Stowe and I would never let that happen to you. You are part of this family. Calvin and I will protect you." Although Harriet was a petite, soft-spoken woman, Lucy was comforted by her words and the intensity that reflected in her eyes.

"Lucy, out of respect for you, I've never asked you about your past," Harriet said. "However, I think it's important for white folks to hear it so we can try to understand some of the tribulations you have been through."

A look of pain washed over Lucy's face. "Oh, I don't know Miss Harriet. I get sick when I think about my life on the plantation. The things I had to do. The things they made me do," she said as her voice trailed off into a barely audible whisper.

Harriet reached out and grasped Lucy's shoulder. "I just received a message from Mr. Stowe asking if we could manage to host a young colleague of his at dinner this evening. I believe this would be an excellent time for all of us to hear your story." Harriet looked deeply into Lucy's eyes. "I need to hear your story."

Lucy nodded shyly. "I will try, Miss Harriet."

When the Stowes and Robert, their guest, had finished dining later that evening, Harriet announced they would forego the usual card game they frequently played when entertaining. "I beg your indulgence, gentlemen, but I wish to present a topic of uttermost importance."

Harriet turned towards Robert. "May I be so presumptuous, Mr. Brighton, as to ask your opinion of the slavery issue?" Calvin looked stunned that his wife would be so audacious as to ask such an impolite question of a guest, but he knew she must have a good reason to speak in such a manner.

Robert waited a moment, expecting Calvin to change the subject, but both Stowes sat patiently, waiting for his answer. He took a healthy sip of tea to clear his suddenly dry throat.

"Well, Mrs. Stowe, if I may be blunt," he paused, waiting.

Harriet smiled and nodded for him to continue.

"Slavery, in my opinion, is an atrocity that has been imposed upon the Negro people. I do not understand how Christians can partake in such an abominable practice against their fellow human beings."

Harriet looked relieved. "Most excellent. Thank you for your candor, Mr. Brighton. I can assure you that this household echoes your sentiments, and please forgive my forwardness in bringing up such a controversial topic."

Calvin leaned forward. "My dear, that was a most unusual request of a guest. Why did you ask him that?"

Harriet turned and gestured toward the doorway where a lone figure stood, nervously swaying back and forth. "I believe it is important to hear Lucy's story. If we are to understand and campaign for change, then we have to know what we are fighting against."

At first Lucy was reluctant to speak, needing gentle encouragement from Harriet. However, the longer she spoke, the words started to pour out in a torrent of emotion like a swollen river that had just burst its dam. The expression on the faces of the Stowes and their guest changed from sympathy to pity to shock and eventually to anger as they listened to Lucy's story.

Lucy told them enslaved children were expected to work as soon as they could carry a basket to the fields, usually about age four or five. The slaves' days were filled with labor from sunrise to sunset. They were allowed almost no respite from their work, whether it be toiling in the fields under a scorching sun or maintaining the grounds of the plantation.

Harriet's face grew ashen as she heard Lucy's description of a white foreman's deviance. She covered her mouth with one of her hands in an attempt to not gag in revulsion.

"Mr. Charles, the foreman, he liked to take us girls to the grove," Lucy said. Her face scrunched in pain at the memory. "I was just a child the first time he took me to the grove. He called it his treat. It hurt bad, that first time. My mama cried so hard that night."

Lucy stopped and wiped away a tear. "Mr. Charles would give everyone more food if we didn't tell Master James when he took a girl to the grove. Us girls learned to lie still with our eyes closed. It didn't last long. Sometimes Mr. Charles would let the treat girls go back to our cabins and rest. He said it was a reward for being good girls."

Harriet got up from her chair and hugged Lucy. "Oh my dear girl, I am so sorry you were hurt by that horrible man. It is such a tragedy anyone has to suffer such indignity." Calvin cleared his throat and declared he needed some air. Robert looked away and wiped his eyes with a kerchief.

When they gathered back at the table, Lucy told them how she escaped. "When I turned fifteen, I think, Mama overheard Mr. Charles and Master James talking about selling some of us girls. Master was disappointed there were so many females. Said he wanted more males to get more work done.

"Two nights later, three of us girls and two boys slipped out and headed to the river. It was the night before church so the white folks wouldn't miss us right away in the morning. Old Joe drew us a map. He said he had worked on three plantations close by so he knew the land.

"We went straight west and then north. Joe said the white folks always look north first, figuring that's where runaways head. We managed to get to the Ohio after hiding during the days and running at night. The ferryman was right where Old Joe said he would be.

"At first the boys didn't trust him 'cause he was a white man, but he knew the signal. We whistled three times then two times then once. He answered the signal with one then two then three whistles — just like Old Joe said he would. The ferryman took us across the river and told us about a house where the people would take us in and help us."

Just as Lucy stopped to compose herself and take a breath, all four people jumped when someone furiously knocked on their back door. It was most unusual for a visitor to do that at that hour of the evening. Lucy started to get up to go answer it but was stopped by Calvin. "Stay here. I will see who dares to intrude on us at this hour." He turned and looked at the others. "Perhaps it is best if you remain quiet until I see who it is."

Calvin picked up an oil lamp and carried it with him to see who was making such a racket. "Who's there?" he called out as he opened the door just a few inches. "Why Tommy Morrison, what are you doing at the back door this time of night?"

Fourteen-year-old Tommy was shaking and panting. His eyes were wide with fear. "Beg your pardon, Mr. Stowe, sir, but Mama told me to get here fast as I could and make sure I wasn't seen from the street."

Calvin gestured for the youngster to enter. "What's the matter? Is someone ill?"

Tommy shook his head violently. "No sir! Slaver bounty hunters just came to our house. They had a warrant for poor Jed, our handyman. Said they had a right to take him and others back South. Mama told me to get here right quick. Them men are going house to house. They're heading this way, sir. Mama thinks they want to take your maid."

Normally Calvin would have corrected the youngster's grammar, but Tommy obviously had run almost a mile in the dark to deliver the message, and the gravity of the situation overruled any educational lesson.

Calvin guided Tommy to a chair, poured him a cup of water from a pitcher, and called for the others to join them. After quickly repeating Tommy's message, Calvin turned to his guest. "Robert, you're not part of this. You may retire to your home, if you so wish. The only favor I ask of you is not to alert the bounty hunters about Lucy."

Robert stood up. "No sir, I will not retreat from my duty. Tell me what I can do to help!"

"Thank you, but I do not know what we can do," Calvin said, frowning at the impending threat to Lucy that was approaching their home.

Harriet leaned down to speak to Tommy. "Thank you, dear boy, for your courage. Now, be careful going home and be sure to thank your mother." Tommy grinned, then slipped out the back door to make his way back home.

The men jumped when Harriet clapped her hands. She smiled as an idea formulated in her mind. "Mr. Brighton, you have a horse and buggy tethered outside, do you not?"

He nodded. "Yes, I do. Please call me Robert, ma'am. Why do you ask?"

Harriet turned to Calvin. "The trunk my aunt sent us last Christmas with all those clothes is still in the attic, is it not?" Before Calvin could answer, she turned and faced Robert while she reached out for Lucy's hand. "Are you, kind sir, willing to transport a very valuable package out of harm's way?"

Robert looked dumbfounded for a moment, but then understood what was being asked of him. "Yes, of course. I would consider it an honor to help get Lucy out of harm's way. I have an uncle and aunt upstate who, I'm sure, will help take care of her and see to her safety."

Lucy just stared in wonder. Other than the ferryman, never before had she met white folks who were willing to help her. "M-m-mrs., I don't know what to say," she said, wiping away tears.

Harriet clasped both of Lucy's hands in hers. "The only thing you need to do, my dear, is gather your belongings. I will pack some nice warm blankets for you to lie on and to put over your head. I am so sorry that old trunk may be musty, but it's the best we can do with such little notice."

Turning to her husband, Harriet flashed him a quick smile. "Lucy will need some money to help her get settled into a new life. Do we have much in the rainy day account?"

Calvin gave a quick nod, grabbed the lamp and headed for the basement to find the money that was hidden away in a pickle jar. Less than a half hour later, Calvin casually walked out the front door and paced up and down the porch while he puffed on his pipe.

Seeing nothing out of the ordinary, he scurried back inside. A few moments later, he and Robert carried out a large trunk and carefully heaved it into the waiting carriage. Harriet gave the young man a hug. "Godspeed, sir, and please take care of our Lucy."

Robert tipped his hat to his hosts. "You have my word." He then untied his horse's reins, sprang onto the seat and drove the carriage off into the night.

Barely an hour later, the Stowes heard another rap on a door. This time it came from the front of the house. Calvin took his time to answer. "Who goes there?" he called out, then opened it cautiously.

Three rough-looking characters greeted him. The skinniest of the trio, a tall scarecrow of a man with an unkempt beard, approached Calvin, and stuck a wanted poster in his face. The poster was a poorly done drawing of a Negro girl.

"We been told you have a Negra maid that may be a runaway. We have a warrant here that says we got the right to reclaim lost property to the rightful owner. Why don't ya'll call her out here so we can take a look? See her papers if she's got any."

At that moment, Harriet appeared at Calvin's side. "Oh, are you looking for our maid? Why that ungrateful girl took my best shawl and all my egg money when she disappeared last week!" Harriet shook her head in mock despair. "My Aunt Margaret knitted the shawl. It was my favorite. That ungrateful thief!"

Calvin shook his head. He was slightly amazed at his wife's performance. "Please, sir, if you find that girl would you be so kind as to return my shawl? I would be ever so grateful. We might live across the Ohio, but Southern chivalry is well known to us!"

The tall man stared at Harriet for a bit, then shrugged. He stepped to one side and spit a wad of tobacco juice into the bushes. "Sorry to hear that ma'am. Never know what them runaways will steal. She been gone a week you say?"

Calvin gave a puff on his pipe and slowly blew out a smoke ring. "Actually, my dear I think it was eight days ago. It was when you came back from your church ladies sewing group."

Harriet stared off into the distance. "Oh heavens, I do believe you are correct, my dear. My apologies, good sir. It was a week ago this past Tuesday."

"Hmmph," the tall man grunted as he rolled up the wanted poster. "Do ya'll know where she might be headin'?"

Calvin shook his head, but Harriet gave a little jump. "I think I do, sir! It all makes sense now. She was always asking about Canada. I didn't give it much thought until now."

The tall man mumbled something under his breath. "Appreciate your help folks. Doubt we'll find that girl now." He and his comrades started to leave when Harriet called out. "If you do catch her, remember my shawl, sir." The tall man chuckled, tipped his hat to Harriet, then waved for his companions to follow him down the street.

Harriet waited until the men had disappeared into the night before she uttered a most un-Christian oath. Calvin grinned broadly, then let out a heavy sigh of relief.

As they went back inside, Harriet hugged Calvin and buried her head in his chest. "I don't care. I'm not asking forgiveness for what I just said." Calvin wrapped his arms around her. "No need to, my dear. No need to."

The next morning as Harriet stared out the window of the sitting room, her mind swirled with the events of the past night. Lucy's stories had sparked something inside her.

"We've lived in Cincinnati for three years and never visited Covington," Harriet said almost to herself.

"What? Covington, why?" Calvin asked, not bothering to mask his surprise. He had been sitting at his desk, preparing the day's college lesson plan. "That's in Kentucky. We would have to cross the Ohio."

Harriet cocked her head slightly, a gesture usually reserved to relate her impatience. "Yes, I'm aware Covington is in Kentucky, across the Ohio, my dear. I have seen maps and spoken to people who have traveled there. They tell me it is quite a charming place except for one thing."

Calvin knew better than to challenge her intelligence. It would be a losing battle. "My apologies, my dear. But again, why Covington? I hear the ferry ride can be quite the adventure." He shook his head. "What in heaven's name does Covington have that Cincinnati does not?"

Harriet paused, then met his gaze full on. "They have a slave auction the third Thursday of every month. I wish to witness this travesty of Southern commerce." Calvin stared at his wife in shock, no words exited his mouth.

This time Harriet allowed herself to smile. It was not often Calvin was at a loss for words. "Let's book a ferry ride and visit the charming South."

Calvin's mind raced. *What is going on? Why does she want to see a slave auction in Kentucky?*

As if reading his thoughts, Harriet walked over and patted his shoulder. "The more accurate the information I gather, the better my stories will be."

Calvin's eyebrows shot up in surprise for a moment, but he quickly regained his composure. After last night, he vowed nothing about his wife would ever surprise him again. "I will book the tickets today, my dear."

3

"Come to church my dear, it's been six weeks now since the funeral," Calvin said as he gently patted his wife's shoulder. "The members of the congregation miss you. They all send you their love. You need to get out. It's communion Sunday. You always take comfort in partaking of the sacraments."

Harriet sighed as she gazed out the window from her chair. The colors of the leaves were starting to glimmer in their golds and reds in the autumn sun. It had been over ten years since the family had moved to Brunswick, Maine, for Calvin's new job. The horrible sight of the slave auction the couple witnessed in Kentucky still burned in her soul, but her passion had been quelled with all the responsibilities of raising children and maintaining a household.

"Oh Calvin, little Sammy would have loved to be playing outside today." She looked up at her husband. He could only nod as tears filled his eyes.

Harriet reached up and squeezed his hand. "I am sorry my dear, I forgot how much you miss him, too." Giggles from outside caught her attention. Despite the grief of losing her eighteen-month-old son, Harriet managed a smile as she watched their twin four-year-old daughters toss the pretty leaves over each other's heads.

"Life must go on, I suppose," she murmured while wiping her eyes with one of her dainty handkerchiefs. She rose from her chair and hugged her husband. "Tell the children they have an hour to dress in their Sunday finest. This is a beautiful day to go to worship."

Harriet's arrival was met by loving hugs from the church women and gentle handshakes from the men. The pastor, a round, congenial fellow, beamed with joy when he spotted Harriet seated with the congregation. He welcomed everyone on this crisp autumn morning.

Despite her best efforts to pay attention to the good pastor, who had a tendency to drone on a bit, Harriet found herself thinking about the troubling news she had just read in the newspaper. The anger in her swelled as the ramifications of the Fugitive Slave Act, recently passed by Congress to placate the Southern states, swirled in her brain.

According to the new law, bounty hunters could capture slaves, who had escaped to safety in the North, and transport them back to their former owners. The law was not popular with many in the Northern states, especially church women. The sight of black women and children being bound and forced screaming into prison wagons was horrifying to these women of conscience.

Harriet took a deep breath and tried to shake the image of these unfortunate souls being dragged away. As she gazed up at the pastor, who was reciting the words to the sacrament of communion, a vision of a shackled young black woman stared forlornly back at her. The woman, who looked eerily similar to their former maid Lucy, held out her hands and mouthed the words: "My baby. They stole my baby!"

A sadness burned into Harriet's soul as a voice breathed in her ear: "Write my story and tell others. We are human beings, just like you. All we want is our freedom!" Harriet sat up with a jolt like a person who had just woken from a bad dream.

Her sudden movement caught Calvin's attention. He leaned over and looked at her with concern. She smiled and whispered, "I am well, my dear. I know what I have to do now." Calvin nodded ever so slightly and smiled at her. He had seen that determined look before and had a feeling his wife was embarking on an important mission.

After the service, when the family had navigated through the waves of well wishers and were settled in their carriage heading back home, Calvin glanced towards Harriet. She was staring intently out the window with her arms wrapped around the twins who snuggled on either side of her. "A penny for your thoughts, my dear," he said, flashing her his famous gregarious grin.

"My stories in the abolitionist magazines were well received, but I have not written much since we moved here," Harriet sighed.

Calvin cast her a sympathetic glance. "You have been so busy with the move, then the twins came, then Sammy was born." He winced the moment he uttered his son's name, knowing it would cause his wife to suffer a wave of pain. "Forgive me, my dear."

Instead of drawing back into a shell of self pity, Harriet squinted while staring straight ahead as if she were surveying the landscape for the first time. "It is time I start writing again. I've always felt such a release when telling stories."

Calvin smiled. "I'm so happy to hear that. People love your stories." He paused. "Well, Northern folks of conscience do, anyway. So, are you going to send them to the magazines as you have done in the past?"

Harriet paused and closed her eyes. The vision in church seemed so real. "No, this will be different. I think it's going to be one long story. A book, maybe."

Calvin started to respond, but their horse stopped suddenly and half reared when another carriage cut in front of them at an intersection. He quickly got the animal under control and uttered an oath under his breath. After making sure Harriet and the twins were fine, he urged their horse onward and returned to their conversation.

"A book? Sounds like an impressive undertaking, my dear," he said. "Will it be abolitionist in tone?"

Harriet nodded. "Why, yes. I believe it will. I have a feeling it may take us on a grand adventure." Calvin grinned and reached out. The couple held hands for the remainder of the trip home.

Caretaker danced around Guardian after returning from its trip to the planet. The entity had been visiting a favorite sentient, a female who was adept at communicating with her fellow organisms.

"This life giver is most impressive," Caretaker said in a vibration to its partner. "It has the rare ability to inspire emotions from those cryptic markings the sentients call words. Others are absorbing her messages and spreading their own ideas in support."

Guardian flashed yellow with concern. "Did the sentient create its own ideas or did you plant them?"

Caretaker abruptly stopped its dance and fired a powerful vibration of displeasure at Guardian. "I only helped open its mind to its potential. The communication is its own unique creation."

Guardian glowed blue and issued a vibration of reconciliation. "It seems we both have been successful. I have identified a male with extraordinary leadership abilities. However, it cannot rise to power with a show of force as with past civilizations. The sentients have developed a most curious method where they choose their leaders by some sort of proclamation. The leader has to be selected by its fellows. Once again, I have encouraged it to offer its services."

Caretaker also emitted a bluish glow. "We have planted the seeds in the sentients. Now it is up to them to take the next step."

This time Guardian circled its partner. "Agreed, but those sentients move so slowly," it vibrated.

Caretaker slowly glowed with a soft pinkish hue. "Patience. We must have patience."

4

"My apologies gentlemen, but he is talking to some folks. It could be a while yet," the young lawyer said of his senior partner's tardiness in keeping the appointment.

The two brothers shuffled in their seats, but said nothing. They had traveled by horse and buggy, then by train for the better part of a day and paid for an overnight hotel room to reach this particular law office.

Looking up from a novel he was reading, the taller of the two smiled. "Thank you, Mr. Herndon, but we have nowhere else to go. Besides, I am almost finished with my book." The shorter brother frowned but kept reading the local newspaper. Its main headline proclaimed in large font: "Congress passes Kansas-Nebraska Act!" The second headline read: "New states allowed to decide slavery issue."

A few minutes later, a cluster of men talking in hushed tones exited a door at the other end of the hallway. Even though he could not hear them, the newspaper reader could see the men were excitedly addressing a tall fellow who stood in their midst.

Eventually, the tall man was able to usher them out the door. He stood, stroking his chin in thought for a minute or so as he watched them depart. Finally, he turned and ambled towards the brothers.

Transfixed by his book, the taller brother shook his head in wonderment. "Listen to this, Levi! This is the last passage." Before his brother could object, Henry started reading:

"A day of grace is yet held out to us. Both North and South have been guilty before God; and the Christian church has a heavy account to answer. Not by combining together, to protect injustice and cruelty, and making a common capital of sin, is this Union to be saved ..."

Before Henry could continue, a deep voice interrupted and recited the last half of the final passage:

"— but by repentance, justice and mercy; for, not surer is the eternal law by which the millstone sinks in the ocean, than that stronger law, by which injustice and cruelty shall bring on nations the wrath of Almighty God!"

Henry looked up in surprise, then reread the paragraph. "That is correct sir! That is exactly what it says. Have you memorized all of it?"

The tall man chuckled. "Too many words for this hound to remember. But certain passages are too powerful to forget. *Uncle Tom's Cabin* is a persuasive book, is it not?"

Henry nodded. "Yes, sir, very powerful indeed. And written by a woman yet!"

A smile spread across the tall man's broad, craggy face. "A very intelligent woman at that. I could not have written it so eloquently. Mrs. Harriet Beecher Stowe makes a resounding case against keeping our fellow human beings as slaves."

Levi held up the front page of the newspaper. "This does not sound like progress to me. Letting states decide on their own whether to permit slavery."

The tall man frowned. "Agreed, good sir. This is a dark day for our young nation."

Mr. Herndon cleared his throat. "Pardon me, sir, but these gentlemen have traveled a ways to speak with you about a legal problem. Mr. Lincoln, this is Mr. Henry Nelson and Mr. Levi Nelson of Osage. They are embroiled in a land dispute with a neighbor."

After greeting the Nelsons with the perfunctory handshakes, Abe chuckled and wagged his finger at Mr. Herndon. "William, have I not scolded you about calling me sir. Makes me sound like a gentleman." William blushed but said nothing. "Well, the Nelson brothers come to me with a land dispute. Nothing the original surveyor's report shouldn't be able to clear up. You know I did some surveying in my younger days."

Levi smiled. "That was one of the reasons we chose you, sir, er, Abe, I mean. We knew you could read the survey and pass fair judgment."

Henry turned ashen at his brother's brusque response. "Yes, that is true, but you also are well known for your honesty."

Abe grinned, then gestured for them to follow him into his inner office. After all were comfortably seated, he took his time reading their written complaint. "This is interesting indeed, sirs. You claim one Frederich Nelson and family have encroached on forty acres rightfully owned by you? Interesting. Is this a family dispute?"

Levi snorted. "No sir, not at all. Our families are not related. We filed our claim first. These Swedes do not even speak English well. They pretend to not understand, but I'm sure they do. They understand enough to have a judge in their pocket!"

Abe glanced up from the papers. Both brothers stared at him intently. "So, this other Nelson family appears to be illegally farming forty acres of that which were awarded to you in this land deed. By the date on the document, you rightfully should be in possession of this land."

Levi nodded. "What can be done? Magistrate Johannson was recently elected and has been sympathetic to the other family's claim."

Abe leaned back in his chair. "Well my good sirs as a circuit judge, I am happy to write a ruling alerting the good magistrate as to his error and instruct your local sheriff to make sure the Frederich Nelson family cease and desist from their claims or risk being charged with trespass and perhaps theft."

Both Nelsons smiled at the news. "Thank you, sir!" Henry exclaimed. The more stoic Levi just nodded his approval.

"You are on the right side of law," Abe said. "It is my pleasure to right a wrong."

As the two brothers were leaving the office, Henry turned and looked back at the lawyer. "So, sir, what do you make of the slavery issue? What is to become of those poor souls?" Levi started to admonish his brother but was cut off by a wave from Abe.

"I honestly do not know, my friend. I served in the House of Representatives for a short time. The Southerners are most adamant about keeping their way of life no matter the human cost. I fear it will become more unpleasant before it is resolved."

The three men shook hands again. They all wished each other well and went about their business. The brothers made plans for their trip home, and Abe returned to his office to mull over his future.

5

Harriet was so startled she almost dropped the bowl of batter she was stirring. She had just started preparations for the evening meal when Calvin unceremoniously rushed through the front door and made his way hurriedly to the kitchen. The color had left his normally ruddy face. His hands gripped a newspaper so tightly that it looked like he was wringing out a dish towel.

"Calvin! Whatever is the matter? You left for work only three hours ago!"

He took a deep breath. "Oh my dear, I fear the worst has happened. This was published yesterday." Without another word, he handed her the April 13, 1861, issue of a newspaper.

In large, bold type running down the middle of the Boston Evening Transcript's front page were headlines Harriet had prayed she would never read:

WAR BEGUN
The South Strikes the First Blow!
The Southern Confederacy Authorizes Hostilities.
Fort Moultrie Opens Fire on Fort Sumter at four o'clock Friday afternoon.
Major Anderson Returns Fire when Other Forts and Batteries Engage in the Conflict.
The U.S. Fleet not heard from when the attack began.

Harriet slumped into a chair and shook her head in disbelief as she read on. She wanted to stop but couldn't help reading the awful news. "Oh my Lord, I didn't want it to come to this," she said in a trembling voice as tears welled in her eyes. "Oh Calvin, this is horrible news! Why can't the Southern states adhere to legislation and the courts like civilized people?"

Calvin knelt beside his wife and put his arms around her. "This was the powder keg that finally exploded. All those states had seceded, and there may be more. The chance of peaceful resolution has been dim since Mr. Lincoln was elected last fall. I'm afraid we're in for a bloody affair."

Harriet swayed back and forth. She couldn't stop shaking. "Do you think, do you think I caused this? The book?"

Reaching up, Calvin gently touched her cheeks with both hands. "No, don't say that. Your book educated many Northerners about the barbarity of slavery. Besides, some of the Southern states have been rumbling about seceding for over ten years now. They tried to impose their views on the rest of union when the Kansas-Nebraska Act was passed."

He took the newspaper out of her hands and held up the front page. "The North didn't start this! A Southern battery fired on a Union fort. This war is on their shoulders."

Harriet slowly got up from her chair and went back to stirring her bowl. Nothing was said between them for several minutes. "Men will die, will they not? Many men?"

Calvin could only shrug. "Depends how much fight either side wants to put up. Could be a skirmish or two. Maybe Union forces will squelch the Southerners and break their spirit or maybe ..." His voice trailed off as he stared out the window.

When he looked back at Harriet, she stared at him intently, waiting for him to finish this thought. "Or maybe it will be a long war that will only stop when both sides agree to peace. The conflict may create two nations."

Harriet sighed, then dabbed at her eyes with a kerchief. "It is a travesty that men will be killed in a fight to free their fellow human beings. Families will lose sons, fathers, brothers. Where is the Christianity in all this?"

Her theologian husband rolled up the newspaper and tapped it against his knee. "I honestly don't know what God thinks when we fight among ourselves and kill our fellows. He may turn away in disgust and wait for the fighting to stop, then try to work through the survivors."

Harriet took her frustration out on the batter as she stirred it faster and faster. "God help us. I fear a great cloud has descended upon the nation."

Henry and Levi waited patiently in one of four long lines being processed by Union officers. The chatter among the men ranged from hopeful bravado to measured nervousness about marching into battle.

"I wish they would hurry it up," Levi grumbled. "Them Rebs could walk all the way to LaSalle County and shoot us in our tracks before they issue us a gun."

Henry shook his head. "I said you didn't have to join this fight. Besides, someone should stay here and look after the home place. Got to make sure those Swedes don't try to steal our land again."

Levi snorted. "If anyone should stay home, it's you. Alice and you have only been married for three months. She's going to miss you terribly. Someone's got to look after you."

A gruff voice erupted from the table in front of them. "Come on, men, keep it moving," yelled a round man dressed in a blue sergeant's uniform. "We need all these enlistment papers signed by nightfall. We march to Louisville in the morning."

Henry looked at his brother. "Last chance to leave." The stoic Levi folded his arms across his chest and stared back.

"The farm should be in good hands with Alice's family. Her father and brothers promised they'd look after things."

Levi nodded. "They are good people." He then pointed toward the table. "You're next. Time to answer Mr. Lincoln's call."

An hour later the 104th Illinois Infantry Regiment, consisting of 700 LaSalle County volunteers, divided into seven companies, assembled in somewhat disorderly lines in a field just outside Ottawa, Illinois. The enlistment sergeant was correct. In the morning they would march out, headed for Louisville, Kentucky. Training, uniforms and weapons would have to wait until they reached their destination.

Secretary of War Edwin Stanton carefully read the handwritten document the President had just handed him. Smoke from his pipe drifted out in slow puffs as he studied Mr. Lincoln's case for continuing the war with the rebellious Southern states. The wisps of smoke stopped abruptly when the secretary read the words that would change the lives of millions of people:

"...That on the first day of January in the year of our Lord, one thousand eight hundred and sixty-three, all persons held as slaves within any State, or designated part of a State, the people whereof shall then be in rebellion against the United States shall be then, thenceforward, and forever free; and the executive government of the United States, including the military and naval authority thereof, will recognize and maintain the freedom of such persons, and will do no act or acts to repress such persons, or any of them, in any efforts they may make for their actual freedom."

Edwin glanced toward Abe, who stood staring out a window deep in thought. He re-lit his pipe and finished reading. "Well Mr. President, you didn't dance around the issue, I will give you that. This may fuel the Southerners' desires to continue the fight."

Abe didn't say anything for several long minutes. "I expect not, Mr. Secretary, but they forced our hand in this fight and, by the will of the Almighty, we will bring them back into the Union and end that evil practice. We will prevail, will we not?"

Mr. Stanton slowly nodded. "Yes, Mr. President. Yes we will. We have more resources, more factories, more supplies and most importantly, more men. Our generals will eventually be able to overpower them."

Abe turned back to gaze out the window. "Yes, yes, we do have more men. All those souls who will be used as fodder. May God have mercy on us for putting our fellow countrymen in harm's way."

Mr. Stanton emptied his pipe into an ashtray on Abe's desk, then stood up to leave. "War has always been a sad and ugly business, Mr. President. Oftentimes both victor and loser pay a terrible price." He started for the door, but stopped and looked back.

"We haven't always agreed on strategy, Mr. President. I expect there will be times in the future when we will have our differences, but you will always have my full support, sir. The sooner we win this fight, the sooner the nation can start to heal."

Abe paused, then reached for a bell to summon an aide. "Let's pray it is so, Mr. Secretary."

6

Levi was relieving himself behind a tree, when trumpet blasts shattered the early morning peace. Instead of that annoying reveille, the tune for troops to awaken for morning roll call he had heard for the past four months, the horns were sounding calls to arms. Levi uttered a curse and ran to fetch Henry.

The regiment's captains were shouting instructions for the troops to line up. Down in the valley outside Hartsville, Tennessee, a brigade of Kentucky infantry was marching toward their positions. Even though the rebels were hundreds of yards away, the strains of "Dixie" played by flutes could be faintly heard in the crisp December air.

The 104th's captains had managed to mount and were riding behind their companies, exhorting them to load and aim. From either side of the Illinois troops, regiments of the 106th and 108th Ohio were assembling as well.

Henry and Levi stood in the second row behind the first line of their kneeling comrades. They aimed their Springfield 1861's and waited for the order.

Captain Andrews' steady, deep voice reminded them of their training as he rode behind them. "Steady now, lads. First line, reload after you fire. Second line, fire while first line reloads. Get ready men!" Moments later, screams of "fire, men" could be heard up and down the ranks.

The first shots of the Springfields sounded like thunder rolling down the valley. Henry, Levi and their second line cohorts held off, then fired when the first line reloaded. Explosion after explosion crashed through the air as the Union and Confederate troops exchanged volleys. Soldiers on both sides collapsed intermittently as they were hit. Screams of pain added to the awful din.

High pitched shrieks erupted from the rebel ranks as they broke formation and charged the Union line. Somehow Captain Andrews' shouts could be heard above the bedlam. "Steady, men. First line, fire! Second line, hold, fire! Look men, the Rebs are wavering. For God and country, keep firing."

Sure enough, the Confederate charge had stopped, and the troops were slowly retreating under the relentless Union troops' fusilade. At that moment, a regiment of Rebel cavalry rode in, dismounted and joined their comrades in the charge.

For the first time, Captain Andrews exploded in frustration. "Where in the bloody hell are 106th and 108th?" At the sight of the Rebel cavalry, the Ohio regiments disobeyed orders, broke ranks and retreated.

Seeing the Union flanks exposed, the fresh Confederate troops surrounded the 104th Illinois and closed in. Captain Andrews, up to that point a pious man, let loose with a stream of obscenities aimed at the cowardly Ohioans. "Goddam you toe-picking sons of bitches! Goddam you all to hell!" Andrews never finished his next curse. A minie ball from a Rebel sharpshooter hit the captain square in the chest, knocking him off his horse.

Seeing his captain lying dead on the ground, Henry shouted for the company to keep firing. Levi grimaced, took a deep breath and carefully aimed up and down the Rebel line. Finding what looked like an officer wearing a white-plumed hat, Levi fired. The hat flew off when his target collapsed to the ground.

As the Rebels advanced, one of the lieutenants shouted for them to fix bayonets. Before the inevitable charge came, the regiment's bugles sounded recall. Sergeants and lieutenants shouted for the Union troops to cease firing.

Now surrounded by superior numbers, the 104th's commander surrendered to the Confederate general. All firing ceased when the regiment raised the white flag.

While the Union troops were milling around nervously waiting for their orders to line up, Levi gestured for Henry to join him. "Quick, give me your money. We'll bury it here under this boulder," he said as he knelt and began digging underneath a large nearby stone in the field. Henry started to object, but the look on his brother's face stopped him.

"What do you think them Rebs are going to do? They're going to take everything, our weapons, money, food." Henry needed no further prompting. "Wait, leave a coin or two in your pouch so they won't suspect anything." Henry just nodded while he rolled up the small amount of cash in a kerchief and buried it alongside his brother's money.

Levi carefully put back the square of sod he had cut out for the hole, then stomped all around it. The ground already was a mess from the skirmish so their efforts blended in. "If we get the chance, we'll come back and get it," Levi said somberly. "If we don't make it back, at least the Rebs won't have it. Remember, it's a half day's walk due west of Hartsville."

Before Henry could reply, the regiment's buglers called the troops to line up for assembly. It was time to turn themselves over to the victorious Confederates.

Union Commander Colonel A. B. Moore saluted the two Confederate generals, then handed over his saber, the traditional military act of surrender. Confederate General Reginald Morgan returned the salute and took the sword. Another Southern General, Amos Burke, barely brushed his hat in a half-hearted gesture and sneered at the Union ranks.

"One of these rats killed General Hanson," he snarled while holding up a broad-brimmed hat with a white ostrich feather attached to it.

General Morgan shrugged. "Lots of shots were fired, General. Besides, Hanson made himself a pretty good target by looking like a damn peacock. Many men on both sides fell today. Do you have a count of your dead, sir?"

Colonel Moore reached for a sheet of paper from one of his captains. He frowned as he read, "Forty-four dead, sir, and about one hundred and fifty wounded, according to this report. I ask for permission to bury my men."

General Morgan nodded. "Permission granted. Your men also will have the honor of burying our dead." He turned to General Burke. "How many did we lose today?"

The other general squinted as he stared at a piece of paper an aide had just handed him. "Sixty-two dead and well over a hundred wounded. Damn those blue bellies."

General Morgan gestured toward Colonel Moore. "Have your men grab their shovels and get to work, colonel. You have a lot of bodies to plant."

By late afternoon, all the bodies from the battle were buried, and the wounded from both sides were looked after. General Morgan said a quick prayer for all the dead, then called for the troops — Confederate and Union — to move out. It was at least a three-day march to a prison camp at Murfreesboro, and Morgan wanted a head start before any possible Union reinforcements could catch up to them.

That night after their forced ten-mile march, Levi and Henry lay exhausted among the members of their captured regiment. Most of the men snored fitfully as they curled up next to each other.

Levi reached over and poked Henry's shoulder. "You asleep?" Henry rolled over and yawned, "Almost, what is it?" Levi's eyes shone brightly in the near full moon. "We need to escape, brother. There's no telling how long they'll hold us in a prison camp."

Henry propped himself up on an elbow. "We can't! They'll send soldiers after us and shoot us as escapees." He leaned in closer so only his brother could hear him. "Besides, every man in this outfit probably is thinking the same thing. Best take our chances in the camp rather than being hunted down with no food or weapons."

Levi reached out and grabbed Henry's shirt collar. "We got to get out of here. We could rot in that camp. Someone's got to get back to the farm. Can't let them Swedes take it over again."

Henry grabbed Levi's wrist and twisted it until he was free from his brother's grasp. "No!" he hissed. "It's too dangerous. We're better off together."

But Levi was not about to be dissuaded. "Maybe they'd go after two runners, but how about only one? Can't imagine they'd be too bothered about one lone Yankee runaway. I think it should be you, brother. Get back to your Alice and to the farm."

Henry lay back down and covered his eyes with his hands. He missed his new bride terribly and was worried he'd never see her again. After several long minutes, he propped himself back up again. "No, it's got to be a fair decision who's going to try to escape." He groped around for a stick, broke it into two uneven lengths and dropped the pieces into his cap.

"How's that fair?" Levi protested in a hoarse whisper. "That's just damn luck."

Henry nodded. "Yep. But I'll trust the good Lord to pick who runs and who stays. Short stick stays." Once Henry invoked the Lord's name, Levi knew his more pious brother would settle for that one lucky draw or nothing. Levi grimaced, but reached into the cap and pulled out a stick. Henry did the same thing.

Both Nelsons took a deep breath, then compared their sticks. Levi shook his head at the result. "It's not fair, Henry!"

But, his brother just waved him off. "You always were faster than me. Besides, you're a better woodsman than I am. God chose the right man to run. Now you just have to find the right time."

Levi flung his stick away. "God had nothing to do with it! It was just pure luck or bad luck, however you feel about it." Henry just shrugged, rolled over in his blanket and tried to get comfortable enough on the cold ground to catch a few hours of sleep.

7

Early the next day, when the sun was barely peeking through the trees, Levi called for a guard. "I need to do my business in a terrible hurry," he pleaded. The guard called for his sergeant, who scolded the soldier to hurry up and keep his weapon trained on the blue coat.

As they walked into the woods, the rebel soldier started to whistle a familiar tune. Levi wracked his brain where he had heard it. As he squatted and plotted his escape attempt, he remembered. Church! He had heard it in church.

Now he cursed under his breath. Of all the luck to be stuck with a Methodist Episcopal rebel. It should be Henry who should have come. His younger brother had an uncanny way of remembering all those hymns, which Levi found a bit boring. Henry usually sang with a faith-filled gusto, but Levi mumbled along and was ever so glad to be released with the admonishment to "go in peace."

After a few more minutes of stalling, the guard called him. "Come on, blue coat, finish up. I don't want either one of us to get into trouble." Something about the guard's voice was different. It was soft. He almost spoke with a chuckle.

When Levi finally reappeared, the guard motioned with his hand to return to camp. He held his gun casually at his side, almost as if it were a walking cane. "Say, Rebel, what was that tune you were whistling? I could swear I've heard it in church."

The guard stopped. "You a Methodist Episcopal?"

Levi grinned. "I am, but I have to confess sometimes Ma had to drag me by my ear to get me in church."

The guard erupted in a high-pitched laugh. "Ma had to do the same thing with my brothers. I didn't mind so much. Kind of like the singing."

Levi nodded. "Yes, the singing kept me awake. I swear Reverend Evans could go on for an hour or more. He liked the sound of his own voice too much."

A big grin flashed on the guard's face. "Yes, Reverend Harrison preached for almost two hours one time. Pa said he caught a good nap. That hymn is called "Like Sheep We Went Astray.""

The words were hardly out of the guard's mouth, when a vision of Reverend Evans leading his home congregation in one of the pastor's favorite hymns floated into Levi's brain. The words starting pouring from his mouth:

> *"Like sheep, we went astray,*
> *"And broke the fold of God;*
> *"Each wandering in a different way,*
> *"But all the downward road.*
> *"How dreadful was the hour*
> *"When god our wand'rings laid,*
> *"And did at once his vengeance pour*
> *"Upon the Shepherd's head!*

The guard stared at Levi. "You weren't lying, blue coat. Them words are powerful true." Name's Darius Williams by the way. Yours?"

Levi did not like getting to know the rebel he was plotting to kill in order to make his escape, and he was having a hard time hating the lanky soldier with the easy smile. Talking with him reminded him of chatting with his neighbors at the general store in Osage. "Levi, Levi Nelson."

Both soldiers paused. The air of good will between them was a welcome relief from the strain of yesterday's battle. Darius shifted uncomfortably on his feet. "Sorry to do this, but

I got to get you back to the others right quick. The sergeant will think I deserted or you ambushed me and will come looking for us."

Levi looked off in the distance. His stomach tightened as he made his decision. "I'm not going back with you, Darius. I've had enough of this fighting. Yesterday was my first action. I killed men and saw men get killed. A couple were my friends and neighbors." He paused and stared at the ground. "I, I didn't want to join up. But I did so's I could look after my brother."

Darius's smile melted into a frown. "Come on now, I got to get you back. Don't make me shoot you."

However, Levi refused to move. He finally looked up at the nervous rebel. "I was planning to get the drop on you. Kill you if necessary so I could escape. I don't like killing men. Makes me sick in the stomach. All I want to do is get back to the farm."

An icy silence fell over the two men. Finally, Levi slowly rose to his feet. "I'm going to leave now, Darius. If you're going to shoot, make it clean so's I don't linger much. That's all I ask." He turned and started to walk away, half expecting to feel a searing pain in his body, followed by a report from the rebel's rifle.

Darius shakily raised his weapon and aimed at his departing prisoner. Taking a deep breath, he cocked the hammer, but stopped when two glowing lights appeared out of nowhere and looked as if they were dancing on Levi's shoulders. He watched in awe for a few seconds, lowered his rifle and called out, "Stop! Please!"

Something in Darius's voice made Levi halt. "You're going to need vittles and a gun to get back home." Levi slowly turned around and watched in shock. Darius approached with his arms stretched out bearing the rifle as if it were a gift. The rebel removed a pouch from his belt as well as his canteen and handed them over.

Levi gaped in astonishment. Relief and gratitude coursed through his body. Apparently, this was not his day to die. All he could do was nod his appreciation. He finally managed to choke out a thank you.

"Ma would never forgive me if she knew I kilt a fella Methodist," Darius said in his soft drawl. "Got to do something to make my sergeant think you got the best of me or he'll bring me up on charges."

Levi frowned. He needed to escape quickly before the other rebels came looking for him, but he didn't want to abandon the soft-spoken Southerner who had given him a potential chance for freedom.

"You're going to have to look like I bushwhacked you," Levi said as he brandished the butt of the rifle.

Darius stared for a moment, then shut his eyes. "I'd appreciate it if you don't kill me, Yankee."

Levi shook his head. "I'm done killing, rebel. This is going to hurt something awful for a while and may leave a scar." Darius gave a quick nod. Levi made sure he had a good grip, uttered, "I'm so sorry, my friend," then jabbed the rifle butt at Darius's forehead.

The rebel dropped to the ground with a groan, but made no other sound. Blood splattered down his face from an ugly gash. Levi gathered the rest of his supplies and disappeared into the forest.

Henry couldn't stand the suspense. Less than an hour after his brother and a tall guard left on a supposedly urgent toilet mission, a rebel sergeant sounded an alarm. Six Confederate soldiers charged into the woods on orders to find the two missing men. Henry prayed he would not hear the dreaded sounds of rifle fire.

However, the only noise came from his fellow prisoners as they woke up grumbling and complaining about the meager rations handed out by their captors. About a half hour after the six rebels had departed, three men emerged from the woods. Two of the gray coats held up another who stumbled woozily between them. The wounded man's head was heavily bandaged with a blood-soaked cloth.

A rebel sergeant charged over to the three. "What in damnation happened here?" The two soldiers who were assisting their wounded comrade, gently lowered him to the ground. Henry edged through the other prisoners to see what was happening.

"Looks like the Yankee jumped him, grabbed his rifle and belted him in the head," one of the soldiers reported. "He's got a real nasty gash. Was barely sitting up when we found him. He's so dizzy, couldn't say what happened or where the Yank lit off to. The other four are trying to track him down."

The sergeant leaned down and examined Darius. "Dammit, Williams, I knew I shouldn't have let you alone with that Yankee. Well, get him over to doc and have him take a look. We got too many wounded to haul as it is. Dammit! Now I got to report this to the general."

Not long afterwards, General Morgan rode down the line on his roan stallion. "Get those four men back here," he yelled at his junior officers. "If they haven't found the runaway by now, he's gone. We've got eight hundred prisoners. I'm not worried about one lone Yankee. Buglers, sound recall. We leave as soon as those men are back."

No sooner had the general issued his order when a lone rifle shot echoed through the trees. A few seconds later, three shots returned fire in quick succession. "Sounds like our boys found that Yankee runaway," the sergeant said, flashing a toothless grin at the general.

Morgan was about to answer when another lone shot rang out. This time, no return fire was heard. "Let me know when our men are back," he ordered. "We don't need to tend to another wounded Yankee. If he's not dead, finish it." The sergeant nodded and saluted.

Henry's stomach convulsed in a violent flip when he heard the shots. He envisioned a scene where Levi most likely had fired first. The three shots that followed most likely came from his Confederate pursuers. Hopefully Levi had dropped one of his pursuers.

The lone shot that answered back was the most ominous sound. Did one of the rebels finish off his brother?

The silence that followed was the most unbearable for Henry. The exchange of gunfire did not bode well. Four rifles against one were not good odds. Henry doubled over and collapsed on the ground in silent grief. A couple of his fellow soldiers knelt down and patted him on the shoulder.

A half hour later, when nothing more was seen or heard from his men, the sergeant sent four more troops to find their missing comrades. They had been gone only a few minutes when all the Confederates returned.

Henry was elated to see the enemy soldiers helping two badly wounded compatriots. "What in damnation happened here?" the sergeant yelled as he rushed over to his men. He took a quick look at the injured men and called for stretchers.

One of the original four stared at the ground, saying nothing. His companion shook his head. "Damn blue belly shot Ezra in the knee. We returned fire, but he tricked us with a decoy. Tied his jacket on a tree branch. We thought it was him. He got behind us and then dropped poor Thomas here. After that, we didn't know where the hell he was."

The silent rebel soldier nodded and finally looked up. "We waited for a bit, but Ezra and Thomas were hurt bad and needed tending to. Then the Yank called out. He told us if we helped our friends and stopped following him, he'd be on his way. Otherwise ..." the soldier's voice drifted off.

"What?" the sergeant snarled. "Finish your report, soldier."

The first soldier shrugged. "The Yank said he had the drop on Robert, here. Had 'em in his sights. Said he would kill Robert, then I'd have to decide which of these hurt fellas I could help. The Yank said all he wanted to do was skedaddle. So we laid down our rifles and set about tending to Thomas and Ezra. They was hurt bad. The blue coat was true to his word and left."

Henry couldn't believe what he had heard. Somehow Levi had warded off his pursuers and escaped. He was overwhelmed with a flash of elation. But that immediately was quelled by the reality he was still a prisoner who was being marched south.

A day later, as the captured Union troops gratefully collapsed to the ground after another grueling march, a tall figure suddenly loomed over Henry.

"You Nelson?" asked a rebel who sported a large bandage over his head. Henry nodded and slowly swallowed what was left of his ration. He was sure the soldier who had escorted Levi into the woods was going to seek revenge for being wounded and humiliated.

"It's a good thing Reverend Evans taught you a hymn or two," the Southerner said with a wink. "Also sounds like your brother is a pretty good shot. He could have killed those two boys." Henry could only stare in disbelief as Darius shuffled away without another word.

8

Harriet tsk tsk'd as she read the local newspaper's daily account of the war. Calvin lowered the paper he was reading and looked at her over the rims of his eyeglasses. "What has upset you this time, my dear?" he said with a half smile. Lately, Harriet's protests over the snail's pace of the war were growing louder and longer as her patience was taxed.

"The Confederates have won another battle," she said bitterly, closing the pages with a frustrated flurry. "The rebels captured several hundred of our boys and chased even more for ten miles until they turned back across their lines. This is not acceptable!"

Calvin shook his head. "We knew the Southern states would put up a fight. War can be unpredictable." His answer, however, did not placate his distressed wife. Harriet rose from her chair and paced around the room. After a few minutes even the ever-patient Calvin was starting to be bothered by her constant movement.

"Well, if you're so unhappy, perhaps you should travel to Washington. I'm sure Mr. Lincoln has no other advisers who can give him such wise counsel."

Harriet stopped immediately and stared at her husband. "An excellent suggestion, my dear, even though it was expressed in a sarcastic tone that I do not care for! I believe I will do just that. Of course I will send a cable to the White House and wait for an invitation to visit."

This time, it was Calvin's turn to stare. He had intended his remark to appeal to her common sense, not spark that famous fire of hers. Now, most likely, she soon would be embarking on a mission to talk with the President of the United States.

Very few women were influential enough to pull off such a scheme; however, Harriet was one of them.

She humored her husband with a half smile, then strode into the study to write a letter requesting an audience with the president. Calvin could only shake his head as he watched her leave, thinking, *Oh what have I loosed upon poor Mr. Lincoln.*

>>>>>

Harriet tried to calm her nerves while William Seward guided her through the White House. She had been shocked to see the Secretary of State waiting for her when the carriage driver pulled up to the most famous door in the country.

"Mrs. Stowe, I presume. Welcome to the White House," Seward said pleasantly as he took her hand and guided her inside. Not usually at a loss for words, Harriet nodded and forced a smile. She had not expected a member of the cabinet to greet a guest. "Please follow me, if you would be so kind. Mr. Lincoln is in his study."

After navigating through a warren of rooms and dodging servants as well as various determined-looking officials hurrying past, Mr. Seward stopped in front of a doorway and gestured for her to enter. "Mr. Lincoln, Mrs. Stowe is here to see you." He nodded politely when she thanked him, then went on his way.

Abe, who had been sitting and warming himself, rose awkwardly, unfolding all six foot, four inches of him. He towered over Harriet, who had to stand on her tiptoes to reach five feet. "Why, Mrs. Stowe. Right good to see you," Abe said with a smile and waved for her to join him by the fire.

"Thank you for seeing me, Mr. President. I am sure you have pressing issues to deal with due to the war raging on. I appreciate you taking the time to speak with an ordinary citizen."

Abe said nothing for a moment while he exposed his wrists to the fire, enjoying the heat as it soaked into his body. "Why Mrs. Stowe, you are certainly more than an ordinary citizen. You have written a might powerful book. I have read it and so have many of our fellow Americans."

His comment caught her off guard. Of course she knew thousands had read *Uncle Tom's Cabin* and its sequel, *A Key to Uncle Tom's Cabin*. But hearing a compliment from the president took her breath away for a moment. "Thank you, Mr. President. It was a story that demanded to be written. I felt people needed to know what an atrocious crime has been forced upon our fellow human beings."

Abe nodded. "You will get no disagreement from me. Now, Mrs. Stowe, what brings you to Washington on such a cold and dreary day? Are you here to advise me or scold me for some unknown offense I may have caused?"

Harriet paused, but the twinkle in his eye and his soft, matter-of-fact way of speaking put her at ease. "No offense at all, Mr. President. I just wanted to lend my voice to encourage you to take action on emancipating those poor souls who are in bondage. Pray tell me, what is your opinion?"

The president sighed as he stared into the fire. "I am a believer of emancipation, Mrs. Stowe. I am sure I have moved too slow for some and too fast for others. It is coming, I assure you, but the moment has to be right. The mood of the country has to be ready to accept it. Believe me, madam, the time draws near."

Harriet sat back in her chair and relaxed a bit. His sincerity had put her at ease. She even allowed herself to sip from the tea service that had been delivered when she first sat down. "Thank you, Mr. President. I know I have written articles urging you to act on this faster than you have. I appreciate your candor."

Abe leaned back, grinning at his guest. "From my recollection, you have written a great many words criticizing this old backwoods mule and my reluctance to move quickly."

Despite the strength of her conviction, Harriet found herself blushing with embarrassment. "I apologize for any grief I may have caused you, good sir. That was not my intention. I was only offering my opinion and hoped my words would be taken as encouragement."

His laugh startled her. "Why Mrs. Stowe, I have received much more serious accusations for lack of character and low intelligence by much less talented writers than yourself. At least you have honest intentions and offer well thought out arguments for your cause."

Harriet allowed herself to chuckle. His good nature was contagious, and she felt at ease with him. Abe leaned forward. "I understand your son, Frederick, has enlisted. Much to my dismay, my Robert is insisting that he serve. It is a heavy burden to be responsible for other people's sons but awful terrible to have my own son be put in harm's way."

It was Harriet's turn to stare into the fire. "What a painful price is being inflicted upon families across the land," she whispered. "One doesn't grasp the terror of war until one of the babies you, at one time, held in your arms marches off to join the fray."

For a moment, the titles of the outside world — president and famous author — were stripped away. Both of them commiserated with each other as parents concerned for their sons.

While taking a sip of tea, Harriet stole a glance at the president. The sight of a tiny flame dancing on one of Abe's shoulders almost made her drop her cup. She watched in wonder as the mysterious light floated over and skipped on the opposite shoulder.

Normally, such a discovery would have brought a cry of alarm. Perhaps an ember had drifted from the fireplace and alighted on the president. However, Harriet had seen such an anomaly before.

Once or twice, while looking in a mirror at home as she fixed her hair, Harriet had seen such a mysterious flame floating around her head. At first she thought it was a trick of a reflection, but the movements of the mysterious light seemed to suggest an intelligence.

Harriet was so absorbed in watching the light, which now had formed into an orb, on Abe's shoulder that she did not notice him staring in wonder at her. "Mrs. Stowe, do you perchance believe in fairies?" he asked in a hushed whisper. Normally, such a question would have been met with amusement or even derision, but she was at her wit's end to explain what she was seeing.

"Most times I would say no, Mr. President, but not today." He nodded and seemed relieved. "Do not be afraid or think me at a loss of my senses, Mrs. Stowe, but I swear on my mother's grave that the most luminescent lightning bug that I have ever seen is dancing a most delightful jig around your head."

Harriet gasped. "I did not want to say anything that would have you question my sanity, Mr. President, but a tiny flame seems to be skipping on your shoulders as well. At first I thought it was a spark from the fireplace, but I confess to having seen such a light before."

Abe let loose with a great sigh of relief as he sat back in his chair. "It seems each of us has an extraordinary friend. Perhaps a guardian angel."

Harriet shuddered. "As long as they are not demons tormenting us."

Abe gave a quick wave. "So far, our friends have not burned us nor caused any harm. I will continue to think favorably on it until proven otherwise." He smiled. "Your fairy seems to have vanished."

She nodded. "As well as yours, Mr. President. It just floated away and disappeared. This has been a most momentous day, indeed," Harriet said, still shaking her head in disbelief.

An aide knocked on the door frame, then stepped into the room. "Beg your pardon, Mr. President, but several telegrams from the generals require your response."

Abe waved the aide off. "I do have a question for you, Mrs. Stowe, if I may be so forward. I am curious. Where did you get the inspiration for that magnificent book of yours? I have noticed at times when I'm writing, it feels like someone else has taken over."

Harriet folded her hands and thought for a moment. "I did not write it. God wrote it. I merely did his dictation."

The president smiled, then pointed in the air. "Or perhaps it was the fairies. Far be it from we mere mortals to understand the other realm."

Harriet stood up and offered her hand. "Indeed, Mr. President. Thank you for allaying my fears. I will not forget our discussion."

Abe grinned and leaned down to speak softly in her ear. "Do not be afraid of your fairy, Mrs. Stowe. I believe it is a sign of good luck."

Before Harriet embarked on her trip home, she sent Calvin a note: "I had a real funny interview with the President . . . the particulars of which I will tell you."

≫≫≫≫≫

Once home, she told Calvin about her strange but satisfying conversation with the president. He was speechless about the discovery of the fairies, but never spoke a word of it to anyone.

A few weeks later, Harriet had a story published in several magazines. She eloquently wrote about her full support of the president based on his character and intelligence.

In the last passage, she praised him as only a great writer can do.

"Among the many accusations which in hours of ill-luck have been thrown out upon Lincoln, it is remarkable that he has never been called self-seeking, or selfish. When we were troubled and sat in darkness, and looked doubtfully towards the presidential chair, it was never that we doubted the goodwill of our pilot — only the clearness of his eyesight.

"But Almighty God has granted to him that clearness of vision which he gives to the true-hearted, and enabled him to set his honest foot in that promised land of freedom which is to be the patrimony of all men, black and white—and from henceforth nations shall rise up to call him blessed."

9

Henry smiled as he read the latest letter from Alice.

"My dearest, I thank the Almighty for sparing you in the battle. My heart is so happy the Confederates eventually traded you and your fellows for some of their boys. I hope the conditions at Camp Chase suit your needs for the moment. Everyone sends their most sincere regards and prays for your eventual safe return home whenever this terrible war finally reaches its conclusion.

"The family recently had the most pleasant visit from a good friend of yours. I believe he said his name was Elihu. He said you and he knew each other as boys in Albany, New York. He had just returned from a most taxing trip. His gray eyes were heavy from exhaustion, but otherwise claimed to be in good health, though he looked a bit gaunt to me. He wishes you well and looks forward to seeing you again."

Henry put the letter down for a moment while he pulled out his kerchief to wipe his eyes and blow his nose. Elihu was his father's name. It also was Levi's middle name. This was Alice's way of telling him that Levi was safe and had made it home in one piece.

He knew Alice had to be careful with her words because Levi was now a wanted man. Despite Levi's heroic escape from the Confederates, his brother had not bothered to rejoin the Union army. Instead, Levi somehow made his way home without being captured by the rebels or snatched back up by Union forces.

Henry and his fellow prisoners of the 104th Illinois infantry had been lucky. Instead of being marched straight to a prison camp, they were held for a short time, then exchanged for a batch of Confederate prisoners. The freed soldiers eventually found their way to Camp Chase in Columbus, Ohio. Unfortunately, Levi's efforts had gone for naught, and he now was listed as a deserter.

With a heavy sigh at the ironic turn of events, Henry picked up the letter and continued reading Alice's letter.

"The family wanted to do something special for your birthday. In the next few weeks a very special package will be delivered to you at the camp. Mr. Elihu was very helpful with suggesting what would be most useful to you. He even chipped in some money. He joked that he found it under a rock.

"I will close for now, my love. I miss you so greatly, but know you have embarked on a most noble adventure. I pray for your safety every day. Until next time.

"All my love. Yours forever,

"Alice."

An unfamiliar corporal poked his head into the barracks of the 104th Illinois infantry, then called loudly, "Nelson, Henry! See the postmaster right away. There's a couple of fellas who have a package for you. They refuse to leave it with anybody but you."

Henry grinned as he pulled on his boots. It must be the birthday package Alice had told him about. He hurried over to the small building that served as the camp's post office.

The postmaster was arguing with two men sitting in a wagon. "I told you boys. You can leave the box with me. I'll make sure this Nelson fella will get it," the weathered old sergeant with a huge belly yelled.

However, the men in the wagon were refusing to give up their cargo. "No sir! We ain't in the Army," the wagon driver replied. "Pa said to make sure we deliver it directly to Henry and no one else."

Henry stopped when he recognized the voice, then slowly walked around to get a better look at the delivery men. He and his brothers-in-law stared at each other momentarily, then erupted in happy laughter. "Lucas? Peter? What in God's green acre are you boys doing here? Did you come all the way from Illinois with this package?"

Lucas, the driver, let loose with a yell and launched himself off the wagon. Peter stood up, a big grin spread across his freckled face. "Henry, you're OK!" Lucas shouted as he wrapped Henry up in a bear hug.

Peter scrambled down off the wagon. "Happy birthday, Henry. I know we're a little late. We had to wait a might to catch a train 'cause of all the war commotion. We rented this team when we got to Columbus." The younger of the two brothers blushed a bit when he saw the sergeant's face turn beet red at his description of the war effort.

Henry laughed. "Yes, there's a lot of commotion with the war isn't there, sergeant?" The postmaster threw his hands up and mumbled something about "damn, ignorant civilians."

After more hugs and handshakes, the two brothers pulled the three-foot box off the wagon and set it on the ground. "Open it, Henry, it's from all of us!" Peter said, shifting from foot to foot excitedly.

Lucas reached into the wagon, pulled out a crowbar and handed it to Henry. "It's your birthday. You should get the honors." It didn't take Henry long to pry off the lid to reveal a rifle wrapped in cloth. At least a half dozen boxes of ammunition surrounded it.

"What's this? A rifle?" Henry asked. He picked it up. It was lighter and shorter than the Springfield he had been using. "You know the Army issues weapons, right?" he said shaking his head.

"Not like this one they don't," Lucas crowed. "Stop beefing and pull off the cover!"

Henry gasped as he held up the gleaming weapon with the brass receiver. "Oh my gawd, it's one of them new rifles I've been reading about," the postmaster blurted. "You lucky bastard. Those things can shoot all day!"

Peter clapped his hands as he danced around the box. "It's a Henry. Get it? A Henry repeater. Best rifle they make."

Lucas pointed at his brother. "Calm down, will ya? Of course he gets it. He ain't slow like someone else I know." Peter stopped his jig and flashed an obscene hand gesture at his brother.

Henry reached into the box and pulled out a piece of paper that extolled the weapon's virtues. In huge letters, the flyer announced it was a "rifle you could load on Sunday and shoot all week long."

Lucas picked up one of the ammo boxes. "It'll take 16 rounds with one load plus one in the chamber. You should be able to pick off a lot them Rebs with this baby."

Peter glanced at the sergeant who was still admiring Henry's birthday present. "Uh, tell him what, uh, Mr. Elihu said," he said softly, trying not to draw undue attention from the postmaster.

Henry looked up from his new prize. "Yeah, your friend, Mr. Elihu suggested you should make sure to keep it clean," Lucas said. "Dirt might clog it up. He said to keep your Springfield handy just in case."

The brothers sobered up and stared uncomfortably at the ground when Henry looked away as tears filled his eyes. He swiped his face with his coat sleeve and continued to admire his present.

Lucas reached out and grasped Henry's shoulder. "It's the best the family can do for you right now. We all want you to come back alive, especially Alice."

The normally acerbic postmaster dabbed at his eyes with a kerchief, then cleared his throat. "I'll need you boys to move this team and wagon over to the stable around the corner. You can tie up the horses temporarily. I'll make sure they get some feed and water." He turned to Henry. "They can't stay long, but I'm sure you can grab some vittles in the mess hall with your friends."

Peter grinned. "Yeah, I could eat! Thank you, sir." The postmaster just shook his head. "I'm a sergeant, not a sir." He turned and headed back inside to sort mail. The others could hear him grumbling something about "damn, ignorant civilians."

10

Harriet didn't hear the rapping at her front door right away. The famous author was so intent on what she was writing that the only thing she focused on her was her thoughts. However, the incessant pounding finally wormed its way into her consciousness.

She glanced at the clock and scowled — 9:17 a.m. This was much too early for someone to be calling on a Monday. "Who on earth could be making such a racket?" she muttered to herself while she grabbed a shawl and made her way to the front door.

Opening the door cautiously with the chain lock still affixed, Harriet peeked out. "Why, Mr. Murphy. What brings you here at this hour?" she asked while unlocking and opening the door. She was surprised to see the city's chief telegraph operator nervously shifting from one foot to another.

Murphy tipped his hat. His eyes were wide with excitement. "Beg your pardon, Mrs. Stowe, but this couldn't wait. I didn't want to trust this with one of my careless delivery boys," he said in his soft, Irish brogue. With trembling hands, he handed her the telegram.

Harriet gave him a puzzled look then gasped when she read the message:

To: Mrs. Harriet Beecher Stowe

I am happy to inform you that this awful war that has plagued our nation for too long is ended.

Gen. Lee surrendered to Gen. Grant yesterday, April 9, in Appomattox, Virginia. All hostilities are to cease immediately. You should soon see your son at your door.

Please pray for healing for this great nation of ours which has suffered most grievously.

Your friend,
A. Lincoln

"Oh my Lord, Mrs. Stowe! It's true, isn't it? The war is over!" Murphy could barely choke out his words. Tears streamed down his round, ruddy cheeks. "Our boys can come home, can't they?"

All Harriet could do was nod. She put a hand to her mouth to stifle a sob. "Yes, yes, Mr. Murphy. All our sons will be coming home."

Murphy exploded in a roar. "The war is over! The war is over! Lee surrendered! Praise Jesus, praise God and praise Mr. Lincoln." Remembering his Catholic upbringing, he stopped yelling for a moment to cross himself, then started dancing a jig in the middle of the street.

Almost immediately people started pouring out of their houses to see what all the uproar was about. Murphy soon was joined by a chorus of children, women and men shouting, clapping, hugging and crying. Harriet dabbed at her eyes as she watched the celebration of unbridled joy.

An hour had barely passed when a carriage slowly made its way through the delirious crowd. Once Calvin made it to the front gate, he sprang from the seat and ran to his wife, sweeping her up in his arms.

"Oh Calvin, no, no not here," Harriet protested but gave way when Calvin kissed her in front of the crowd, which erupted in a happy, collective shout. Someone in the crowd, possibly Mr. Murphy, yelled: "Three cheers for Mrs. Stowe. Hip, hip," and the crowd boomed, "Hooray!"

The normally shy Harriet started to protest, but was stopped by Calvin. "My dear, this is a most auspicious occasion. May I have the honor of this dance?" Harriet offered a mild objection, but the normally reserved Prof. Stowe was not to be denied. She took his hand and soon the couple was waltzing on the front porch. More shouts of "hip, hip, hooray" and laughter filled the air as their friends and neighbors allowed themselves to bask in the glorious moment.

The celebration slowly spread through Northern cities as word got out. The reaction in the South was much different. The news was met with sorrow, grief and anger as well as relief. Many of the great cities in the Confederacy had sustained terrible damage as the Union Army swept through the rebel states. The scars from the war would last for generations.

Robert was ready to call it a night after combing through hundreds of letters addressed to his father. Many of the writers were asking for favors or complaining about some offense which had been perpetrated on them during the war.

He rubbed his tired eyes and leaned back in his chair. Only five days had passed since the war ended, but the son of the president had been allowed to return to the White House to lend his assistance. He had chosen the mail room, along with dozens of other young men, to help handle the flood of correspondences.

With a tired sigh, Robert decided to open one more letter. He paused when he saw the military stamp and return address of Goldsboro, North Carolina. His eyes lit up while he read the simple but direct request of a Union soldier from Illinois.

Robert put the note on top of a stack he deemed worthy of his father's attention. Abe was sitting at his desk, writing replies to previous letters as well as issuing orders on how to stand down after the cessation of hostilities.

The president looked up when he saw his son enter the room. "I see you have even more work for your Pa," he said with a smile.

Robert plunked down the stack on his father's desk. "Here are the letters that the other clerks and I recommend you address as soon as you can, sir."

Abe looked up. Even though his hollowed out eyes gave away his exhaustion, Abe managed a chuckle. "Sir? I like Pa better."

Robert stood at attention and saluted. "As long as I am a captain in the Army, I am required to refer to my commander-in-chief as sir." Abe shook his head and let loose with a boisterous laugh. Robert grinned and sat down when Abe pointed to the chair next to his desk.

"Well, Captain, I may have to get to these tomorrow unless there is pressing business. Your mother has requested my presence for a performance at Ford's Theater this evening."

Robert shrugged. "Nothing appears to be of immediate importance. That top letter is interesting. It's from a soldier who you did business with back in Springfield. It's a touching request."

Abe nodded. "These old eyes are getting blurry. I'd be obliged if you would read it to me." Robert scooted his chair closer to Abe's desk and turned up the oil lamp.

To the Honorable President Abraham Lincoln.

From Pvt. Henry Nelson of Osage, Illinois, currently serving with the 104th Illinois Infantry

Dear Mr. President:

I don't know if you recollect meeting me and my brother back in '52 when we asked you to handle a land dispute for us. You and I talked about the book that Mrs. Stowe wrote. My brother, Levi, was the quiet one.

Well Mr. Lincoln, I am writing to entreat you to consider a pardon for my brother, Levi. We was attacked by the Rebs outside Hartsville, Tennessee. Our company had turned the Rebs but two Ohio companies retreated and left us exposed. We had no choice but to surrender or be killed.

The second day as we was being marched South by the Rebs, Levi managed to escape. Before he got away, he wounded three Rebs. He shot two in the leg and clubbed another. I doubt the two Rebs he shot ever returned to duty. They was hurt pretty bad.

Levi got himself home safe. Been farming the ground we bought together ever since. He never returned to duty so he's listed as a deserter. My brother never wanted to join the fight but did so to look after me. I'm pretty sure he dropped a few Rebs at Hartsville, including one of their generals.

I've heard stories about deserters being rounded up. They've been hung or sentenced to prison. I beg you to spare my brother. He did the best he could. While I was away, he sent many boxes of ammo and other supplies to my company.

I have served my three years and saw my share of action. By the grace of God I never suffered any injuries. I did spend some time in hospital when a shell exploded near me. I don't hear so good nowadays, but otherwise am in good health.

I asked Capt. John Tracy to witness the action I seen so's you know I'm being straight with you.

Mr. President, I always thought of you as a fair man. One more time, I hope you see clear to spare my brother. He's a good man. I look forward to getting back behind the plow with him and not worrying about being shot at.

Your humble servant,

Pvt. Henry Nelson.

Robert paused and glanced at his father. Abe had turned toward the fireplace. His eyes were closed. "Pa. You awake?" he asked softly.

Abe stirred and moved back behind the desk. "Yep, heard every word."

"Well, the letter ends with a note from Captain Tracy," Robert said. "Hmm, appears the Illinois 104th saw a lot of action. Here's what the captain wrote:

I, Capt. John Tracy verify that Pvt. Henry Nelson was engaged in the battles of Hartsville, Chickamauga, Lookout Mountain, Mission Ridge, Resaca, Peach Tree Creek, Utoy Creek, Jonesboro and Bentonville. His regiment participated in a great many skirmishes, in which they lost men.

Abe didn't wait for Robert to finish reading. He reached for a sheet of paper and scratched out a message with his quill pen. "I remember those boys. Far be it from me to sit in judgment of a brave man. If his brother can forgive him, I'm not going to insist on any punishment."

The President handed the paper to his son. "I'd be obliged, Captain, if you could telegraph this pardon to the War Department right away. Now, if you excuse me, I have an outing with your mother." Robert stood, saluted his father one last time, then left to carry out his mission.

11

Harriet was tired after an evening of socializing with friends in her home. It had only been five days since the announcement that the war was over. Everyone had been in a joyful mood. Shortly after 10 p.m., Harriet finally got a chance to sit down at her dresser and prepare for bed. She had just set the oil lamp down and started to comb her hair out when a flash of light startled her. The orb she had seen from time to time over the past few years appeared above her head.

This time the magical light was acting strangely. Instead of the usual white, dancing light, it flickered between a dark blue and gray color. It did not dance, but bobbed up and down slowly.

To Harriet's surprise, a soft yellow flame appeared beside her orb. The second light looked like the floating ember that had danced on Mr. Lincoln's shoulder during their conversation. In what almost appeared to be a gesture of affection, the two mysterious lights touched for a moment. The new flame flared in a burst of white light, then slowly faded into nothingness.

Harriet's orb glowed in that melancholy hue. It slowly appeared to land on her shoulder. A few moments later, it disappeared in a shower of sparks.

She didn't know why, but a great sadness overwhelmed her. Harriet pondered what had just happened, then eventually returned to her bedtime routine. Calvin had just walked into the bedroom to start preparing for bed when a loud banging sound startled the couple.

"What on earth?" Calvin muttered. "It sounds like someone's pounding on the front door. Who could it be at this time of night?" He picked up the lamp he had just set down and carefully made his way downstairs.

Harriet sat up in bed and shivered as a feeling of dread slowly crept into her soul. When Calvin reached the front door, she heard him angrily challenge whoever had the gall to bother them at such a late hour.

A few minutes later, Calvin shuffled slowly into the bedroom. His face was contorted in a most sorrowful expression. He stopped, let out a trembling sigh and held out a telegram.

At that moment, Lincoln's fateful words to Harriet about the end of the war echoed in her mind: "Whichever way it ends, I have the impression that I shan't last long after it's over." Without looking at the piece of paper Calvin held out to her, Harriet doubled over in sorrow. She looked up as tears streamed down her cheeks. "Oh Calvin, Mr. Lincoln is dead, isn't he?"

Calvin didn't ask how she knew. He simply took out his kerchief and handed it to his wife. "Oh my dear, this is terrible news. The president was shot in a theater. It seems he doesn't have long to live. The authorities are searching for the assassin."

Harriet dabbed at her eyes. "Oh Calvin, what a terrible price Mr. Lincoln has paid for preserving the nation." Calvin could offer no words of comfort to his wife. All he could do was hold her.

A solitary man stood at the edge of the small Illinois village as President Lincoln's funeral train chugged along on its way. He had ridden his horse for half a day to make it on time.

The nine-car train had slowed as it made its way through the village so mourners could pay their respects to the fallen president. The train bore the caskets of Abe and his son, Willie, to be interred in nearby Springfield.

The engine picked up speed a bit as it cleared the outskirts. Most of the people had gathered along the tracks in town. The man wore a Union Army blue coat and cap. The ex-soldier stood at attention and saluted as the train rolled past.

Robert Lincoln had just stepped out the back of the caboose onto the small platform to get some fresh air. The train was nearing the end of its seventeen-hundred-mile trip from Washington, D.C. Thousands of mourners had stood somberly along the tracks as the train made its way on its solemn journey.

Abe's son and the man locked eyes. Robert nodded his appreciation and returned the salute. The former Union soldier stood at attention until the train was well out of sight. He held up a piece of paper he had been clutching in his hand and read it out loud.

From:

War Department of the United States of America
Attention:

All who read this shall be apprised that Levi Nelson of Osage, Illinois, has duly been pardoned for any crime levied against him during his service as a soldier in the Union Army's conflict with the Confederacy.

Let no authority seek him out or sentence him to any punishment henceforth.

So ordered on this day of our Lord, fourteenth day of April, 1865.

A. Lincoln, President of the United States of America.

Levi slowly folded the piece of paper and tucked it in his coat pocket. "Thank you, Mr. President," he said softly, gazing down the tracks. Soon afterward, Levi mounted his horse and turned toward home. It was May 1, almost time to plant corn.

EPILOGUE

Even though they had been expecting the visit, the jolt of energy from the arrival of Searcher and Other almost jettisoned the planet's cloud of entities halfway across the small solar system. However, they had been forewarned and given the luxury of two solar seconds to merge into a protective orb.

After emerging from the orb, Guardian and Caretaker flashed the white welcome sign. The two original entities emitted vibrations of greeting. It was a homecoming, not unlike parents returning from a long trip and being welcomed by their children.

Searcher orbited the third planet from the sun, taking a long look at the world it had helped form and give life all those millennia ago. It blinked down to the surface, tasting oceans, mountains and observed the massive cities that had spread across the world.

It returned to the others and flashed the yellow of concern. "The planet tastes sour, but it still holds life," Searcher vibrated. "The sentients have multiplied in numbers I did not extrapolate. It is a testament to the planet's vibration that it has not died. It must not have been cleansed since I exterminated the monstrosities."

Guardian addressed the newly arrived entities. "The planet indeed has been cleansed. The higher beings have endured floods, famines, other organisms, earthquakes, volcanoes, disease."

Caretaker emitted a green glow of pride. "The sentients have proven to be resilient. They come back stronger and multiply in faster numbers than before. The judgment was made not to exterminate all life. However, many times it appeared the sentients would bring about their own extinction.

"Guardian and I interceded many times to alter their vibrations, but the sentients' self-determination always changed the direction of our intentions. One leader persuaded his followers to exterminate millions of his fellow beings. Only the intercession of other sentients outside his influence stopped the slaughter."

Other drifted over to Caretaker and flashed the blue of sympathy. "It is problematic to change the nature of living beings. The sentients and their fellow organisms are descended from creatures that had to fight for their existence. The sentients are survivors, but they carry the blood of their bestial ancestors in them."

Searcher flashed an agreement vibration to its longtime companion. "Intercession had been effective with the sentients only a few times. When organisms gain or are granted self-awareness, they will evolve and go in unpredictable directions. Of all the worlds we have monitored, only a minuscule number have formed and followed the path predetermined for them."

A rainbow flash of colors emitted from Other. If it was a sentient, the reaction would have been taken for laughter. "All those worlds that followed a predetermined direction turned stagnant and stopped evolving. They all were cleansed."

Caretaker flashed the orange of concern. "Even when enlightened ones are placed in their midst, the sentients follow briefly, then change the messages to fit their needs."

Other transmitted a question vibration. "That is an interesting concept. Explain the success of the enlightened ones."

Guardian moved alongside Caretaker to show its support. "Over millennia, the cloud has selected individuals who would illuminate and lead the sentients to create efficient and sustainable societies."

Other and Searcher vibrated their encouragement for Caretaker to continue. "We sent them mathematicians and engineers. They built magnificent buildings, but did not improve the lives of their fellow sentients. Astronomers were encouraged to flourish. They misinterpreted signs and allowed the useless slaughter of their fellow sentients. Philosophers were born, but many of their words fell on deaf ears."

Guardian interjected. "Brilliant generals and kings arose, but greed destroyed most of them. Succeeding generations of their offspring almost always brought down the empires. A few almost succeeded in uniting the peoples of the world, but their dynasties eventually dissolved. Seeing these attempts fail, a different approach was attempted."

Caretaker emitted a strange vibration. It started out as pride, transformed to disappointment, then resurged with hope. Searcher and Other were intrigued.

"I tasted thousands of sentients and found a few that offered a hopeful future. One was pure logic. Another one opened its mind and tried to communicate with us.

"One of the most hopeful of the enlightened ones was a being who exhibited perfect love for its fellow sentients. But jealousy arose, and the sentient was exterminated in a brutal manner. A massive movement sprang from this leader, but the message and intentions have been twisted and manipulated by the imperfect beings.

"The success of the enlightened messenger of love encouraged the search for another with a true heart. One was found some hundreds of solar cycles later. Yet another movement was born, but the teachings and words of this leader also have been misunderstood. Followers of both of these enlightened ones have done both commendable and dissatisfying things to their fellow beings."

Other circled Caretaker. It vibrated confusion. "I tasted hope, if I recall that emotion correctly, from a previous message."

The younger entity continued. "Instead of creating one enlightened one, the cloud has been fostering many enlightened ones among the sentients. Successes and failures have been recorded. As many enlightened ones that are created, also dark energy beings rise up to challenge them."

A light pink glow emitted by Other surrounded Guardian and Caretaker. "Life creates a balance, young ones. When an enlightened one appears, others will rise up to oppose it out of fear and jealousy. Those sentients will only change when they are threatened or challenged as a species."

Searcher vibrated its approval to the younger entities. "Great patience has been shown by your cloud. Life on this planet will not continue if an edict of cleansing is approved or if the sentients kill themselves slowly by poisoning the planet.

"The great experiment has been a success. This world has spawned life on numerous planets. All life forms, including the troublesome sentients, have been successfully transplanted elsewhere. The instinct to survive is exceptional here.

"Millions of planets were seeded with life from this world. Most attempts failed, yet thousands have prospered and evolved."

Caretaker danced around the two original entities. "The sentients have finally ventured from their world. Their efforts are slow and clumsy. It may take another millennia until they reach other planets."

Searcher emitted a strong vibration of doubt. "To reach their kin on other worlds, those sentients will have to work together as a species. That is your challenge. If a cleansing is needed, so be it. This planet has served its purpose."

Guardian and Caretaker merged briefly. "We remain here to witness the success or failure of the sentients."

Other transmitted a vibration message to Caretaker: "Encourage the enlightened ones. They are this planet's only hope of survival."

Searcher and Other tasted the planet one last time, then flashed their final message to Guardian and Caretaker. "We entrust the care of this planet to you. Join us when the sentients leave their nursery to become explorers or when they exterminate themselves. A myriad of other planets require our care. We will not return to this one."

The original entities formed into a glowing orb and blinked away.

NOTES FROM THE AUTHOR

Writing *A Most Promising Planet* proved to be fun as well as a lot of work with researching some of the various periods of history. The enjoyable part was interweaving fictional characters into historical events.

Since the lines of fiction and reality are blurred, I thought some readers might enjoy knowing what I delved from historical accounts as well as other tidbits of how this book came about.

The Architects of Sentience: First of all, the heading for this section was almost the title for the book. However, this title came in a distant second to *A Most Promising Planet* during an online poll. The architects title was born out of a brainstorming session with a group of writers. The young woman who suggested using the word "architects" said she liked the idea of the entities being the builders of our world as well being responsible for creating and influencing humans.

The people who liked this title were quite adamant. That got me thinking about using "Architects" as a common theme for the other sections. I like how it turned out. I believe it gives the book even more character and helps the sections stand out.

As I said in the Foreword, the story in this section was influenced by my visit to the Tewa Pueblo's Cultural Center in New Mexico. The pueblo's creation story made sense with its folklore of how the Earth actually developed. Those mysterious entities blinked into my imagination when I started writing. I didn't plan it, they just appeared on the page, and I was off on an interesting adventure.

The Architects of the People: I've always been fascinated by what actually happened when Neanderthals (what I call the light skins in the story) and Homo Sapiens (us, the dark skins) met for the first time.

The extinction of Neanderthals after being exposed to Homo Sapiens suggests they were subjected to violence or disease on a fairly quick, massive scale. However, there must have been cooperation or possibly coercion between the two groups.

In a Feb. 4, 2020, article for smithsonianmag.com, Katherine J. Wu wrote: "New research published last week in "Cell" … (found) People with African ancestry actually have close to 0.5 percent Neanderthal DNA in their genome. (It also) found that Neanderthal DNA makes up roughly 1.7 and 1.8 percent of the European and Asian genomes, respectively." So, Neanderthals still live — in us. They are our distant ancestors.

The Architects of the Word: Being involved with writing for most of my adult life — as a former journalist and now independent writer — of course I've been interested in how words have shaped our culture. What better way than to look at who wrote the first words and how they were used.

Research revealed the ancient Sumerians of the Middle East are credited with being the first culture to use symbols to form words on clay tablets that have been discovered over the years. The Sumerians influenced the Babylonians and later Egyptians.

I found an interesting online source — http:// sumerianshakespeare.com — that told about a mysterious clay tablet that apparently made no sense when it was transcribed. One archeologist finally noticed some odd marks at the bottom of the tablet. When he used those seemingly innocuous symbols to read the tablet, they revealed possibly the world's first political satire — "The Great Fatted Bull" — about a cruel king who eventually gets his comeuppance.

I found the names of two kings who were brothers. One ruled for a short time and was succeeded by his sibling, who ruled for many years and was described as one of the great kings in Sumerian texts.

The Architects of Omnipotence: What happens when you mix the Greek gods of mythology, aliens and my entities of light? Why, this section of course. I've been fascinated by mythological tales from around the world for a long time. Those gods of legend were the first super heroes and/or villains.

If such beings did exist, I'm sure they would have put up more of a fight to stay in control than how some texts describe their downfall. So, why not include aliens and the entities to explain it all?

The Architects of Revenge: The idea for this section is inspired by Po'pay, a holy man of the Tewa people who organized a revolt against the Spanish invaders.

He united many of the pueblos as well as other Native American in the Southwest with the common language that they had been forced to learn — Spanish. According to records, Po'pay did kill his son-in-law, whom he suspected of being a traitor. I changed the character's name out of respect because I obviously blended historical accounts with fiction.

This hero came up with the idea of using five knots on a cord as the way to determine when the attack on the Spanish would begin. Many Spanish were killed in the revolt, but several thousand were "escorted" by the native people without harm to the Mexican border.

Of course, the Spanish eventually returned to the area and defeated the Native Americans. They did change their policies of enslavement in part due to the influence of a priest who helped barter peace.

The Architects of Justice: While growing up, my mother liked to tell the story of how her grandfather, Levi, and his brother fought in the Civil War, were captured by the

Confederates and escaped from a prison camp. Later in life, while doing research for this book and hopefully a future work, I found their enlistment papers. Yes, both served during the war and were captured after the battle of Hartsville. The Ohio regiments retreated, leaving the Illinois soldiers' flanks exposed, which led to their capture.

According to records from the Illinois Historical Society, the account of my ancestor's actions were quite different from family folklore. It seems great gramps was not the hero as my kin portrayed him, but I decided to stay loyal to family history. Who knows what really happened? I hope Levi appreciates how I portrayed him in my version.

Abraham Lincoln and Harriet Beecher Stowe did meet during the Civil War, but there are no records of their conversation. My ancestor and his family lived within a reasonable traveling distance from Springfield, Ill., where Lincoln lived at the time. Why not have them meet the great man?

The account of the Stowes helping a black servant girl escape from bounty hunters looking to nab escaped slaves appears to be true. Calvin and a friend reportedly helped the girl hide in a chest. The friend then hauled her away to safety.

As with all the tales in the story, my entities either influenced or witnessed some of these moments in history. Perhaps they're still watching us.

ABOUT THE AUTHOR

M.L. Williams is an award-winning ex-journalist. He retired after battling deadlines to write stories inspired by his imagination. Williams lives in Cedar Rapids, Iowa.

He spends his time reading, writing, wandering around the yard acting like he knows what he's doing and enjoying his role as Grandpa.

A REQUEST

Dear reader:

Thank you so much for taking the time to read my book. I hope it was a worthwhile experience. If so, I would greatly appreciate it if you would write an honest review and indicate a rating on amazon.com or goodreads.com. It can be as simple as one sentence. Reviews help authors know how they are doing and also can influence potential readers.

I also would enjoy hearing from you — pros and cons. Feedback from readers is another way for writers to learn if they are doing a good job. Following are the various sites you can contact me.

Happy reading!

M.L. Williams

mlwilliamsbooks.com
mlwilliamsbooks@gmail.com
www.facebook.com/mlwilliamsbooks
www.pinterest.com/mlwilliamsbooks
www.instagram.com/mlwilliamsbooks/
Twitter: @MLWilliamsinCR

Made in the USA
Columbia, SC
27 May 2021